Burn Barrels and Weed Whackers

An Old Guy's Musings on Country Living and Days Gone By

Joe Ulrich

Many of these musings reflect experiences related to country living. Others represent chapters in a life, times of sadness, and observations from afar. Although most are based in fact, a few are purely fictional. I'll leave it to you to decide.

Table of Contents

America's Worst Invention

Ever since the Pilgrims landed at the Hard Rock Cafe, smart folks in our country have been inventing terrific stuff. Everyone knows that it was an American who invented the cotton gin, the telephone, the airplane, and breath mints. We're all proud of those accomplishments. There is one, however, that stands as a mark of embarrassment to us all. I regret to say it was an American who invented the weed whacker.

He gave it the vanilla-sounding name of "string trimmer." Those of us who have used his machine have given it many other names, most of which could not be printed here. It was an invention only slightly less heinous than the guillotine or the roadside bomb.

Anyone with a piece of property knows all about the following routine, which begins on an autumn weekend morning.

It's a little after nine, and you've sipped the last of your coffee. You're feeling uneasy over the battle that awaits. As you savor the last of your sweet roll, Marge keeps up her tactic of thoughtfully mentioning day after day that you have been putting off trimming the lawn for several weeks. Your shoulders slump. She's onto you, but you knew that. Today is the day. You venture a quick glance outside. Although it's sunny, weeds obscure your full-grown German Shepherd. You take a last glance at the sports section and see that the big game has a 1 PM kickoff. You know it's the big one: the game you can't miss.

It's almost ten before you've changed into your jeans before slinking out to the garage. There you reluctantly search for your weed whacker. "Now, where did I stash that darn thing?" you mutter. You find it; partially hidden behind a stack of empty bottles you keep forgetting to return for deposit. You reach around the bottles with one arm, and manage to pull it out, just as a leaf rake tumbles down against your head. Not a good omen. You lay the weed whacker on the garage floor, and notice no cutting string is sticking out of either of its two holes. Ugh. And where is that new roll of string you bought last spring?

After a quick trip to the neighborhood hardware store to buy more string, you check the instructions. You've changed the string a bunch of times before, but every time is like the first day in school. A glance at your watch shows it's a few minutes past eleven. You cut the string following the instructions. You're starting to make progress! But how to hold both strings to keep them from unraveling, while pushing it into that doohickey with the springs in it? (Hint; it can't be done unless you hold the string with your teeth).

The Force is finally with you. You spit out the string, it's on, and you pour the right mix of gas into the tank. Now it's time to get it running. How many yanks does it take to get it started? You've tried and tried. Now you're winded. Your heart is pounding like you ran up the steps of the Statue of Liberty carrying a moose carcass. Another glance at your watch. It's just a few minutes till noon. Well, maybe there's enough time if all goes smoothly, but it will be tight.

Finally the darn thing turns over and begins running, amid a cloud of blue smoke. Just as you reach down to lift it up, the engine coughs and dies. You unleash a fusillade of cruel oaths. Now it's an hour until kick-off. Too close for comfort. You glance up and see your neighbor Ed has happened by. At the wrong time, as usual. Ed is one of those guys who keeps his lawn absolutely immaculate, and whose car is always washed and shiny. You dislike him fiercely. Ed considers your plight, and offers a joke about your mechanical skill. You fail to detect the humor. He comes over, adjusts the choke, and starts it on his second pull. You don't want the thing to stop running now, so you swallow your pride and politely wave a thanks, put on your protective eyewear, your protective earplugs, your ball cap to keep the gnats out of your hair, and maneuver the strap over all of your protective gear. When you finally get the strap over your shoulder, you remember. Your other neighbor, Bruno, had borrowed your weed whacker and used it last. Bruno is 6-foot-8, so the straps are so long that the cutting part is dragging along the ground. Not good. So the strap comes off over your eyeglasses, earplugs, and ball cap. You tug at the adjuster, not sure whether to let more out, or pull it in. Sweat is running down into your eyes. You again fantasize about what you would do to the guy who invented this thing. An ice pick and a ball peen hammer come to mind.

It's twenty to one, and you're finally ready. Phew. You begin whacking the weeds over by the garden. Your machine is humming, and grass shards are flying. All your effort is now paying off, and you're finally getting at it. You're in the groove. Moments later, you notice it's not cutting as well as it was. In fact, it's not cutting at all. You reluctantly shut it off. You notice no string is showing from either of the holes. You reach over your shoulder, and unharness yourself over your protective eyewear, protective ear plugs, and ball cap.

Feeling a burst of superhuman strength, you grab the friggin' weed whacker and toss it fifty feet beyond the gladiolas; it comes to rest with a thud against the trunk of a maple tree. Your neighbor Ed, who is waxing his Lexus, looks over, amused.

You slam the garage door, and stumble into the kitchen, avoiding Marge's steely gaze.

At the fridge, you crack open a cold drink, then plop down in your easy chair. Whew. Just in time for the kickoff.

An Old Guy's Football Dreams

I looked more like a scarecrow than a football player. But my skinny arms and legs didn't scare anyone. Back then in '64 we wore black leather helmets so ponderous that I ran like a bobble-head. My black high-top cleats weighed about ten pounds.

I was the worst high school football player ever. And that was how many years ago? So why do I still have dreams that I'm playing on my old high school team?

Once it was more than a dream. The head coach for my suburban New Jersey team may not have been the most successful in the school's history, but the crew-cut no-nonsense coach was wise enough to put me in a game only rarely.

It was mid-season, with only one win to show for it. We had gotten our buns hammered in all the others. Our one win was against hapless Cliffside Park. He didn't let me in until the fourth quarter when we were drubbing them, 34-6. Coach Alvord was no dummy.

Our next game was against the heavily favored Hackensack Comets. So it was with surprise that Coach advised me an hour before the game that I'd be on the kickoff team. Depending on the coin toss, it could be the opening play! I'm glad he didn't tell me the day before; I wouldn't have slept a wink. I'd be hauling in the game-winning touchdown catch right in front of our screaming fans!

But it wasn't to be. How well I remember the Saturday afternoon of the game. It was sunny and dry with a bright blue sky; perfect for football. Our home bleachers were filling up. We had finished the warm-ups; doing deep knee bends and tossing the ball around, trying to look cool. My sister Lynn and her hubby were in the stands watching. I wanted to impress them. Our band was playing joyously. I made sure I was facing the home sidelines with my helmet under my arm, so the crowd could notice me, and see that I would be "starting."

Since I wasn't a favorite with the girls, I figured I had to make the most of this situation. I wore a clean white jersey with number 81 in black numerals. I took a quick glance up into the stands to see who was watching me. I saw little kids chasing each other around and parents chatting with one another. I didn't notice anyone intently studying my every move. No girls swooning over number 81. Hmmm. From the field I could catch a whiff of sauerkraut and fries. Soon our cheerleaders were screeching out their final pre-game cheers. I listened, straining to hear my name. And there it is! "Joe Ulrich, he's our man, if he can't do it, no one can. . . ."

Now I'm too nervous to pay attention to the National Anthem. And I have to make sure the cheerleaders see me, especially Michele, the cute one who sits behind me in homeroom. Now our marching band, bedecked in black and red, plays their hearts out with our fight song. Coach yells a few words of encouragement. I join the kickoff team as we charge out onto the field. A chorus of cheers rings out from the stands!

I'm positioned near the right sideline, next to our bench and close to the bleachers. I line up with my teammates on the chalk of the yard marker. I lean over and put my right fist down on the grass. It feels clumpy. My helmet threatens to pull me over face-first. My heart is pounding hard; I'm too nervous to remember what Coach had told me about covering the kickoff. I lower further into my stance and scowl, looking as mean as a skinny 140-pounder could. I know I'm gonna run faster than ever before.

The referee moves the whistle to his mouth, and looks up and down our line.

I hope all the pretty girls are watching me.

The ref moves his arm to the straight-up position. A quick sensation hits me: maybe I have to pee.

His whistle blows.

I'm off! I slip, but then I dig my cleats into the turf and charge toward the enemy. I'm running faster than man has ever run. My helmet bounces up and down, almost obscuring my vision.

The ball comes down to a Hackensack player far ahead of me, to my left. He looks like a big guy, and he's fast.

I tear down the sideline. I hope they're all watching me.

The runner sprints, then angles across the field, right toward me! I prepare my body for tackling. He's closing ground, now ten yards away.

All of the sudden, I sense a shadow from the side. A Hackensack blocker slams into me and knocks me "ass over tin cups." I see the blue sky above, briefly, before my helmet slams into the turf. Then all is silent.

I have no idea how far the runner got, or whether he scored. I didn't hear the crowd, and I didn't smell the sauerkraut. Humbly, I pulled a grass clod off my faceguard and tried to appear nonchalant as I trotted back to the sideline. Coach Alvord spotted me just before I disappeared into the safety net of my teammates.

"Ulrich," he said, "don't ever let someone hit you like that." I nodded knowingly, then moved to a familiar seat at the end of the bench.

Geez, I hope none of those pretty girls were watching.

The Joys of Country Living

What could be more fun than burning your trash?

Lately we've had prime trash-burning weather: the ground is either soaked or snow-covered. The walkway to the burn barrel hasn't been blocked by mountains of snow. And there's been enough wind so that smoke from the burning papers and kitchen droppings wafts out of our yard and over to the neighbors'.

Most of this past summer I had to refrain myself from doing the burning. Too dry, or too windy. Or both. Having to summon the local volunteer fire brigade when flames start licking their way toward our garage is not high on my favorites list. It can get out of control all too quickly. That's why a seasoned trash-burner not only selects the right weather to strike the first match, but also must have a safe, yet sporty, 55-gallon drum to contain the burning. Rust-colored ones are quite popular around here. Then I go for the tried-and-true method of standing the burn barrel solidly on the ground. You may see some that are set at a 45-degree angle, like a surface-to-air missile launcher. That's too high-tech for this country boy.

Springtime is also a fine time of the year to burn trash. Mornings are best, when the grass is still wet. There are some who would argue that evening is better, right after dusk. Later, after the fire is out, often a bear wanders by to do a taste test on that thick black muck that fills the bottom of the barrel. Last week's chicken bones get him salivating. Raccoons may tip your barrel over to lick the pan that the cherry pie came in.

My buddy Johnnyboy recently was being considered for the coveted Black Belt of Trash Burning, at a national competition held at an undisclosed but smoky location. Unfortunately, he was disqualified. It was revealed that last autumn he had fired up a pile of tinder-dry leaves during a county-wide burning ban. I recall it being a hot, dry evening.

Not only did he start burning them in a huge pile, but then he casually decided to go inside. There he poured himself a glass of wine, plopped down in his easy chair, and promptly dozed off while watching a fishing program. Fortunately, the township fire sirens stayed silent that night.

I know many will argue that trash-burning contributes to pollution. Heck, I don't disagree. Plastics definitely are a mean culprit, as is rubber. Once it's torched, foam from old pillows smokes it up like a burning oil well in Iraq. Don't worry: I haul all that stuff to the dumpster rather than burn it. Even cardboard emits crummy stuff that stinks. But cars contribute to pollution too, and we drive 'em anyway. Folks shouldn't be discriminated against because they enjoy the sheer thrill of trash burning.

Many years ago, in the days before YouTube and chipotle tacos, everyone who lived in the country burned their trash. You had no choice. Grandma would be out in the yard every evening in her lace-up shoes, striking a match, waiting for smoke to shoot back up into her eyes. Growing up in a more citified area, I didn't know what joy could await me once I moved to the country. It wasn't till after college that I had my first experience with a burn barrel. And, as with other rites of adulthood, my first tries were disappointing. Leaning over into a dark barrel with a single match trying to light a wet orange peel is hardly a recipe for success. But I persevered, determined to master the art.

Most of today's trash burning experts prefer a knot of crinkled-up newspaper to get the fire started. I've learned it flares up fastest if it contains photos of politicians. Once lit, they say to toss in a tad more newspaper before the kitchen garbage bag gets dumped in. As if like magic, the smoke will come billowing up at you, and flames will dart up and singe your eyebrows. Soon you'll be hooked on this exciting pastime!

But all thrills have limits. Seasoned trash-burning experts all warn against sprinkling Boy Scout water (i.e. gasoline) into a burn barrel before tossing in a lit match. I tried that once, back when I was a novice, in a vain attempt to dispose of a few college textbooks. A light coating of snow was on the ground that afternoon. Before the match was struck, I dumped a cup of Sunoco regular onto the books. Then I tossed a lit match into the 55-gallon drum, turned away, and ducked. A giant KA-BOOM shook the yard. Out of the top of the burn barrel flew a Biology textbook, landing in the snow. It barely had a scorch mark. My neighbor shot a glance over to me, then shook his head. He yelled a comment, something to do with my posterior.

Obviously that guy had a lot to learn about having fun in the winter.

Up Your Dog's Nostrils

Dogs come in many sizes and colors. Just like people, huh? But every pooch has their own good qualities. In retrospect, my wife Linda and I should have gotten our dog Fika (FEE-kah) trained to do Search and Rescue, or other productive endeavor, because she has one heckuva nose on her. Taking her for a stroll on a leash is a struggle, even after five years, because she goes into "stop mode" every few feet to sniff dried-up rabbit pee, deer droppings, a tick turd, or other gem of the great outdoors.

Not all of the dogs in my life have been like that. One canine critter I had in the mid-Seventies, a rescued beagle-looking mutt named Ernie, couldn't sniff out a bacon burger in a phone booth. Other former four-legged friends, like my beloved Mattie, couldn't be bothered sniffing around. She spent all her time worrying and warning us about oncoming storms, like if she sensed thunder over Kansas headed our way. With Fika it's all about her nose. She's not a bloodhound though. That breed is the champion of dog sniffers, but they have an unfair advantage over our Labradoodle. Their long floppy ears help fan odors up to their noses.

So what is it with a dog's sense of smell? Researchers come up with some startling statistics (I guess that's their job, though, to amaze us with numbers). They say that a dog's sense of smell is 10,000-100,000 times greater than ours. How'd they figure that out? And what does that really mean in understandable terms? Here's one description: comparing it to vision, many of us can see 1/3 of a mile away (or once could). Using a mathematical equation, some brainiacs determined that at that rate dogs would be able to see 3,000 miles away. See, I told you it would be startling. Of course, many dogs (like our Fika) use that sense of smell to manipulate us. They make believe they can't see or hear you when you're calling them back from the neighbor's yard across the road (sorry, Dean and Pam). Other researchers say dogs can smell a single drop of liquid in multiple Olympic-size swimming pools. Or they can detect one rotten apple in two million barrels. It must have taken one helluva big warehouse to do that test.

As we all know, dogs' incredible sense of smell is utilized nowadays to sniff out drugs, save people trapped under rubble, or locate dead bodies. One of the reasons they can do so is that unlike us humans, pooches can wiggle their nostrils independently and can sniff continuously, whereas we have to breathe in and out while we're sniffing. If you want to check this out for yourself, give your nostrils a wiggle test in front of your bathroom mirror. If you practice wiggling every day for a year or two and get them to move independently, you have what it takes to become a YouTube sensation.

Dogs also have something we don't have called Jacobson's Organ, which detects chemicals that advertise mating readiness and other sex-related details (not sure where to go with that one).

With all that capacity for detection, dogs have to be able to discriminate smells to be fully trained and effective. If its job is to track down Susie, a little girl lost in the woods, the dog has to be able to overlook odors from a cat, a coyote, or a discarded taco wrapper on Susie's path to concentrate on the trail.

How far away can a dog detect a smell? Researcher-type dudes have looked into that one, too. It figures, huh? Get ready for this: under perfect conditions, they can smell objects or people more than ten miles away. My buddy Bob, who rarely showers, can be detected at twenty. But even at that, dogs aren't at the top of the Sniffer Hall of Fame; bears can detect a smell more than twice that distance.

The world of medicine has been turning to our four-legged friends more and more due to that keen sense of smell. One test showed that dogs can be 97% accurate in discovering cancer in blood samples. That's remarkable! They also can sniff out prostate cancer (no surprise there, that's where they have their noses all the time) and other cancers. They have also been proven to be effective in detecting diabetes, tuberculosis, and malaria. Predicting seizures has been successful with some people, as has predicting migraines. Probably other maladies too. I've heard there has been success in detecting the Covid virus.

So don't be surprised if the next time you go in for a checkup you are met by a dog accompanying the medical person. The only reason it hasn't happened yet is that insurance companies haven't figured out how much to charge for a dog consult.

Golden Friendships

When we think of anniversaries, the one you'd better remember first is your wedding day. Although we guys may struggle with remembering the exact date, we often have the right month, and are not more than three or four years off. Wives seem to have a better handle on that.

Here's today's question: how do you celebrate anniversaries of friendships? If you're fortunate, those of us who are "long in the tooth" may have friendships that have spanned fifty years, or even longer. Think for a minute. Who are the lucky folks you've had continued friendships with the longest?

A couple times each year Linda and I get together with my "longest" friends, Gunnar and Giz. Gunnar and I date back to kindergarten, close to seventy years ago. Giz is a newer friend. He didn't enter my life until the second grade. We met not too long ago in Gettysburg, where Gunnar went to college. We have maintained contact through the years, usually getting together over Christmas when we head to visit my family in Jersey for a few days. Gunnar retired after a long career as a Lutheran minister, and Giz finally hung it up after teaching at a Catholic high school for a mind-boggling 46 years.

As kids, Gunnar and I lived in, and shared, an imaginary world. We made up baseball teams and leagues, making up names for all our players. We developed our own game in which our teams could play one another. We even traded players back and forth. I remember trading my imaginary veteran left-handed starter Gordon Shale for his young center-fielder Ken Allen. I recall I got the better of that deal. We kept pages of statistics on how each of our players performed. We made up leagues of football teams too, again making up names of all the players. Most of the team names are long forgotten, but I remember one of his teams was the New York Groundgainers. One of mine was the Houston Sams (catchy, huh?)

Making up names in our limitless imagination wasn't confined to the sports world. We made up countries, too. I remember his country was Andraxia, and mine was Kranjovia. Even as kids we must have been peace-lovers, because our countries never attacked one another. We made up leaders' names, as well as battleships, aircraft carriers and fighter planes. I remember naming one of my plastic toy soldiers Lt. Ed Montague. Gunnar's head-of-state was Gia Teca. Maybe we made up more things, too, but it's all forgotten. I doubt kids do that today. Or, more likely, no one other than Gunnar and I were ever that nerdy. Giz knew about our name games, but he wisely stayed out of it.

Giz, though, joined us in a more educational bent in coming up with a more esoteric game called "Asking Questions." It could be called the forerunner of "Trivial Pursuit," but we never thought to make a buck off it. After a rousing summer afternoon of wiffleball, we'd sit down on Gunnar's porch with an iced tea, and ask each other questions about history, geography, or who knows what. Egad, were we nerdy, or what? Thank goodness we three guys found each other, or we would have been total outcasts. Having such a solid basis for friendships with them made me value and treasure subsequent friendships through the years.

Sometime this summer I'm planning on a few days in Cooperstown with my buddy Flash, who I roomed with in college. He and I go back a little over half a century. Sports has been the magnet that's held us together for the duration, dating back to our intramural teams in college. In those days we both tried to pass ourselves off as athletes, playing on our ragamuffin team which we named "Poland's Best." During our senior year Flash and I were the first ever to announce Grove City College football games on the local campus radio station. When I say local, I mean it. The station's signal was not much stronger than a mouse's heartbeat. But we have great memories from that time; even broadcasting from out-of-state games at Hobart and West Virginia State. Flash and I remain in contact regularly, often recalling watershed events in our lives, like hitch-hiking to the Friday night dances at neighboring Slippery Rock.

Howie is yet another fifty-year friend. We celebrated our anniversary with a camping trip, something we did many happy (and wet) times through the years. He and I also go back as far as college days. Not only did Howie become a dependable and fun-loving friend through the years, he gave me a priceless gift by making me part of his wonderful family. His parents camped with us till they could hardly walk anymore, and his brother Bob is only a year away from his fifty-year friendship achievement award. Howie and I talk weekly; we do train trips together, and just about anything else that sounds like fun.

Another fifty-year friend was once the ranking hippie on the Grove City campus. That was back in the late Sixties. Bill had a wild head of frizzy hair, an acoustic guitar to play Dylan, and an incisive, questioning mind. He's settled down in Asheville now, cut his hair some, but has continued to make great music and artistic paintings. We chat for hours every now and then, sometimes about his '57 Chevy. His "gray ghost" would go through sixteen quarts of oil on his trips back to Pennsylvania from North Carolina.

Then there is Gary, a guitar-pickin' dude with whom I stayed up many times till the early hours doing Kristofferson or Leonard Cohen stuff. And Willie, who used his Fifties movie camera and tape recorder, as well as his sense of humor, in unique ways that were years ahead of his time.

How about you? Who have you been friends with the longest? What made your friendship special? Why don't you surprise them by sending a hand-written note, giving them a call, or even better, getting together to celebrate your years of friendship.

The clock is ticking for us with golden friends. Don't put it off too long.

A Mechanical Mind

The American male is well-known for his ingenuity, and for having an incredibly clever mechanical mind that enables him to fix everything that goes kaput with the house and car. That includes adjusting carburetors, fixing leaks in the bathroom faucet, getting the old tractor running for one more season, and figuring out why the furnace isn't pumping out any heat.

Well, I should say that "most" American males can do that stuff. Not me. I can't do hardly any of it.

Way back when I was a kid, maybe ten or so, Dad envisioned some hope for me, and even bought me a Craftsman screwdriver set for my birthday. Sorry to tell you this after all these years, Dad, but that sort of disappointed me because I was hoping for a Lionel box car for my train set. Sixty years later when I lean over to reach a rusted-on bolt with a socket set in hand I still have trouble figuring out which way is tightening, and which way is loosening.

Somehow I must have learned a few things, because by the time I was twenty or so I could change the oil in the car. I did a fairly decent job of that when things were relatively simple, like with the old '55 where the filter was easily accessible. Still I always spilled a puddle of hot black motor oil on the garage floor, and often on my jeans and sweatshirt too. I got it on my socks more than once, and even into my shorts. Yowzers on that one. That was long before cars began getting seriously complicated.

When I tried to change the oil in my SUV a few years back, I had to squeeze myself under the engine and look straight up at the oil filter, lurking just inches above me. I didn't want to jack up the car to give me more space, because I always have had visions that the jack would collapse, pinning me to the pavement as I tried in vain to yell for help because my lungs were collapsed by the transmission on top of me. And as for using those little ramps you see in the auto section at WalMart, forget it. I was always afraid to run the car up on them, because I was sure they'd either collapse, or I'd run the car clear off the end. So, images of impending doom paraded before me as I bravely squirmed under the engine, praying the brakes wouldn't suddenly let go. I reached up with one of those flimsy oil filter wrenches, and tried to turn it. Darn. Wrong filter wrench. I shimmied out from under the engine, and went to the garage to get another one. That one fit better, but the filter still wouldn't turn. I tried yanking it, but it was too tight. Ugh. I tried again, but the wrench was already oily. I grabbed it for all I was worth and gave it my best yank. The f&^%(^g wrench slipped and I slammed my knuckles against some other big metal thing hanging under the car. When my hand slipped, my head shot up and slammed against the car frame. I let loose with a succession of phrases for which Mom would have paddled me. Glancing down, I saw blood mixing with dirty black oil on my hand. As I reached to wipe it off on my sweatshirt while still lying down, hot oil began dripping down onto my forehead. As quickly as I could, I shimmied out again from underneath the car, muttering ugly phrases. As soon as I got the oily mess off my hands and the bleeding stopped, I called Bill at the local car repair shop. I haven't crawled under a car since.

While on the subject of car maintenance, I recall once being brave enough to go down to the auto parts store to pick up a replacement air filter. The guy behind the counter, Herm, had about six homemade tattoos on his Stallone-like arms, his hair tied back in a ponytail, and a sneer like a member of the Manson gang. He asked "what engine do you have in it?" I replied "a big black one under the hood." Herm found no humor in my reply, rolled his eyes, and probably wished he could crush me like a bug. Or the time I went to another auto parts store (to avoid Herm) only to find what appeared to be his twin brother at the counter. I bravely asked for an oil filter, and he replied "How many cylinders ya got in it?" How the heck would I know? It would be like guessing how many rings in a tree. Besides, he's the one that's supposed to know all that car stuff.

I always dread the coming of spring because that means I'll have to get the old lawnmower running again. Sounds simple, but it's always a pain in the butt for me. Last year on one of the first sunny days, I rolled it out of the barn into the sunshine. I poured some gas into the tank, flexed my muscles, and yanked on the pull cord. Once. Twice. Maybe fourteen times.

My heart was pounding like I just ran a marathon wearing a mink coat. Nothing. I let it set for a while, walked up to the house for a cool drink, then came back down to the barn and looked it over again. After about six pulls, it began chugging. Briefly. Then it stopped amid wisps of smoke coming from the engine, and a yucky smell like I burned up the wiring. Upon looking closer, I found the engine compartment full of bits of paper and pink insulation. I unlatched something and saw two baby mice squirming around the smoking engine. Egad, this repair stuff is not for me.

My lack of mechanical wizardry first showed itself at an early age, much to my dad's chagrin. He wasn't an expert mechanic, but he could get basic engine stuff fixed. This had to do with changing the muffler. About once a year he would come home after supper following a long day at work. After he grabbed a bite to eat, he'd show me the new muffler he bought at Sears. It was a big long silver thing in a brown cardboard box. He'd jack up the Chevy in the driveway. I guess he wasn't afraid it would fall. He'd then crawl under the car and begin hacksawing the rusted-out muffler pipe, then bang on the muffler with a sledge hammer to get it off. Perhaps he thought his twelve-year-old son was enthralled with the idea of handing him muffler clamps when he asked for them. Poor Dad. He was trying to teach me something I would find useful in life. But my mind was elsewhere, off dreaming. I was thinking of batting averages, and whether the Dodgers would beat the Braves that night.

"Where's that clamp I asked for?" he'd ask, his hand reaching out from under the car.

"Umm. Here. Sorry, Dad."

He never seemed to get mad at me for being a mechanical doofus, though at one time I left the sledge hammer lying in the yard after a muffler job. He admonished me, saying "that's the sign of a bad mechanic." He couldn't have been more prophetic. I should have surrendered my Craftsman screwdriver set right then. Hey, even today I'd rather have gotten that Lionel train car.

They Called It Junior High

Those of us older folks often reminisce about high school days. Some of us look back longingly. Others wonder how we survived the experience, because we just didn't fit in. Perhaps you join me in the latter category. But I must say that even worse than high school, were those three years of purgatory we spent at what was then known as Junior High. It was all one jumbled mess. Could it possibly have been worse? I doubt it. There were so many things I was crappy at, or that drove my anxiety up as high as where DC-7s were flying. Where to start? One of the worst for me was school dances. I never left the safety of the wall against my back. Just anticipating a dance was enough to have about 300 zits pop out on my face. And as for classes, algebra, or whatever they called that nonsense, was the pits. Who cares what "X" equals? In the next problem, they would change "X" anyway. Geometry was no better. Do you recall memorizing its "theorems?" Cut me a friggin' break. I'd have to say that gym was my favorite class, but having to wrestle other guys on the mats? Yuck. Everything was sticky and sweat-covered, and I had arms like swizzle sticks.

But the absolute worst for me was science class and the day my teacher, Miss Podesta, made the dreaded announcement. She said we would have to do a Science Project. She said it would be a big part of the grade. I should have said "goodbye" to any chance of graduating right then and there, and hopped a freight for Idaho. And as for someday becoming a scientist? You gotta be kidding me.

What made a Science Project really hard was that you were expected to actually put your mind to work and think of something new. Something scientific. You were supposed to think of it yourself, and do it all yourself. In my case, my mind was so totally wrapped up in baseball that there was no room for any other type of thinking to occur. To make matters worse, for some reason they had stuck me in a class brimming with "A" students. Talk about a mismatch.

Some of my classmates eagerly jumped at the challenge, and probably went home and started working on it with gusto right away, even though it wasn't due for six weeks or whatever. To my way of thinking, that would be after the start of Spring Training, so why waste energy thinking about a future Science Project when a new set of baseball cards would be available down at the corner store any day now?

The day was drawing nearer for submission of Science Projects. In class a week or so beforehand Miss Podesta asked each of us what subject we would be presenting. As we went around the room, each classmate came out with something which made me scrunch down lower and lower in my chair. I don't remember exactly, but one of the class brains said something like he is trying to send an electric charge from a car battery up his TV antenna to a cloud to make it rain. Another egghead said he would be mating white mice with dark mice to determine what colors were dominant, or whatever. I think a girl said she is teaching her cat to sing Norwegian folk songs. It went on and on. By this time I was almost prone on the floor. Finally it was my turn. I nervously stammered, saying I had a few ideas that I was still working on. Nope, I doubt Miss Podesta bought it.

Soon the dreaded deadline approached. Of course, I hadn't started anything. Heck, I hadn't thought of a topic yet. But I knew all the batting averages of my favorite players. I checked the calendar. Egad. Tomorrow would be the day to turn in our Science Project. Ugh. At some point after supper that evening, I reluctantly turned off my transistor radio. My dad had come home only a short while ago from a long hard day of work. I sheepishly went downstairs where he had just sat down in his easy chair to relax and read the Daily News. I give myself credit; at least I let him eat his supper first. My voice quivered as said I needed to turn in a Science Project. Tomorrow. And could he help me? And maybe help me think of something? To this day I'm not sure why he didn't just pack me up and drop me off at the nearest homeless shelter.

But Dad had world-class patience, I guess, and we went downstairs to his workshop. I'm not sure who suggested it (probably Dad) and it was decided to make a toy car. Fine with me! So we began. The underside was cut out of a piece of scrap plywood about 10" long. He probably had me cutting it out with one of those saws with a skinny blade; I don't remember. We found two sets of wheels off another toy car, and added them with two long finishing nails for axles. It ended up supposedly being a racing car with an open cockpit. I don't remember what the body was formed out of, but we covered it with aluminum foil. It was kind of craggy looking. Perhaps "crude" would be a better description. I'm not sure how long it took before Dad was able to go back upstairs and return to his newspaper. I studied the car, my "Science Project." At least it was something. Phew! With that crisis behind me, I hurried back up to my bedroom to listen to the scores.

I don't remember bringing my project to school, but I imagine I wasn't bragging on it, especially when other kids had bells and whistles and mortars and pestles and all kinds of scientific-looking stuff. They talked about specific gravity, AC vs. DC electricity, chicken eggs, and who knows what else.

Maybe I was nervous; maybe I was relieved: I don't remember. But I had gotten through that horrific Junior High crisis. I think Miss Podesta gave me an "S" on my report card for Stressed.

Only A Twenty-Minute Job

How many of you have been victims of this prank? I know I have. Many times. A household job has been waiting for your attention for a couple weeks. Well, call it a couple months by now. You sit at the computer and find out all about the job; everything that's needed, step by step. You even go on YouTube and watch a video or two that apply to your task. The do-it-all dude on the video says "it's only a twenty-minute job." Really?

Here's my tale of woe: over the winter Linda has been pointing out, gently, that the kitchen faucet is leaking. Not only leaking, but sending a fine spray out the back of it. The spray lands on the wallpaper that she labored over installing, not all that long ago. After studying the matter, I thought I had calmed things down. You see, I had solved the problem temporarily by placing a plastic cutting board behind the faucet, so it wouldn't spray on the wallpaper. The spray would hit the cutting board, and drip its way back to the sink. No wet wallpaper. Job done, I thought. Perhaps temporary; maybe for the next year or so. Or till we sell the place.

After a few additional gentle reminders that the faucet really needed to be replaced, yours truly decided one morning to man-up and swing into action. A replacement faucet had been selected and brought home. I looked through the directions, expecting to read how to do it. Alas, there wasn't a word to be had, just a series of boxes with hieroglyphics using arrows and numbers that purportedly showed how to do it. No explanations whatsoever. Sensing a rare blast of testosterone, I decided I could handle it, and reviewed the YouTube videos again on how to do it. Linda would be gone till the afternoon, so it seemed like a convenient time to tie up the kitchen for "twenty minutes."

I gathered the "few tools" pictured on the instruction page, and hung a portable light under the sink. The dog was lying in the adjoining mud room, one eye open periodically, bored and snoozing. The first instruction diagram showed arrows pointing to close the shut-off valve under the sink, which I would need to do before disconnecting the line to the faucet. Here I gotta brag a bit; even I knew to do that. But that's where my "twenty-minute job" began going awry. When I turned the plastic hot water valve to "off," the water wouldn't stop; it kept flowing. Freakin' bad valve; I'll need to replace it before going any further.

Okay, I can deal with that. I turned off the water, fired up the pickup and woke up the dog. She jumped in the back seat, and off we drove six miles to the neighborhood hardware store on a sunny Saturday morn. The helpful hardware man there showed me a new type of metal valve fitting. He said it was a "snake-bite" or a "shark-bite" or something. I took his word for it. Heck, I wasn't going to bite it. I brought it home and installed it, slicker than snot.

The next task was to remove the faucet. To do that, I had to lay on my back in a yoga position never before attempted by a human, while reaching up over my head to unfasten the faucet. My wimpy arms felt like they were imploding. But, wait a minute. Something's not right here. I had watched three or four YouTube videos showing how to "easily" remove that same brand name of faucet. My faucet must have been one-of-a-kind, because the mounting on mine was different from any I'd seen. By now, the "twenty-minute" time frame was thrown clear out the window, well past the septic field. I'm already two hours into it.

One of the videos suggested using a basin wrench. A what? Actually, I remembered I had one of them, but where? Thirty minutes of digging around in the garage unearthed this homely contraption that looked like it had been designed by a committee of social workers who'd never picked up a wrench. So I got back into my yoga position and reached up with the basin wrench. Then another problem. Oh shit. Which way do I turn the wrench? How come I can never figure that out? Lefty-righty or lefty-loosey or something like that. When I'm lying upside down, is everything reversed? Just when I thought I had it, the wrench slipped and came tumbling down toward my noggin. Using my best tae-kwan-do move, I swatted it aside with my hand when it was an inch from my eyeballs. Whew.

That did it. Deep breath. I need to take a break. I'm at three hours, it's past lunchtime, and I need a sandwich. I hated to glance outside because it's the nicest afternoon we've had in months. Rotten planning, huh? But I got back at the job, assumed the position, and decided if I tried to use the flippin' basin wrench again, it would likely fall down and knock out at least six teeth. And my benefit package doesn't have a decent dental plan.

After trying just about every tool I owned, I managed to get the darn thing loose by prying it with a whatchamacallit I found in the garage.

Success! I yanked the old faucet out, the taste of success on my lips. I had the urge to toss the damn thing out onto the driveway and pound the crap out of it with a sledge hammer. Then I noticed how rusty it was. Egad, have we been ingesting all that junk? No wonder my I.Q. has taken a dive.

The new faucet went on rather smartly. Because the hot water shut-off valve had been leaking, I studied the cold-water shut-off, and decided I'd be wise to put a new one there, too, since if one of them went bad, I ought to replace the other one also.

So I hopped back in the truck, the dog jumped in her normal seat, and back we drove to the hardware store. I bought another of those new-fangled snake-bite fittings, went home, and snapped it on, slick as could be. I turned the water back on, and was standing triumphantly over the sink, stretching out my back for the first time in hours, admiring my fin-ished shiny faucet. It was then I noticed a spray of water under the sink. Son of a &@#$%^& !!

Linda waltzed in the door just as the dog was absorbing a verbal barrage aimed at whoever designed these things. By this time, I had six hours into the twenty-minute job. Now it was dinnertime and Linda, sensing she'd waded into a black sea of emotions, wisely suggested we go out to eat. You got it, girl. I need a burger and a beer.

The following morning I made trip number three to the hardware store, with the dog in the back seat, to show them that their newfangled valve was bad. He took it apart, agreed with me, and said the "O" ring was the culprit. Wasn't it a bad "O" ring that doomed the space shuttle Challenger? You'd think they would have learned by now. Anyway, he gave me a replacement for free, and it worked jim-dandy.

Twenty minute job? The guy who told me that ought to be beaten with a basin wrench in his private parts. What made it even worse is that I knew the dog was laughing at me.

Will You Be My Friend?

Perhaps you saw that Mr. Rogers movie. Just seeing it advertised brought back memories of those first tenuous steps through the world of friendships. Do you remember your first attempts at befriending other kids?

My first try at friendship was around kindergarten time, when a kid named Bobby Morris came over to our house. Bobby and I must have been in Sunday School together, and one afternoon his mother dropped him off at our house, since he lived across town. I remember he and I sat in our living room on a white flowered couch and watched a show on our tiny black and white TV set. Did we talk at all? Who knows? I don't recall how many programs we watched. When the visit was over and Bobby got up to leave, my mom noticed something. Bobby had left his mark. He had peed on the couch. No, I don't think he was invited back. We'll put an "X" on that first attempt at friendship.

I took chance number two with another Sunday School classmate, a quiet kid named Eddie Kirstein. This time it was me who was invited to his house. So perhaps my popularity was on the upswing. He lived only a couple blocks away, and being that the world was a safer place back then, my mom allowed me to walk over there myself. Eddie told me he lived on nearby Prospect Avenue. He didn't give me a street number, but said he lived at the house with the brown milk box. That was enough direction for me, and at the appointed time in the afternoon off I went. Well, I walked up and down Prospect Avenue, but where was that brown milk box? Nowhere to be found. Heartbroken, I made my way back home.

It wasn't long before a new kid moved into our neighborhood. Back then I was a skinny runt, with thick glasses. His name was Cliffy; he was bigger. And more aggressive. Their back yard was adjacent to ours. The main problem with our friendship was that Cliffy seemed to enjoy beating me up. One time he must have damaged my glasses, because my dad had to go talk to his father. I remember his dad; he was a big coarse man with that nasal New York City accent. He was a rugged longshoreman in the harbor. Not a dude to mess with. He gave Cliffy the message to lay off that skinny kid with the glasses. He got the message; the beatings stopped. We hung around some after that and played ball together, but we weren't really friends.

One afternoon sometime later, I went with Cliffy and some other kids to the movie theater downtown. That was maybe a mile away, so someone's mother must have dropped us off. Cliffy and the others got to goofing around in the theater, so I moved to another seat on the other side. When the movie was over, I looked to leave with my buddies. Where were they? The lights were turned on and the place was empty. My pals had not stuck around for the rest of the show, and taken off. I was alone. Forgotten. Heartbroken once again, and feeling lost, I stood in the aisle by the theater entrance. I remember it was sunny outside. To make my way home by myself was out of the question. How long did I stand there, sniffling and wondering if my world was coming to an end? After what seemed like hours, my mom appeared. She had seen the other kids back on our street, but "no Joe." She must have hurriedly walked downtown to get me. I think you get the picture that meaningful friendships were proving elusive.

But my luck was changing. Back then, kindergarten was only half a day; at least that's how I remember it. My teacher's name was Miss Body. That's true; I wonder how she dealt with that! Anyway, I liked to get to school first, because there was only one red wagon. I could get on it and ride it around our class room. Another kid wanted it too. His name was Gunnar, he was bigger than me too, but fortunately, he never tried to beat me up. This friendship blossomed, as we remain the best of friends today, almost seventy years later. Another life-long friendship began a year or two later when I became pals with Giz. So two enduring relationships were kindled.

But all was not well with friendships. I recall another face-off in about fifth grade. Ricky, who was another bigger kid, and I were playing with those little plastic soldiers all us boys seemed to have. We were playing one summer afternoon in my mom's flower garden in the front yard, throwing "dirt bombs" at each other's men. For some reason long forgotten, Ricky took offense, and started pounding on me. Like all the other kids, he was stronger than me. My pathetically skinny body didn't scare anyone. I don't recall if I was either crying or screaming, but my mom appeared at the front door to break up the tussle. Ricky got on his bike and rode home, sensing victory. My mom got the last word in with me. She was annoyed we had roughed up her bed of marigolds, and let me know it. Not a good day for the kid.

Cub Scouts got me involved with more kids my age. I got along well with some. Not so with others. One mean kid in particular was just known as Gibbons. He was bigger, too. If we were slow to leave the evening meetings when they were over, he would follow one of us out and use us as a punching bag. The "us" was usually me. So I got to be good at darting out, and hiding behind a tree until Gibbons came running by, puffing loudly, searching me out. I don't think I ever told Mom about him.

By this time in my young life, lessons learned pointed me away from a life of physical confrontations. I had no choice but to choose pacifism. Luckily, I had a friend at home, too. My sister Carol, who was three years older, and I got along really well. We both recall playing "cowboys and Indians" under the kitchen table. No doubt we had been fueled by watching Roy Rogers and Dale Evans on Sunday evenings.

Looking back, I have been incredibly fortunate to have friendships lasting over sixty years. But it was not without its struggles. I guess it's no wonder some of my first feeble attempts at fisticuffs turned out the way they did. Cliffy, the big neighbor kid, went on to become a college basketball star at Long Island University. Ricky, who pummeled me in the fifth grade, eventually signed a minor league baseball contract with the Detroit Tigers.

And as for me? If you glance below my bald dome, you'll see I'm still a skinny runt wearing glasses.

Just Another Decoration?

On a recent visit to my hometown, I ran into an old school chum who I hadn't seen in years. All us guys called him by his nickname back then, Zirk. He was pretty much an egghead as a kid, usually studying rather than playing ball with us. Today he is the internationally-acclaimed researcher Dr. Zirkon P. Kybosh of the University of Kranjovia.

Zirk proudly told me about his work. As he spoke his story became so fascinating that I asked him to take me to his research lab, where the story continued. At U of K he is Chair of the Department of Flea Market Studies. There they have developed a method of taking what might seem to you and me to be an everyday item at a flea market, and tracking it back to its original owner. When he said he could show me an example, I jumped at the chance. Zirk said the process he developed is the Universal Old Stuff Tracking System, now known as UOSTS. He said exactly how they do it is pretty much Top Secret to keep the process from being accessed by unfriendly foreign governments. "You see," he added proudly, "the government gives us a lot of dough for this incredibly important work."

I nodded, visibly impressed.

My old friend was really excited now; he asked "Did you ever wonder who owned that Elvis oil painting, that black velvet one you bought at the flea market last week?"

I told him my brain has been so busy thinking about soybean futures that it never occurred to me.

"Come with me," he said, with a knowing smile. Inside his impressive lab, Zirk took his time selecting an item. "Do you know what this is?" he asked.

"Yeah, it's a wreath," I replied. "A Christmas wreath; it's got Rudolph on it. Looks like it's seen better days; kinda ratty-looking."

"Indeed it is," Zirk continued, pausing before referring to his computer screen, and then glancing at a complicated-looking machine with a number of dials on it. "I chose this one to show you because it came from your area. This was handmade back in the fall of '68 by Yoselda Johnson, of Wetmulch, New York. She had it for a few years, then stuck it in her attic, forgot about it, and after she passed away her daughter Sarah took it to her home near Sugar Grove, Pennsylvania. Let's see . . ." I watched as Zirk twirled a few dials. " That was in '73. In the summer." Zirk studied his screen for a few moments, then continued. "After keeping it for two years, Sarah put it out on the curb with her other trash. That's when things started to get interesting."

By now I sported a quizzical look.

"A guy driving by noticed the wreath, stopped, picked it up, threw it in his gray Plymouth station wagon, a '62 we think, and took it home. That was Jasper Cringe of Bear Lake. His wife took one look at it, thought it looked crappy, and stashed it under their bed. When their divorce became final, she put everything he gave her out front for a yard sale.

"Mrs. Eleanor Farquahr of Blockville, New York, bought it at the sale. We're not sure how much she paid for it. Maybe thirty-five cents. We're still researching that," he continued. "Mrs. Farquahr displayed it each year during the holidays, hanging it on her front door. That is when things got even more interesting."

"Huh?" I was getting lost in the details.

"You see," Zirk continued, "a troubled teenager from across the tracks, Albie Croom, snuck up to her house one night after dark and stole it off her door. He gave it to his step-mother, Olivia Mae Shankle, as a Christmas gift. But Olivia Mae wanted to throw it in the trash the minute she saw it. That hurt Albie's feelings big time; but that's another story. She put it in a box to go to an auction house. By now, it is the fall of '88.

"The years go by quickly for Christmas wreaths," I wisely observed.

Zirk referred down to his notes, and then the computer screen. "At the auction, the high bidder was a middle-aged lady, Miss Josie Jugash of East Scandia, Pa. She had a collection of wreaths that were her pride and joy, which she loved to show her visitors. Actually, not many people stopped by her place; but that's another story. She kept it for years, even refurbishing it. That's when Rudolph's nose got touched up. Days later, disaster struck. Miss Josie lost her life in a tragic wheelbarrow accident. Then her stuff just laid around the house. For years nothing happened. Her nephew finally cleaned up what was left of her belongings, and threw the wreath in the township dumpster."

Zirk paused, looking back down at his computer screen. "End of the wreath story, you think?" he asked, not really expecting a reply. "Not quite," he continued. "In checking through UOSTS, we find that the truck driver picking up the dumpster was Harlan Fenwick Jr. Research indicates the wreath caught his eye. It was lying on top of some white kitchen trash bags that were all gooey. So he grabbed it, wiped the worst of it off, and took it home to give to his live-in girlfriend, LaTonya. By now it's 2006; a week before Christmas."

"Zirk, you guys know everything! I'm beyond impressed!" I blurted out.

"Well, his girl LaTonya wasn't impressed. But it wasn't the wreath that started the big argument between them, it was Harlan's drinking. Late that night she kicked Harlan out. But that's another story. Two days later, some big dude named Parnassus Poindexter moved in with her. Come spring after she kicked Parnassus out, she held a yard sale in front of her trailer. We believe that was just before she moved to Jamestown with another new boyfriend. At the sale, Jimbo McCoy's wife Lizzie bought the wreath, offering only a quarter. Ol' Jimbo usually rents a few tables at that flea market just outside of town. She gave it to Jimbo as a birthday gift. The wreath then hung on a nail in his barn for two years, nestled above a bunch of croquet sets he had picked up along the way. One Saturday morning he took it off the nail, and hauled it to the flea market. He and Lizzie had a two dollar tag on it when Sally, one of my student interns, noticed it. She got him down to a buck-fifty, and brought it here for research purposes. Here at our lab, we unleashed our powerful Universal Old Stuff Tracking System on it. The rest, as they say, is history."

"Words escape me," I remarked in awe. "I've learned so much about this wreath."

"Your response is exactly why I have devoted my professional career to UOSTS" continued Zirk. "People just don't understand the historical significance of every item at a flea market or a household sale. We need to understand that each rusty oil filter wrench and each plastic spaghetti strainer has a story. We need to respect them. Especially holiday items, like this wreath."

With that, I thanked Zirk, my mind overwhelmed by the fascinating life of this Christmas wreath. We said our goodbyes, planning to meet again.

I needed to hurry home to hang that black velvet painting of Elvis over my bed.

The Annual Winter Bird Count

Every December a devoted group of local birders gather their scarves and mittens, grab their binoculars and a tally sheet, and head to the wintry outdoors for the annual bird count. Those hardy folks help track the ups and downs of the local bird population, by species. It got me thinking how my family history is forever entwined with that process.

Years ago, during the lowest point of the Great Depression, my dad's Uncle Bill developed an obsessive interest in birds. Exotic birds. Despite the heartbreaking economy of the times, Uncle Bill (I'll call him that for this story) was doing quite well for himself running his roofing business. It was based in Jersey City, located across the Hudson River from Manhattan, and not far from the huge Jersey Meadows wetlands. He never lacked for work, often doing big roofing jobs on local municipal and state buildings. Rumors are that he had an "in" with the local political machine.

The Depression hit the New York/New Jersey economy like a hammer hitting glass. Thousands of men lost their jobs. On many street corners, you could see a man who lost his job selling apples for a nickel trying to support his family. But not Uncle Bill. He had bucks. Here's how he was different: some nights after getting home from work, he would page through the monthly National Geographic magazine. His attention would be consumed by an exotic bird in some far-off part of the world. Uncle Bill would then get hold of a specialty animal supply house in New York City. He'd tell them he wanted to purchase that special bird which had caught his fancy. For that, Uncle Bill would leave a deposit of a hundred dollars or more. That was huge money during the Depression years, especially for a bird! Weeks or months later, he would be contacted by the animal supply house. They had his bird, they would tell him. Uncle Bill would then drive into the City, pay whatever else was needed, and carry his caged feathered friend home.

Uncle Bill's family lived in a brick two-story row house in Jersey City. Their back yard was tiny by many of our standards. Up against the back of the house he built a line of bird enclosures, which he would keep warm with hay and with heat from the house. The birds were safe from predators, being off the ground, in cages, and all secured by a locking system he devised himself.

His flying menagerie grew. At the peak of his collection, he had several dozen exotic birds from South America, Africa, Hawaii, and elsewhere. He took great pride in caring for his birds, and spent time with them every evening after he got home from work. Indeed, they were his beloved pets.

Another aspect about Uncle Bill's colorful life was that he enjoyed refreshments offered at the neighborhood tavern, located just down the street. He was a "regular," and was known as the life of the party. How much of a partier was he? Well, when Uncle Bill went out every Friday night, he didn't only have fifty cents in his pocket or a buck in his wallet like most other guys. Years later, his son told me his dad always had ten one hundred-dollar bills stashed in his shoe. Again, this was during the depths of the Depression!

To digress from the bird story, one night he came home from a night on the town to find that his thousand bucks was missing. Stolen? Fell out of his shoe? He never told his wife he lost the money. Pretty good move, I'd say. And another tale about Uncle Bill. Once again, it involved a night of partying. He had way too much to drink, and ended the night at home by bending over the commode and barfing. When he woke up the next morning, he didn't have his false teeth in his mouth. He realized he must have flushed them down the toilet. Having done the plumbing job himself years previously, he remembered there was a trap in the pipe in front of the house. So he dug up the lawn, located the trap, and found his false teeth there. He washed them off with soap and water, and popped them back into his mouth.

Okay. Back to the birds. One summer evening Uncle Bill was once again well "into the cups," and came home tipsy late on a Friday night. Instead of securing the bird cages when he got home, he must have fumbled with the locking mechanism, leaving the cages ajar. On Saturday morning after his head had cleared, he went out back to tend to his birds. To his horror he saw that the cages were all open and empty. Every exotic bird had flown off, perhaps to the nearby Jersey Meadows.

It's unlikely Uncle Bill ever saw any of his prized collection again. But if bird lovers happened to be down in the Meadows doing a bird count that morning, an incredible surprise might have awaited them.

Claude

Not too long ago, I had a working lunch with Aggie, a seventy-ish woman from California, and we began sharing stories about WWII heroes in our families. I began by telling her about my Uncle Chet, who as a 21 year-old was shot down and killed while flying a P-47 fighter over France. After she patiently listened to his story, Aggie began to tell me of her Uncle Claude.

Claude grew up in northern Maine and had dual citizenship in Canada and the U.S. He spoke French fluently. While he was in high school, WWII was raging across the globe. As soon as he turned 18, he volunteered to serve. He had a decision to make: to wear the uniform of the U. S. Army, or Canada's? He chose the latter.

By then it was the spring of 1944, and the invasion of Europe was imminent. Following basic training, he served in Canada's infantry. By late May, the armies were finally ready. The Allied invasion of the French beaches occurred on D-Day, June 6th. The Americans landed at two beaches, the British at one, and the Canadians at another. Claude bravely stormed ashore with the Canadians amid enemy gunfire. Though the beach was horribly blood-stained, Claude made it safely.

Claude fought his way inland with his mates. Only a few days later, in the midst of a battle with the enemy, he became isolated from his unit. Then a German shell hit nearby and he fell, badly wounded. Hours passed. He wafted in and out of consciousness. With the battle still raging, he was found by a French peasant farmer as Claude lay bleeding in a field. The farmer went back to get his wife and his wagon. They put themselves in extreme danger by returning to the battlefield, then carefully lifting Claude onto their wagon. Then they brought him to their meager farmhouse.

All around them was the chaos of a heated battle. The family could not transport him to a doctor. They nursed him as best they could, using whatever they had, trying to help him recover from his dreadful wounds. At times he was conscious, and could converse with them in French. He gave them his home address and family name. He asked another favor: if he did not pull through, to contact his family to let them know what had happened.

The French family did all they could for him in a loving manner, but the extent of his wounds was beyond their care. When Claude closed his eyes for the last time, they were both at his side.

Weeks later, Claude's family received a telegram from the government, advising them of his death in battle. His mother was heartbroken, not knowing if he died alone in a faraway land. Day after day brought tears.

It was another year before WWII mercifully came to an end. The French family held onto Claude's family information. But communication overseas had become an impossibility for them due to their lack of money, their isolation, and war-ravaged communication lines.

The French family didn't forget. A year after the end of hostilities, a letter arrived at Claude's home in Maine. It had a French postmark, and arrived a few days before Thanksgiving. The letter told of Claude's last few days on Earth, of his love for his family back home across the sea, and of how the peasant family tried to help him.

The letter was passed around the table as the family was gathered. They were greatly touched by the love and care he had been shown after falling in battle. Tears fell in buckets. All cried except Claude's mother. She had passed away before the letter arrived. She had gone to her grave never knowing if Claude had died alone, far across the sea.

Claude's story is a lesson to remember for all of us. We need to reach out to one another, and to love and cherish everyone in our family. And we need to be thankful for every day we share the gift of togetherness.

April Means Baseball!

When the month of April comes round, rich baseball memories return with pleasure. To us silver and gold folks, there is no month more associated with a single sport than April. March Madness has made a big impact with basketball in the last twenty years or so, and, yes, football may have taken over as America's premier sport. But to those of us "long in the tooth," the "thwack" sound of a wooden bat smacking a baseball is dear to the heart, and deep-seated in our genes when April rolls around.

As a kid, my transistor radio would always be close to my ear as I listened to early April's spring training games from Florida. Just the names of locations like Bradenton, Vero Beach, St. Petersburg and Clearwater had a magical quality when I'd listen to the games and conjure up the action on those sunny diamonds. As a northern kid, I'd zip up my jacket, dab at my runny nose, and dream about what it would be like to be down there with my heroes during spring training. I'd evaluate the player trades made over the winter, and dream of the "can't miss" rookies who would help my team win the pennant.

As soon as the snow was gone from the field in late March and early April my pals and I would head to the ball field and start hitting them out. In the brisk air, there would be "bees in the bat" as you'd connect with a fast ball. You'd blow on your hands to warm them up. Guys standing in the outfield had their jackets on with their collars turned up, and one hand in their pocket.

With the arrival of warmer weather in mid-April, the year's new baseball cards would be for sale at the neighborhood store. You'd be giddy with excitement! A nickel would buy the thrill of a new pack, which would quickly be ripped open. You'd get your first whiff of the slab of bubble gum as you'd go through the half-dozen cards. You'd quickly move a Jerry Kindall or a Ted Lepcio card to the bottom, eagerly seeing if you got a Hank Aaron or maybe even a Willie Mays. Your buddy would be next to you. You'd say "what did ya get?" and, just your luck, he got that blue and white Gil Hodges card that looked great. "Wanna trade?"

By mid-April each year the big league season would start for real. I recall that some of the games were on TV, but I mostly caught them on the radio. The Majors played a lot of afternoon games back then, and at times when you got home from school you could catch the final score right away, as you eagerly swapped your school clothes for your ball-playing clothes. Your mom would ask you how school went that day. You'd quickly answer "good" as you gulped down a cold glass of milk and snatched some cookies. Then you'd grab your mitt and be out the door in a flash.

By the time you rode your bike home at suppertime, your jeans would be dirt-spattered. As you darted in the back door, the aroma of the chicken your mom was frying up smelled delightful. You were starved! You tried to hide the hole in the elbow of your flannel shirt that you got sliding into second base. But your mom spotted it right away. She always did.

Each night after supper, as soon as my dad put the paper down, I'd check the standings, easily memorizing them. Next were the league leaders in home runs and runs batted in. Those numbers would stick in your head much better than those in the math problems you stumbled through in school that day. In my room I'd give my homework a half-hearted try while the game was on the radio in the background. But study would be interrupted by the sound of a loud "thwack" and the crowd cheering as a long drive headed for the wall. Gone! Way to go! Between innings I'd get back to the homework while the familiar commercial jingles for beer, cigarettes, and coffee played in the background. Then the book would be put down for good. Lying in bed at night, I would catch the final score before falling off to sleep, dreaming of that bang-bang play at home plate.

Those thrilling April days of yesteryear: how I loved them!

The Saga of Refrigerator Magnets

Here's how it all started. Early one morning a few weeks ago I was sitting in the kitchen sipping coffee and considering whether I should actually do something productive for the day. Our pooch Fika was curled up asleep nearby. Lost in meaningless thought, I glanced over to our refrigerator, and noticed a few colorful magnets. Are they new? Who knows? Maybe they had been there for weeks. Maybe months. Guys don't notice details around the house, I'm told by someone who knows.

I set my cup down and counted them. Twenty-four. No wonder some looked new to me. This one of our great-niece Ashley, how long has that been up there? And the moose magnet from New Hampshire? As I worked at prying my eyeballs open while the caffeine kicked in, it made me wonder who invented refrigerator magnets, and how long they've been around adding their tacky touch to American kitchens.

As usual, the internet is the go-to source for this type of critically important information. Let's go back to the beginning of magnets themselves. What civilizations used them first? One source has it being the ancient Greeks. But there's a fact to consider before you picture Pliny The Elder in his gleaming clay kitchen with the Mrs. proudly gazing at his collection of refrigerator magnets. The refrigerator wasn't invented until 1913, and not popularized for another fifteen years. So what did Pliny do with magnets, not having ordered a fridge from Sears yet? Dunno.

Another source credits the ancient Chinese for the first use of magnets. Rumor has it that occurred on a Tuesday morning, only weeks after a neighbor down the street invented Chinese checkers. Those remarkable findings pre-dated by many centuries their development of the Covid-19 virus.

Inventing magnets led to the development of the compass, which revolutionized how brave people explored the World by crossing the ocean in tiny ships. It may be only conjecture, but it wouldn't surprise me if some of those explorers were planning how to eventually mount GPS screens in today's SUVs. One thing is sure; their forward thinking paved the way for mankind's ultimate invention: the refrigerator magnet.

According to internet sources, it was in the Sixties when an American mold-maker of some renown named Sam Hardcastle (yup, that's his real name) decided to make some extra dough. The dude must have been hot; he was approached by the space industry to come up with a magnet that was flexible and non-abrasive. I guess he scored big on that one. His next idea was using magnets to sell whatever products people wanted. He set the world on its ear when he developed advertising magnets, the first step toward their entry into our kitchens. So remember to thank Sam for the magnets from personal injury lawyers that come attached to your phone book.

But the job wasn't quite done yet. Sam passed the hat along to William Zimmerman of St. Louis, who patented our most modern colorful fridge magnets in the Seventies. If Mr. Z. gets a penny for each fridge magnet in existence, I'd imagine he has accumulated a few bucks. He must have been a guy of talents; in 1948 he invented the first Hi-Fi record brush, which was made of Chinese goat hair (there's that Chinese connection again). It's reported he sold that invention to RCA, making a bundle on that too.

Getting back to your fridge, someone did research and found the average person views their refrigerator door forty times per day. To come up with the idea (and time) for that study probably meant the researcher had nothing more productive on their to-do list. That's almost 15,000 times per year to look at advertisements for pizza and hot dog shops. No wonder we're all getting fat.

Since those magnets do such a great job of holding photos, at times you'll be challenged in deciding how many photos are too many. I thought it might be helpful if I provided some guidelines in choosing what type of photos to keep up there. I polled countless women shoppers at the grocery store the other day to find who was most likely to be found on their Whirlpools. Grandchildren/great grandchildren were clearly number one, followed by pets, and then other family members. Occasionally, husbands were even mentioned.

To add contrast, I spent the next day talking with guys at construction sites, bars, and repair shops, asking them whose magnetized pictures were least likely to be found on their refrigerators. Several of the guys were unable to identify which room their fridge was in. Not surprisingly, photos of ex-wives would be the least likely. Another one I heard frequently was photos of their probation officers.

Here's an idea: when no one's around, take a couple magnetized photos of kids off your fridge. Then sneak into a house down the street and switch them with a couple of theirs. Mount theirs on your fridge. See how long it takes someone to notice.

If ever.

Giving Thanks for a Back-up Dog

It doesn't have to be late November to give thanks, and consider all our blessings. If you're like Linda and I, you're so fortunate you have too many to list. For eleven years we had been incredibly blessed to have shared our home with a "rescue dog" named Mattie. She joined us from a series of nightmare experiences in her previous life. Mattie was a mutt, in the most lovable sense of the word. I would come to call her our "Perfect Dog." A forty-pound brown-colored short-haired critter, she had a mixed heritage which she wore well, starting with her four white feet. Her original "owners" had kept her chained up outside for over a year, with almost no human contact or stimulation. Life was one cruel, miserable day after another. Her next stop was the Humane Society, where she stayed for weeks. No families chose to make a home for that timid dog lying in the corner of the cage. Then one day her luck turned for the better. A canine-loving lady bravely took her home to see if Mattie would thrive living among her five other dogs. But that proved to be a disaster. Mattie was overwhelmed and failed miserably. So, for her it was back to the cage.

Having known about her failed test living among others, another dog lover signed her out on leave from the Humane Society and by chance brought her into my office. It was a rare quiet afternoon, a good time for us to get acquainted. Mattie stayed for maybe two hours, mostly napping on a rug next to a chair. Timid as could be, she would open her eyes, roll over, and invite her tummy to be rubbed. Okay, I admit it. Right then and there I was hooked. I wanted to bring her home right away.

Alas, we already had a lab mix named Velveeta. After much discussion with Linda, it was decided that given our lifestyle there was room for only one dog in our household. So sorry, Mattie, I hate to turn you down. Perhaps this was not just another lost opportunity for her, could it be her last chance? I was deflated; what would become of her?

Fortunately, she got another audition, this time with a thoughtful man who took her home to see if she would thrive living only with him. But this was intended to be only temporary; he would keep her for two weeks, and if it didn't work out, it would be a return trip to the Humane Society. We learned this was to be her last chance. Once again she faced a trial. The clock was ticking; if she didn't do well in that quieter environment, it could be curtains.

It was at that time when the health of our beloved Velveeta suddenly went south. We had no choice but to put her down. Did Velveeta know that her leaving would open our door to another pooch? After she passed, we made a call to the fellow who was Mattie's "roommate," introduced ourselves, and went for an evening visit. Once again, Mattie and I connected. Linda got a good feeling from her, and agreed that she would be welcome to come home with us.

Mattie was now faced with a new and different environment. Another trial. She cautiously eased her way through our front door for the first time, before curling up on a blanket in a corner of the mud room. Finally, after a long and heartbreaking journey, Mattie had found a home.

But was she truly a perfect dog? Well . . . due to having been so alone in her first year, Mattie missed out on learning basic social skills. Too timid to interact, she preferred being by herself. She didn't know how to play, didn't care to, and never did learn. She was much too serious to spend time playing. At first Mattie wanted no part of any neighborhood dogs. Her preference was being quiet, and keeping to herself. Our home was a good fit for that. Slowly, eventually she let our neighbors' chocolate lab, Bottle Rocket, into her confidence. It felt so good seeing them run side-by-side in the fields chasing groundhogs. They became the best of pals. Bottle Rocket was the key to unlocking Mattie's prison cell of loneliness.

But still she remained timid. For years she would not take fresh meat if it was dangled in front of her nose. We had to set it down in her bowl, and then we'd leave the room. A few minutes later she would sneak over and gently nibble on it. She hated to ride in a car, and would try to burrow under the front passenger seat. Mattie would not walk on floors that didn't have a carpet or rug. There was one room in our house with bare floors that she never entered the entire time she lived with us. So she might have had her eccentricities. But she was always there for us. Linda and I could be gone for hours, and we knew when we pulled into the driveway she would be lying on the front porch, looking up at us with a tail wag as we drove in.

Mattie's forte was as a weather predictor. She hated thunder, and could tell an approaching storm was on its way when it was still over Iowa. If I was out on the tractor and she sensed a storm coming, she would dart out and run circles around the tractor to alert me. When a storm was about to hit, Mattie would force herself into the tiniest places. She tried to hide behind the clothes drier, under the toilet tank, behind the couch, under an outdoor shed, or any shelter she could squeeze herself into or under. And another curiosity; Mattie would not drink water from a bowl. Well, maybe a drop or two at most, if she was desperate. Nor would she drink from our pond. She was always on a mission to find her own puddle. When we would go through a dry summer, Mattie would hunt around out back until she found a seep with dampness that she could lap until she got her fill. She loved rain, and when the snows of winter came, she was in her element.

As she entered her 13th or 14th year, Mattie began having a health problem. We tried one medication after another, but it was to no avail. Then came those days of heart-wrenching choices once again; should we put her down? Can we put this decision off? Is there a chance she'll get better? It became inevitable.

Between tears, we whispered goodbye as the vet gently let her pass from our world. Arriving home without seeing our beloved Mattie lying in her special spot on our front porch was mighty hard to take. Once again, tears flowed. We talked about the future. Linda and I agreed we needed time before getting another dog. But what about this vast emptiness inside our hearts now? No more of our beloved Mattie! What to do?

In hours, our question was answered. Mattie's former pal Bottle Rocket took up residence lying in Mattie's spot on our front porch. Actually his real name is Rocky, but the way he zipped around helter-skelter as a pup I felt I had to give him a nick-name. His "dad" Dean tried to make a bird dog out of him, but Dean said when going out on a hunt, Bottle Rocket would keep nudging into the back of Dean's legs. Okay, so Bottle Rocket was too much of a lover to be a hunter. Pheasants and ducks were not for him.

Bottle Rocket sensed we had suffered a loss. It was his loss too. He saw fit to come over every morning after the school bus took the kids away. With his gentle eyes, he urged us to pet him while his tail wagged furiously. We got to calling him our "back-up dog." A casual observer might say he came over just to get a treat or a biscuit from us. But I know he had a deeper reason. To help us heal. He put the term "rescue dog" into a whole new perspective.

There's so much in life to be thankful for. Let's not overlook those who reach out to us with unconditional love. They may be family. They may be friends. They might even have four legs.

Thanks for being our best friend for so many years, Mattie. And thanks for being there for us, Bottle Rocket, when we needed to be rescued.

The Big Hurl

Those of us fortunate enough to live on dirt roads out in the country know that late March is one of the times we look forward to the most. With the first signs of spring, it's time for the annual tradition of "Raking the Road."

If you're a city dweller or if you live on a country road that is blacktopped, you may not be aware that each winter there is an intense competition that results in your needing to get out the rake. You see, snowplow operators compete for the prized Golden Catapult Trophy, given to the operator who hurls gravel the furthest onto a resident's lawn while plowing the roads.

Our township has two snowplow drivers. The first one, Heather Jo (not his real name) drives the smaller plowing truck. He is more of a Finesse Plower. Our regular driver, Monique (no, not his real name either) commands the big plow. He is the epitome of a Power Plower.

The lower part of our land is on a downgrade. As soon as Monique safely passes our mailbox, usually at about 5 AM, he heads down and throws his big diesel hog into overdrive, and kicks up an array of snow, ice, sod, gravel, branches, and discarded beer cans. Then he continues tearing downhill, spraying his bounty onto our property. Glasses rattle in our cupboard. My teeth chatter. That early morning racket wakes up our pooch, who then feels a sudden urge to go outside and investigate, or whatever. You probably know the routine.

When the weather warms just a tad and the snow cover melts, it's time to measure and rake the lawn from the conglomeration that has accumulated over the winter from the plowing. The rocks need raked, because if the gravel was left in the grass, I'd wing a few across the road when I begin mowing the lawn. I'm afraid I'd break a window, or scalp the neighbor's dog. That could be treacherous to me, since our neighbor Dean is a lot younger and considerably more robust than I am.

With winter fading away, I eagerly headed out with my tape measure to see if we had the "longest hurl" on our road. My best was a hunk of gravel I measured to be 16', 4 1/2" from the road. Not bad. My other neighbor Johnnyboy boastfully claimed a 20' hurl, but he thoughtlessly tossed the chunk of gravel aside before an official measurement could be made..

It's not universally known that retired snowplow operators get together at a local gathering joint to sit in front of a toasty woodburner, drink coffee, talk about their most recent visit to the urologist, and reminisce about their plowing days. Invariably, one of them brings up the famous "hurl" that other drivers only dream about. Some say it was back in the Eighties, but the exact date has gotten hazy. Legend has it that a driver named Big Ivan hurled a hunk of gravel an unbelievable 39 feet! What a hurl! It happened just east of here one sub-zero morning, and the length of his toss was corroborated by two credible sources. History has it the chunk ended up on the widow Johnson's doorstep at 6 AM, just as local handyman Barkley Binkum was hurriedly leaving her house after servicing her water conditioner. The retired drivers shake their heads in amazement at Big Ivan's incredible feat.

There is generally no trophy given for the largest rock that ends up on the lawn once plowing season is over. That's unfortunate, because if there was an award, I'd nominate our plow guy. He would be right up there among the finalists. One snowy morning, I looked out and saw a big dornick as big as a possum carcass on our lawn next to the road. I don't know whether it was Heather Jo or Monique, but it looked like a winner to me.

Our other neighbors have yet to submit their entries for the annual gravel hurl. Although some winters don't have as much snow or plowing, you can still expect notable tosses. I think it was Albert Einstein who calculated that "Less snow to plow translates into higher plowing speeds, which results in longer hurls." At least that's what I think he was most famous for.

The fear of making a final determination too early in the spring is that at least one more snowfall could be forthcoming. I'll think about record hurls on a chilly morning at 5 AM when Monique shifts into high, and floors his big diesel. The glasses in the cupboard will rattle, my teeth will feel it, and the dog will give me a nudge with her wet nose as if to say "you'd better go rake the road again."

Ah, the joys of country living . . . .

Going to Class

Be honest. Do you think about how much you loved your high school English class? Yeah, you know I'm kidding. But we all had to get through it. You may remember the teacher, perhaps an old biddy with a name something like Miss Pringlethorn. She gave you a list of books to read, all beyond boring. One was about a woman named Esther or Evangeline who lived in the Scottish moors, where it was always foggy and drizzling. The book was about 900 pages long. Snore city.

Here's how I would go about it; maybe you did the same. I delayed opening the book as long as possible. My thinking was that maybe the world would come to an end before I had to read it. Then I would have spent all that time with the book for nothing. Soon enough, though, the next day became the deadline. So I hunted around for it in my room after dinner, while Mom clanked around downstairs with the dishes. Eventually I found it, stashed underneath my stack of Sport magazines and old National Geographics. I laid on my bed, turned down Cousin Brucie on WABC, and flipped open to the first page. I could only read about three sentences before I started thinking about baseball. Maybe I'd get through a page here and there. But all the while I'd be wondering who would be pitching in the big game tonight.

Did I have time now at the last minute to read the whole dang book? Get serious! When panic hit, I'd quickly flip through it. Bummer. Not a single picture. Then I'd go to the last page where the young leading lady was saved by a tall handsome dark-haired dude named Richard (never a pudgy bald guy named Cornelius). When it was time to discuss Esther or Evangeline in class, if you were like me you kept out of eye contact with the teacher at all costs. You'd dread being called on so you wouldn't have to answer dumb questions like "why did the author refer to Evangeline's pet sturgeon in the book?"

You kept your head low, only daring to glance up at the clock, hoping you could escape before being called upon. When the bell finally rang to end the class, you slammed your book down and hustled out before she could ask any goofy questions. Equally as important, you needed to find out if they were serving hot dogs for lunch.

In addition to boring books, there was all this darn grammar stuff. I recall that, in order for a word to look right, you had to have a mix of consonants and vowels. I was never sure who made that rule. Nowadays we no longer have to be concerned about it; texting has changed all that. When you say "Consonants and Vowels" these days, it sounds like you're talking about a pair of personal injury lawyers from Buffalo.

For those of you who might not have had your morning cup of coffee yet, here's a reminder that consonants are letters like B, D and F. Good, hard-sounding letters. Vowels are weak-sounding letters like O and I. There are some places in the world where folks don't know how to mix them properly. Hawaii jumps right out at you. They don't believe in the use of hard, manly consonants at all. Wimpy H's and Ls are their best shot. Because they don't use strong consonants, Hawaii has places like Haleiwa and Kauai that even local coconut salesmen can't pronounce.

Taking it the opposite way, look at Sweden and Finland. They are hung up on the letters J, F, and K. Granted, those are good letters if you're playing Scrabble, but who can pronounce places like Hjefko and Gjerrik? And to make matters worse, they come up with totally wrong ways to say the words. For example, we have really good friends who live in the Swedish city of Skövde. Starts out, you think, with a good, solid "Sk" sound. Wrong! They pronounce it Huvv-deh. What happened to the "S" and "k"? And to make matters worse, they somehow purse their lips when they say it. Come on, you silly Swedes! Speak a real language!

So, that takes us back to our original subject. For a lot of us, the struggle wasn't over when you were done with high school, because my freshman year in college I had to take a dreaded English course once again. Our prof was a pipe-smoking guy who always wore a spiffy plaid sport coat. He fancied himself a cool-dude aristocratic intellectual. His imported loafers squeaked when he walked. Let's call him Dr. James Watson the III (that's close to his real name). He loved the "III" after his last name. That was years before football players started wearing that on their uniforms. If he had the chance, I'm sure our prof would have had "Watson III" on the back of his sports coats. About the only thing I remember from his class was that to emphasize a point and further belittle us freshmen, he would sit down at his desk, take out his pipe and go through a routine of cleaning the pipe bowl by clicking it against the bottom of his shoe. Click-click-click. At the same time, without looking up from his shoe, he'd call on you, using only your last name, in a nasty, demeaning tone. It went something like this: click-click . . . "Ulrich!" . . . click-click . . . "Ulrich, discuss, in depth, the underlying and divergent themes Socrates used when he wrote "Hamlet'". . . click-click. Or whoever. Get me outta here.

Compare that to my fondest recollection of my college freshman French class, when the only thing I remember happened one time in the afternoon. As I recall, it was really hot in there, around 3 PM during the last class of the day. After constant jabbering in French, there was a sudden unexpected lull in the conversation. Just then, the girl sitting in front of me let out a stinky. A confirmed pffft. There was no doubt it was her. Me and the guy next to me almost blew a gasket trying to keep from bursting. Those being the most memorable events of college classes might be why I never made the Dean's List.

Oops, I see I've gotten away from the topic. Sorry. Back to English class. I have one pet peeve I have to get off my chest about spelling, so please hear me out. Here it is: I hate when people who run a business try to make their place sound more antiquated or gentrified by adding an extra "e" to its name. Such as, the "Olde Pottery Barn." Or "Southpointe." Or, even worse, the dreaded double: "Olde Towne Tavern." Who gave them permission to do that? In my opinion, those are extra "e"s that should be saved, recycled and sent to Finland so they can stick them between their consonants so they can finally pronounce where they live.

There's the bell. Class dismissed.

Dad's Dust Pan

We all know what we have to do. We gotta get rid of much of the excess stuff we've accumulated over the years. If you have a basement, an attic, a garage, or an outbuilding you've probably been more susceptible over the years to taking something home that might be of questionable value. Some of us country people even have a barn. At least that's my excuse. Hey, we've got the room. Why not?

Okay, how and when did all this stuff accumulate? Looking back, we cleaned out my parents' home and garage twenty-some years ago. Then there were the homes of two sets of aunts and uncles. Then my friend George passed on. Then my brother-in-law. A year ago, Linda's father died. More stuff. So, in our household, inventory has continued to grow. Perhaps the passing of loved ones in your lives has had similar results.

It probably doesn't help that, until Covid hit, I was a sometimes-regular at local estate sales, arriving there early on Thursday mornings "to get a good number" for early access. So I've dragged more than a few things home from those ventures. I call it "the thrill of the hunt." Although I've moved a lot of that stuff on through on-line sales as well as a nearby auction house, a heckuva lot remains. For Linda and me, the question remains: what do we keep for now, and what do we get rid of?

Let's start in the house. The first decisions for "keepers" are easy. There's no way I'm getting rid of Granny Yeager's rocking chair, even though we can't use it because it's too fragile. That Structo garbage truck I got before kindergarten? That's staying. Family photos are also a no-brainer. Current hobby items and collections aren't going anywhere. Special glassware from our parents is here as long as we are.

At the other end of the spectrum, there is some stuff I know I have to toss. Let's look around. Here's a plastic tray from a refrigerator that we junked maybe twenty years ago. I never did find a use for it, not even to store those bent nails I got from Dad. Those round Christmas cookie tins seem to multiply by themselves. Gone. That bowling ball I got for a buck. We don't bowl. Outta here. Okay; making progress. I found a few "must goes."

Should you be interested and if you have money to blow, there are a number of "self-help" books out there to help guide you through the process. Spend thirty bucks for one if you want. But they will only help you with the easy decisions. What about the "tweeners?" Those items with no significant value, either monetary or personal, but for whatever reason aren't on the way out the door. That's the rub.

If you're serious about streamlining your stuff, sifting through miscellaneous items that have made it to shelves in the garage is a good place to start. It's sort of like the backlot of Disney films. Out of sight, out of mind. Over there is a baseball mitt. It's from the Seventies, a Ron Cey of the Dodgers model. Is it worth anything? Maybe five bucks. Oops; this water jug has a hole in the bottom. Okay, that baby's outta here. We've got a big garage, so that means room for lotsa stuff. Looking around the garage, there are tools I've never used (mainly because I don't know how to). Here's a showerhead I took off God knows when. Looks kinda crusty now. All right: heading for the dumpster.

I spot a blue car window scraper hanging from a nail. I've never used it despite greasy spots on its hard plastic. It's really too small to work like it oughta. Easy to throw out? Not so fast! At a closer look, it reads "Chapman Chevrolet, Cliffside NJ." I recall it came with our '55 Chevy, the first "new" car my dad ever bought. Could this scraper be the last remnant of that memorable car? (oh, I guess not. I still have one of its hubcaps. Somewhere. And its license plate). What to do with the scraper? I guess it has to go. For now, I'll put it over there in a box for a potential on-line sale to some Chevy lover. Maybe I'll get five bucks out of it. Ten would be great.

Which brings me to today's final item: Dad's dust pan. It's a rather primitive-looking homemade metal job. It never has worked the way it should, because the lip where you sweep the dust onto is too rounded. I've had it in the garage since we moved here years ago. Linda has probably never even seen it. Being that it's an item that doesn't work, perhaps it seems like an obvious candidate for the dumpster. But hold your horses. I remember Dad proudly telling me he made it in his eight grade shop class. That would have been around 1923. It got me wondering; how many other dust pans are closing in on 100 years old? I considered the historic nature of this item, but knowing there's probably not a National DustPan Museum, and that tough choices need to be made, I swallowed hard and reluctantly tossed it in the bottom of the bag to go to the township dumpster. A good decision, but not an easy one.

Later, as I was driving to drop off the trash, I pondered the matter once more. Maybe I could straighten the lip of the dust pan and make it useful (a thought I've had for many years). Nawww. Stuff has gotta go!

Five minutes later I stood beside the township dumpster. I hesitated before throwing the bag in. A guy pulling up for a drop-off in a new pickup looked at me curiously. He watched me reaching down in the bag, through oily sawdust, past scrunched-up paper towels with gobs of tractor grease. As I slid my hand past last week's rotisserie chicken carcass, my fingers reached the dust pan. I pulled it out. Maybe I'll work on it this summer . . . .

A Summer Road Trip Not Taken

That darned Covid-19! Normally, our summers are spiced with a few long distance trips and exciting events to highlight the year. It never happened last summer, at least for us. Was it the same for you? No trips to the beach, or to Uncle Ralph's woodsy get-away cabin in Hoboken?

I suppose what we missed most was our trip each July to the Annual Weed Whacker Championship Series. Regretfully, this year due to the virus its promoters had to cancel the whole shebang. As you probably know, it moves around each year to a different location. Last year's was a real blast; it was down in Fire Ant, Alabama. The year before it was in Bilgewater, Ohio. It's a great time to get together with others like us who live and breathe weed whackers. Folks arrive in their R.V.s, camp, party, compare and brag about their weed whackers, and thrive in a week under a cloud of ever-present exhaust fumes amid the din of our proud-looking machines.

Each day there are competitions, displays, and everything that makes weed whacking so much fun. Three years ago we were in awe when J. Ferdinand Kaplutz, known lovingly as "the father of weed whacking," made a rare public appearance. In his 90's at the time, he spoke of how he built the first weedwhacker. Ol' Ferd said he got his inspiration after a night of watching horror movies while drinking Tequila. Although he nearly severed his big toe the first time he ran it, he persevered and was singularly responsible for the development of the hobby we have come to love.

At the annual gathering, folks do just about everything with their "whackers." Our tent was next to a long-haired couple from Kentucky. Unkempt and wearing mud-splattered jeans, they passed a bottle back and forth all day long. Like my old hippie buddy Randy, they spent hours grooving to Dylan tunes. Each morning they made their scrambled eggs by whisking eggs with their weed whackers. Those folks took "eating organically" to the next level. Having yesterday's grass shards and bits of mulch mixed in the eggs adds major nutrition to start the day.

Linda's favorite event each year is the famed synchronized weed whacking. How a group of six folks with their favorite whackers can do those dance steps barefoot only inches away from each other is a thing of beauty, what with the sound of their engines choreographed as well. When they all kick up their legs in unison, it's as thrilling as watching the Radio City Rockettes. What precision! They wear their Band-Aids proudly, like battle ribbons. And for a finale, when they do it blindfolded, their shrieks are louder than their whackers!

Another of last year's outstanding performers was a couple from West Virginia, Homer and Harriet. They don't want their last name shared with the public (but I think it's Dimwiss). They have a unique use of their weed whacker, for which they choose their yellow Ryobi sport model. First they have Homer lay on the ground with his mouth open, and toothpaste spread on his three teeth. Then Harriet fires up the Ryobi, and carefully brushes away. After the performance is over, Homer gets up and shows off his spotless front tooth. "I'm proud of doin' it," he says. Even if my gums and lips bleed a bit afterward." But Homer ends with a message for youngsters in the audience. "Don't try this at home; remember, me and Harriet . . we's perfessionals at this."

The Saturday night of the gathering is what our whole crowd eagerly anticipates. At the stroke of midnight, everyone gets in formation, revs up their weed whackers, and parades through the residential part of town with their whackers on full throttle. You can watch the lights come on in every house as we strut on by. The fun lasts till the final gasp of the last machine. He or she whose whacker runs the longest is crowned the Ultimate Winner. Last year's winner was Pennsylvania's own pride and joy, Heather Jane Mildew. For her noble accomplishment, she received a year's supply of orange string for her favorite weed whacker, who she lovingly calls "Mikey."

There will be new performers and presentations at next summer's Championship Series, and for that we're headed out west! Save the second week in July; hope to see you at Holdyer Horses, Arizona!

It's Rachel Calling

Here's how it all came down. I was enjoying a libation with my buddy Lefty, down at the club. It was getting late, we were both tired, but I thought, why not? I'd tell him the story I'd been holding in, waiting for the right time. I admit to bragging; it's sort of a guy thing, I guess. After I set my empty glass down on the table, I began. I said each word slowly for what I hoped would be the maximum effect. I leaned over toward him and began with the words "I heard from Rachel again." With the mention of her name, his eyebrows raised, and he tipped back his ball cap. Then he lowered his head and crushed out his smoke. He turned to me, fidgeting in his chair. I let him know it all. I told him she calls me frequently, at all hours of the day. "She's always upbeat," I continued, "and really interested in me because she always has concerns about my credit card. She sounds like she really wants to help me." I said it all kinda man-proud.

He was silent for a few seconds as he picked at the label on his bottle. "Do you believe her?" he asked, his voice dry, without inflection.

"Of course, why shouldn't I?" I wondered where he was going with this.

Lefty rustled around in his seat as I continued my story. "Sometimes I tell her that I hope she's having a nice day, but the subject always gets back to my credit cards." I told Lefty that I feel like I'm special to her, because even if I'm tied up with something important when she calls, like if I'm carrying out the trash, she takes it OK and calls me back the next day.

I awaited Lefty's response with anticipation. He nodded his head almost imperceptibly, and looked down into his glass. Then he said the words slowly, quietly, from the heart. "Rachel calls me, too."

I was momentarily stunned, then realized it must be some kind of mistake; perhaps another gal with the same name. "Yeah, she calls me," he continued, "and it's about my credit cards too."

A sudden burning came over my chest. The same feeling like seeing your first love, years ago, back at the junior high dance, hand-in-hand with that tall fella with the wavy hair. I just sat there, smoldering, unable to speak.

Lefty's tongue continued loosening. He took a deep breath. "Do y'know Booger Grunderholt, that guy from across the tracks who drives that rusted-out junker?" Of course I did. Everyone knows that slimeball. "Well I seen him at the pool hall last night. We got to talkin'. He was braggin' around and said Rachel called him too."

Booger Grunderholt? That sleaze? Getting a call from my Rachel? Suddenly, it all became too much to bear. I slammed my fist down on the table and almost ran for the door, jostling into Harvey Fribble as I left. As I crunched my way down the snow-covered sidewalk, I heard Lefty yell at me. "Dude, you can read all about Rachel on your damn computer!"

Egad! How could all of this happen? Rachel, calling these two other guys? I thought I was special to her. And how did her calls get reported on the internet? I needed some time to get over this. So I let things set for a few days. I needed to plan out my next move. Dare I look on the 'net for any mention of her?

It took me a while to get my strength up. Finally it was Tuesday, about noon, right after I pushed away the last of my french fries. My napkin slipped to the floor. My fingers shook as I got on line to see what Lefty said I'd find about Rachel.

Indeed, he was right. It wasn't only me she had been calling; and it was more than Lefty and Booger, too. I couldn't believe what I was reading. Altogether, without her telling me, she's been calling 2.4 million other guys, always asking about their credit cards. I feel used. Why so many other guys? What does she see in them that she doesn't see in me?

So here I stand, a week later, acrid smoke wafting into my nostrils as I stare down into the burn barrel. The last vestige of my credit card turns into a gooey black glob before my eyes. How do I get my world back in order? The pungent smoke causes a tear to form. Or was it something else?

Then I hear a familiar sound coming from the house. It's my phone ringing. Could it be?

Bored?

Are you fighting boredom? Here's something to consider. A number of years ago we were driving through upstate New York when I caught a glimpse of a sign on what appeared to be a normal two-story frame house. I thought the sign read "Drain Tile Museum." I did a double-take to make sure I had seen it right. Indeed I had. After returning home I checked on line and the place was legit. Since that time, I thought we'd head back that way to spend the day (or weekend) browsing through the collection of historical drain tiles. Nope, we haven't made it back yet. Like I said, it looked like a regular house. No parking area for buses full of senior tourists spending the day at the museum, picking up drain tile novelties and souvenirs for their grandbabies.

It got me to thinking; what out there is not included in any museum? Especially when cold weather hits, maybe it would be a good idea instead of watching reruns of Perry Mason, to start a museum. But what's still unclaimed?

Someone told me that in Pittsburgh there is a museum dedicated to ketchup. With the Heinz factory down there, it could be likely. Later I found it does exist. Well, now that there is one dedicated to ketchup, how about mustard? I searched. Lo and behold, some place in Wisconsin has laid claim to the Museum of Mustard. How about hot dogs? Yup, you guessed it. There is a Hot Dog Museum; this one is in Ohio. I'm sure there is a museum dedicated to french fries somewhere in Idaho; I won't even bother looking that one up. Okay, how about coleslaw? After checking on the internet, I could find no reference to a National ColeSlaw Museum. I'm thinking maybe starting one of those might be an option on a January night, when the fireplace is crackling and the dog is napping peacefully. I'd guess that museum would appeal to the grilling and tailgating crowds, and maybe the vegans too.

What museum do you want to open? Art? Paintings? Forget about it. Someone already came up with that idea. Every city has one. There's even decent art museums in many small towns. Linda and I have been to one of the most famous art museums, the Louvre in Paris. My main recollection of being there doesn't involve the Mona Lisa. What I remember most is that I couldn't find a bathroom in the place. So if I was to think really big and start the International ColeSlaw Museum, I would want to have clearly marked restrooms, in several different languages.

It's no use trying to be the first to open a museum featuring antiquities. It's been done many times over. And some efforts have been wasted. Do you remember what happened in Iraq? Those ISIS boneheads blew up everything, destroying thousands of years of history. I'm thinking I'd be safe. Who would find my ColeSlaw Museum objectionable enough to torch it?

Locally here we've had a Lucy and Desi Museum for a number of years. More recently, the National Museum of Comedy opened, and it's a winner. How about a Museum of Losers? I haven't checked on that. Or maybe there's someone in your town for whom to devote a museum? Around our little village, there's just normal folk, and deer. You can forget about a deer museum; Michigan already has got that nailed. Maybe you like groundhogs. I'm guessing Punxsutawney has that one claimed already. On the subject of wildlife and hunting, here's a travel hint to keep in mind: if you're driving around western Canada and get bored looking at fields of grain that stretch from horizon to horizon, plan to stop and nose around the Gopher Hole Museum in Alberta.

How about sports? All popular sports have been taken by a combination museum/hall of fame. I'm sure you're well aware that baseball, basketball, football, golf and soccer have long been claimed. Hockey, too, of course. Tennis has one. So does NASCAR. How about frisbee? Already taken! It's actually called the Disc Golf Museum (huh?) in Columbia County, Georgia. The inventor of the frisbee is credited with being one Ed Headrick, actually a very intelligent dude. And here's one for the books: upon his death, Ed's ashes were put onto a frisbee and flung onto the top of his museum! (Hey, you can't make this stuff up.) If

I had flung it, I probably would have bounced off the side of the building and ol' Ed's ashes would have ended up on the roof of someone's SUV.

What sports are left? How about a dodgeball museum? Guess what? Already claimed. Dominoes? Nope, some guy in South Carolina has already got that one going. West Palm Beach has claimed the Croquet Museum. You might want to consider stopping there after taking the grandkids to Disney World, then compare the two places for excitement. As for wiffle ball, the folks in Connecticut who invented the sport opened that one. Give up?

Don't despair. There's one more sporting event I've researched that may yet be available. Here it is: I haven't found any reference to a National Hide and Seek Museum. Think for a minute; it could include a closet, a big overstuffed armchair, and maybe a dark corner. Kids would love it.

But could anyone find it?

Reading The Paper

I don't know about you, but I still look forward to reading the morning paper. Sure, it costs a lot more than it used to, and there is a lot of junk and ads in it, and it has shrunk dramatically in size. But there's a warm and comforting feeling to have the morning news spread before you while you sip your first cup of coffee. Even on winter mornings when there are icicles hanging from my nostrils, I happily strap on my mukluks and head out to the road to grab the paper.

Last Spring I was in New York City, and took a ride on the subway. I hadn't ridden it for twenty years or more. The last time I was on it, most all the other riders had a New York Times, a Herald Tribune, or a Daily News in hand as the car swayed to and fro. This last time, in a car with maybe forty riders, only one guy was reading a paper. Everyone else was glued to their smartphones. Maybe the guy with the paper was locked into the old days. If so, I admire him.

The world has changed. I get it. But I don't have to like it. Back when I was growing up, reading the paper was a nightly routine in our house. After Dad got home in the evening and ate his meat and potatoes, he'd sit in his easy chair and reach down for the paper. It made for a comforting rustling sound as he changed from page to page. I don't recall if Dad paid much attention to the national or international news. This was back in the Fifties, those long-ago days when people still respected the president. Can you remember back that far? I doubt my dad disagreed with anything President Eisenhower said or did. Maybe he wasn't the only one. My mom would look at the paper briefly, to read her "Brenda Starr" comic strip, and peruse the A&P ads to see if hams were on sale this week. I don't remember if my sisters had much interest in the paper, but then it was my turn. I'd eagerly flip to the sports pages to see how the Dodgers did. After I digested that story by reading through it about three times, then I'd page back to see what was up with

Dick Tracy. We all looked at the paper in the living room, with the radio in the background. It was a warm family routine, a sharing.

Back then there wasn't any other way to catch up on what was happening in the world. Dad, always frugal, had splurged part of his salary in 1954 on a tiny Hallicrafters black and white TV set. If Walter Cronkite had made his debut by then, we didn't know about him. The radio had a few minutes of news on the hour, but that was it. If you weren't listening when the clock struck the hour, you missed it. On the other hand, the Daily News or the Bergen Evening Record had stories you could hold in your hand, study, and digest. You could even re-read them if you wanted to. I vividly remember being absorbed by the dramatic photos in the Daily News of the tragic collision of two passenger liners, the Andrea Doria and the Stockholm, off Block Island in '56. I was eight at the time. The pictures fascinated me.

A lot of the local papers have done a flip-flop from years past. Back in the Fifties and Sixties, the front page would have major national or international stories, with local news stuck in the back. Nowadays people glance at their phones to get the headlines, or get it on their computer. And the TV news programs are on continuously, with the news anchor yapping about one story while one or two other stories are zipping by you on the crawler. Too much information, huh? So our smaller papers focus on what's happening locally, which is a good thing for us to keep up with our neighbors. I guess it's a good move for the paper because they sell extra copies when older folks spot photos of their grandchildren playing soccer.

I've done a flip-flop, too, with the paper. As I mentioned above, as a kid I quickly paged towards the back to get the sports news first. Nowadays I'm first drawn to page two. If I don't see my photo in the obits, I figure I'm good to go with finishing the rest of the paper.

Reading the Times or the Record everyday as a kid also helped with becoming familiar with English grammar, and enhancing spelling skills. That guided me toward one of the greatest achievements in my life. Okay, maybe it wasn't covered in the local paper, but it was a notable moment indeed when yours truly bested Mary Ann Rodgers for being the best speller in Mrs. Lockwood's fourth grade class. I recall it being a nail-biter to the end, but I won out (in the interest of self-disclosure, Gunnar, my life-long friend, has stated that it was he, not me, who took the honors in that memorable contest. I take exception to his claims).

Not too many years ago, while still employed, I entered two spelling bees back when an annual event was held locally. But when it came down to the final round, each time I blew it.

Fortunately, that local story did not make the paper.

The Most Difficult Question

This scenario occurs sooner or later to all of us older folks. You're in the food store, or the Post Office, and you see a guy you once worked with. He waves to you with a friendly smile, and greets you by name. He's younger than you, and still working full time. You recognize his face, but can't remember his name even though you saw him everyday at work. Could his name be Tom? Or Ted? You sense what's coming. After a handshake, he hits you with the most difficult question.

"So, what are you doing with yourself now that you're retired?" Tom or Ted asks. Gulp. Quickly you need to formulate a plan. You have to tell him something that sounds remotely productive. You can't just say you've been walking the dog every morning and spending afternoons watching reruns of Gilligan's Island.

"Well, I'm as busy as I was when I was working full time" you finally stammer, forcing a smile. He responds with a quizzical look, like when a president gets asked a question about an international crisis and avoids it by giving an answer about lower gas prices.

"Well, we have a new puppy and it takes a lot of time to train her." You feel that answer might alleviate the pressure for now. His eyes narrow, realizing you couldn't have had that same puppy for all the years you've been retired. He immediately suspects Alzheimer's.

Meanwhile, you are still trying to figure out whether it's Tom or Ted. Or maybe Tim?

He tries to give you some wiggle room. "I bet you spend a lot of time with your grandchildren, taking them to soccer games and all." You'd love to answer that with a quick "Yes," and move the conversation along to a subject less stressful, like terrorists in the Middle East. But if you answer in the affirmative, he'll follow up with a question on how many grandkids you have. That can get thorny, because you immediately recall that you don't have any grandchildren.

You mumble a "Yeah," and immediately turn the table on him. "So what's happening back at work?" you ask, as if you give a fluff. He tells you how wise you were to retire when you did, and that things aren't as good as they used to be (even though he continually complained about everything when you worked with him). You sense he is ready to unload another tough question on you.

What the heck was his name? He worked in Maintenance. No, wait a minute. Accounting?

I recall a helpful hint that worked once before. It was last spring. I was rudely cornered by another former co-worker as I was picking out a deodorant in the drug store. He had the nerve to ask what I'd been up to. I decided to try it again. Glancing at my watch, I reply "Oops, I gotta go. I have to be at the urologist's office in a couple minutes." That's usually a good firm response to end oppressive questioning, because no one will follow up with "What's the specific problem you have that you are going to a urologist?" They may glance down at your private areas, but they won't ask a thing.

This time it doesn't work. He's still standing there, arms folded. The dude isn't finished. "Doing much traveling?" he asks. Will the friggin' questions ever end? The image of your last trip comes to mind. It was to your mother-in-law's. "Oh, a little," you respond, forcing a smile. "Not to Paris or anything like that." You hope the jocular nature of your response ends the interrogation.

But Tom or Ted or Tim's questions are incessant. "Are you still doing a lot of camping?" he probes. C'mon, what's with him? And how does he know that I camp? Your forehead begins to sweat, and you fantasize about being home, napping in your easy chair.

You decide to pull out all stops and take the initiative. You tell Tom or Ted or Tim "By the way, I've taken up studying quantum physics." Now it's his turn to sport a surprised look. "Oh yeah," I continued, "I picked up a book on it at a garage sale. Spent a buck on it. It was written by some guy who should know about it, because he went to college and all. I haven't started to read it yet, but I have it on my nightstand. I'm gonna get to it next, right after I finish the trashy novel I'm into."

Finally, success. His brow furrows while he stares at me for a few seconds. He looks away, then glances down at his watch and responds in a flat voice. "Wow, look at the time. I have to get back to work."

Whew! I catch my breath. As he walks away, a hazy memory stirs within. His name was Todd.

Why Aren't Campers Happy?

Time and time again we hear about someone who "is not a happy camper." You hear it on TV shows, in conversations, and see it in written articles. Always, there's some negative connotation. But why, I wonder, are campers so unhappy?

I decided to research the subject. It didn't make sense to me, since being in the great outdoors, roasting marshmallows over a crackling campfire while singing "Michael, row the boat ashore" is just about the greatest experience in the world. At first, I couldn't come up with any reasons why campers might be unhappy, despite my having done tent camping for fifty-plus years. I even asked my buddy Johnnyboy, who is a lot older than me, but nothing bad came to mind at first.

After thinking for quite a while, we managed to come up with a few minor annoyances that could make someone less than 100% happy about camping. They include: hordes of mosquitoes attacking every inch of your skin; mud in all your gear, including on your toothbrush; tent zippers that jam at 2 A.M. while getting up for an emergency potty run; pulling a dead branch off a tree, only to be swarmed by angry yellowjackets; noticing that a squirrel has eaten through your pack to get at your stash of trail mix; finding the only roll of toilet paper is soaking wet; waking in the middle of the night to hear primeval grunting sounds outside your tent; campfire smoke so thick and acrid you can't stand near it; a thunderstorm so wicked you have to lie on your belly and hold your tent poles from blowing away; finding that your last pair of dry socks are saturated; the guy in the next tent snoring so loud you can't sleep; reaching in your gear bag and finding a snake; and, oh, did I mention mosquitoes?

So I suppose there are some minor inconveniences that lead campers to be less than thrilled about outdoor adventuring. In my search for truth I decided to check on the web to find how long it has been that campers have been so troubled. No one seems to know when the term "not a happy camper" started. Some say it has been in use for twenty years. As mentioned above, we have done a whole lot of camping, and most of it has been incredibly good. But even in my joyous history of camping, a couple of individual events stand out that may have resulted in my using the "not a happy camper" phrase at the time.

It started back when I was in Boy Scouts. My guys and I were camping on a rainy weekend (as most of them were back then) and started a small campfire right next to our tent late one morning. It was one of those big old canvas wall tents that weighed about a thousand pounds when wet. We were wise enough to remove any flammable stuff that might set the tent afire. Pretty smart, huh? Crouched around the small flames, we were starting to feel dried out from the persistent light rain. Then someone (whose name cannot be revealed) stuck a sealed can of sliced potatoes on the fire. A good warm breakfast, huh? We never gave it a second thought. When that can got hot enough, it burst and sent shrapnel and tater shards all over and through the tent and on everyone. No one was hurt, but rumors abound that there was some unhappiness among the campers, directed at the perpetrator of that incredibly stupid deed. Ahem. . . .

A period of joyous camping ensued after that. But it came to pass on an outdoor venture to a rugged local area that an excess of libation occurred one evening. There were six or seven of us guys out there. Sometime after midnight, my buddy Lavern decided he had had enough, and rolled up into his sleeping bag that starry night. He didn't bother putting his sleeping bag in a tent. Over the course of the night, he rolled down a gentle slope into a drainage ditch. And, yup, it had rained a whole bunch the day before. When morning came, Lavern dragged himself out from his sopping wet bag. That boy was clearly not a happy camper. Years later Lavern went on to have a professional career and earn advanced degrees, but he will always be known to us as the guy who slept in a drainage ditch.

Back in the same place a few years later, once again I was camping with a bunch of guys I will loosely refer to as friends. One night they began pumping me full of a wet greenish fluid they fondly referred to as "melon babies." I downed more than my share, and eventually settled down to sleep in the back of my pickup. Sometime later, that green glob in my stomach started moving from whence it came. In due time, I did the worst thing possible while camping. Yes, I barfed in my sleeping bag. The fact that I had shoulder-length hair and a full beard at the time only made the situation more perilous. I suppose I became an unhappy camper. And it was no comfort to see my fellow "friends" pointing at me while laughing heartily as I dealt with the aftermath.

So perhaps there are a few reasons to report that someone is "not a happy camper." But come springtime, we'll take to the woods again. And the lesson to be learned?

Just say "no" to melon babies.

A Village in France Remembers

Talk about a surprise! This whole thing came out of the blue. It was mid-May. A woman in France wanted to get hold of me. Hmmm. These days not many French gals are showing me much interest. Soon we learned her name is Stéphanie, she is 43, and works as a guide at the Normandy-American Cemetery on the northern coast of France. What is this about, I wondered?

A series of emails followed. I learned she is bilingual, and had read a book entitled <u>The Dust of Angels.</u> I had written fifteen years previously about a fighter pilot who was shot down and killed a few days after the D-Day invasion of France. That occurred in June of 1944. She had become enamored of the story, especially knowing that his crash happened in her little village. She became fully engrossed with it, and wouldn't let go.

The pilot was 2nd Lieutenant Chet Ulrich, my dad's youngest brother, who was shot down by anti-aircraft guns while flying the most advanced American fighter plane of its time, the P-47 Thunderbolt. Minutes before being hit he had successfully completed a bombing mission. Chet was killed three years before I was born, so we had never met. But his life story had unfolded in unusual ways, and I had spent three or four years researching it.

Up until hearing from Stéphanie, my copy of the book had been stashed away for a decade, and I had given little thought to it these last few years. But to her, Chet and his story became an obsession. Before getting hold of me, she had filled a three-ring binder with information on him and his military career. She contacted me because she wanted to know if I had any additional photos of him, or any further background information. I replied that I had some pictures and further knowledge that I would be glad to share with her. But why did she want it?

Stéphanie revealed that on the upcoming 75th anniversary of his tragic death in her little town of Isigny-Sur-Mer, she was planning to do a full program about him. And she wanted to follow that up with a ceremony at the Normandy-American Cemetery, where Uncle Chet is sleeping out eternity. She said she, on behalf of her townspeople, wanted to pay homage to him for giving his life for the freedom of the people of France. I was knocked over.

After sending off the photos, my wife Linda and I sat down over a cup of coffee the next morning. The decision came quickly. We had to go.

On the morning of June 14, Stéphanie met us at the train station in Bayeux, a small French city about twenty miles from her village. One of the first things she did was to drive us to the field where Chet's plane exploded upon impact and burned so many years ago. It is believed that he was mortally wounded in the air after being hit. But in his last fleeting moments of life, he may have aimed his stricken P-47 for this field, to avoid hitting a nearby field hospital crowded with wounded soldiers.

Then we were off to other sites of interest to his heroic story. I wished others in my extended family could have joined us for this once-in-a-lifetime trip, but no one else was able to come along.

After hosting us for dinner at her home with her family, Stéphanie took us to a local community hall where she would be doing her presentation. When Linda and I walked into the building, the sight was startling. About forty local townspeople had given up their Friday night to listen to a one-hour program on this 21-year-old American pilot who had died seventy-five years ago. Amazing! She gave her talk in French while she showed a series of slides about his personal and military life. Everyone was gracious, and several of the people asked pertinent questions about Chet. Although I can speak a little French, the locals either conversed in English, or we relied on another man from the village who was bilingual to translate. It became obvious they were truly interested in Chet as a person. They were not there only to take up seats. At the conclusion of the presentation, the town's mayor presented Linda with a lovely basket of products made locally. Many photos followed. When all was done at the hall, and after a visit to a nearby WW2 museum, we drove to a 15th century manor house, now a delightful Bed 'n Breakfast, where the people of Isigny-Sur-Mer had generously arranged for us to stay at their expense.

The day had been a blur of emotions. We had no idea there was more awaiting us the next afternoon. It was Saturday, June 15, seventy-five years to the day since his fighter plane went down. Stéphanie had arranged that we meet her at the cemetery, where she was working as a guide that day. The afternoon was overcast, with a chilly wind rustling the leaves in this reverent and peaceful place of honor.

Linda and I first spent an hour alone at Uncle Chet's gleaming white cross, one of 9,388 graves of American military heroes, situated on a bluff overlooking Omaha Beach and the English Channel. It gave us time to reflect on a life of great promise, cut tragically short. A few raindrops fell, adding to the somber mood. After the rain was over we were taken to the main memorial statue at the cemetery, where a crowd of about eighty had gathered. All these people! Wow! Once again we were amazed! There Stéphanie opened by giving a brief introduction about Chet. Next the town's mayor brought forth a floral arrangement, which he and I ceremoniously placed at the foot of the bronze statue. After a moment of silence, a three-rifle volley thundered overhead. Then, a bugle played "Taps" as the onlookers stood silently by. I noticed several of them dabbing at their eyes. I sure did.

Linda added tearfully "I kept thinking of your dad, and what he would have thought about his youngest brother being honored this way so many years after his death. He would have swelled with pride and love of family." She was right on.

We all walked solemnly back to his gravesite, where once again Stéphanie offered a thoughtful message about Chet to the folks who continued to be part of our group. Then she pushed two small flags into the hallowed ground in front of his cross; one American and one French. Next she placed his photo at the base of the marker, and invited those present to come forward with their flowers. Linda and I were unaware that so many of the townspeople had brought flowers; at least twenty of them came forward, one at a time, to lay a rose upon his grave. Some were children, some were our age. We were overwhelmed by their thoughtfulness. Stéphanie presented us with the two flags to take home. Brushing away a last tear, we walked quietly away from his gravesite.

And then it was over.

Everyone we spoke with during the three days we spent in Normandy was truly thankful for my uncle giving his life for them. And they were indebted to the millions of other young men from across the sea who fought for their freedom. They knew that Chet was only one among the thousands who made the ultimate sacrifice.

For Linda and I, it was an experience like none other. Indeed, the folks in this village remember.

Beware: This Could Be The Year!

Watch out! This might be the year for your high school reunion! Egad. You may be facing your 40th, 45th, 50th, or even worse. Your gathering may not happen until spring or summer, but don't put it off. Time's a-wasting. Start getting ready now.

If I were you, I'd start with anti-wrinkle cream. I've seen it advertised on the internet, so you know it's effective. Getting rid of facial wrinkles will help make a good first impression when you run into that high school sweetheart you haven't seen since you watched Ed Sullivan on Sunday nights. For those hard to fix wrinkled areas, your family doctor can probably recommend a good plastic surgeon. That doc will make you look even better than you did back in the day when you held a transistor radio to your ear listening to the Ronettes.

If plastic surgery is too much for you, at least show up at your gala looking nicely tanned. Although those of us living up north are at a distinct disadvantage to the Florida crowd, here's something you can do. Go out to your garage, and sit next to your kerosene heater for an hour before you go.

My late buddy Carmen said that when he arrived at his last high school reunion, he glanced in the room and thought he was in the wrong place. There were only old people there! Friends, you need to get ready for the shock of seeing your former cafeteria lunch mates as they look now; all bent over, balding, and with white stuff dripping out of the corners of their mouths.

Remember that star athlete? The pitcher whose fastball was only a blur? When you see him now, you notice his weight exceeds his batting average from high school days. You wonder how in heck he struck you out so many times.

You'll need to dress for your reunion in a way that minimizes the weight you've put on in the last half-century. I recommend you forget buying a fancy suit or dress. If you've had trouble saying "No" to cheesecake and brownies all these years, think about picking out an outfit similar to a blue tarp. But if you want something more stylish, keep in mind they're doing some nice things with burlap these days. Breath control will be important, too. You'll need to make it through the entire evening without exhaling. All the better to impress others with how slim you are, and also to hide that nasty "medicine breath" you've had for the last twenty years. So be ready to pop some Sen-Sens.

And how about that cheerleader who was the queen of the class? And snotty as hell? Could that be her who just walked in? You mosey over, just close enough to glance at her name badge. Yup, it's her. Back in high school she held her nose high and mighty. Now she looks like she got run over by a hay wagon. You smile.

At the reunion dinner, you'll probably sit down at a table with old friends for a full meal. A couple cocktails, an appetizer, maybe a glass of wine, salad, rubber chicken, the works. You'll need to do your utmost to stay awake, at least until dessert is served. Hiding a No-Doz or two in your upper lip will do the trick.

If you're still awake, you'll want to leave the table abruptly when the talk comes round to how many surgeries each of your table-mates have had. Here's how to do it: just jump up, pinch your nose closed, and fan the air vigorously above where your buddy is sitting. Then head for the bar. Hey, who wants to hear about gall bladders anyway?

What really will get you is the dancing. Yup, you'll have to do it. Maybe you'll wait for a slow one, but sooner or later the lure of those old tunes, and the urging of your friends, will get you out on the floor. It's tough to remember which dance step was the Locomotion, which one was the Frug, or which one was the Mouse. Before getting too demonstrative in flailing your arms about, I suggest you make sure the class nerd who became a doctor is nearby, and still awake.

When it's getting close to midnight and folks are tired of doing the Twist, a voice in the crowd will call out your name and urge you to enter the Limbo contest. It's probably someone who never liked you, because friends don't ask friends to do the Limbo. Nope, not at this age.

If you make it through this far, some of the guys will meet outside the main room for "men only" talk. Guys will smile slyly, trying to impress while puffing on expensive cigars. Amid the coughing and the smoke, chatter soon begins about which of the girls still look the best. Then, one of the guys will happen to mention that the business he started is doing very well, and he just opened a new factory. In Mexico. You roll your eyes. Eventually, though, the conversation will change to matters of the highest priority; that being how many times each of you gets up at night to go to the bathroom.

Some of the gals will gather to discuss Facebook photos, bragging about grandchildren who are about to get their PhDs from Harvard, or who just took an executive position with a tech giant. On the other hand, there are those of us who prefer to show photos of our dogs.

Someone will take out a class yearbook and mention that the guy who was most likely to succeed didn't make it tonight. Another follows up by saying he'll be out of the state pen by the next reunion. Then there is the girl who was a wallflower. Hardly anyone knew her, she was so timid and shy. Now she is radiant, looking years younger than all the others. Yay for her!

You've got to get ready if this is your year. I wanted to be the first to warn you.

Would You Drive a Cow?

Back in the Fifties and Sixties there were only a few car choices offered down at the local new car showrooms. Ford and Chevy were the biggest sellers, Plymouth a distant third, and not much else after that. Almost all of them were made in the USA, and even Grandma was familiar with the names of the models, since there were only a relatively few, and they had catchy, exciting names.

You remember them; first there were cars named after speedy animals: the Chevy Impala and the Ford Mustang come to mind. Mustang gives the image of being wild, fast and free. That was clearly a better horse name than a Clydesdale, which sounds huge, ungainly, and slow. Not a good name for a sports car. I'm not sure if the Plymouth Fury was named after a horse on TV, or a stormy day. The Ford Thunderbird fits in there somewhere. Studebaker Hawk comes to mind, too. So does the Eagle. Powerful sleek birds were OK for car manufacturers but I don't recall any named the Buick Buzzard or the Chrysler Goose. It's the image that sells cars.

In the last couple of decades, with the proliferation of foreign manufacturers selling in the U.S., and countless new models, companies have had to expand their naming horizons. It didn't take long before they ran out of animal names that had the desired combined image of speed and power to go with a melodic name. Indeed, it would be a struggle for the marketing people if the Chevrolet Cow or the Plymouth Possum were in the showroom. Would you be impressed watching a commercial during a football game showing a powerful pickup truck, the Nissan Rattlesnake?

There were also models named after exotic places, like the Dodge Daytona, the Buick Riviera, and the Parisienne. Even the New Yorker was on the road. Soon, though, all the "easy" exotic places had been named. So they went to some back-up locations, which still sounded pretty good, like the Montana, Dakota, Tacoma, and the Santa Fe. Not bad. But once again, eventually the neat-sounding locations had all been picked over. Industry leaders would have their hands full making the Honda Harrisburg or the Audi Bakersfield sound melodious and sporty.

The next big push was for initials. For some reason, Z, X, and S must have had the best mix of mystery and masculinity, as there was no shortage of vehicle models using those letters. I guess the Jaguar "XKE" sounded more sporty than the "YY." Those more powerful letters sur-faced due to research in advertising. If market research had been started back when old Henry Ford came out with the "Model T," he might have named that first production automobile the "ZK-38." Would he have sold more cars?

During the Fifties, high-falutin' luxury names were popular. The Town Car, the Coupe De Ville, the Silver Shadow, and the Ambassador all had their time in the sun. Diplomat, too. Today it just wouldn't seem right to see someone drive up in something ultra-glitzy called a Cadillac Conglomerate, Lincoln Lobbyist, or Oldsmobile Watergate. (Oops, for-get about the Olds . . they went the way of the Studebaker).

Another more recent phenomenon has had manufacturers com-ing up with upscale futuristic-sounding names, such as the Saturn, the Quest, the Infiniti, the Vision, the Horizon, and of course, the Smart car. I suppose sales would drop off if their names were the Toyota Yesterday, the Kia Relic, or the Subaru Mediocre.

Exciting professions got their chance, too, with the Ford Explorer, the Lincoln Navigator, Mercury Mountaineer, the Ford Ranger and the Astro van. I think Pilot was used, too. And Forester. Even a Matador. No one at the top of GM probably would think the Chevrolet Social Worker would be a big seller, though. It just doesn't have the right ring to it. Nor would the Acura Accountant.

With all these visions, letters, numbers and names already being used up, what does the future hold? China is eager to sell cars here. Rus-sia, too. Maybe even Finland and Zanzibar. And the top auto producers want to change model names every few years to keep their products sounding fresh and new. So, be advised there's a critical shortage of car model names out there. They've gone to totally made-up names. The Camry, the Alero, the Jetta, the list goes on and on. What the heck is a Passat? It sounds like a cat that got pancaked by an 18-wheeler.

Or maybe car models in the future will become like computer passwords; auto manufacturers may let buyers come up with their own password model names, one that only they will know. That would make it tough on police trying to track down a stolen car.

Here I am once again being old-fashioned. Give me a Mustang to drive. It sounds more exciting than a Ridgeline.

Requiem for a Railroad

The "Gateway Pass" was not one of those fancy model train layouts you might have seen featured in the railroad hobby magazines. Perhaps years ago it could have been, but George was not that way. At 84, George was supremely content to run his long trains around the sweeping curves of his huge 12' by 40' H.O.-gauge layout in the damp basement of his rambling old home, tucked away in Pennsylvania's rural northwest. George was short in stature; if you were taller, you needed to guide your head between the floor joists as you walked through. Lighting consisted of widely-spaced 25-watt bulbs. Cobwebs hung down in ragged bouquets. During long Pennsylvania winters, it was downright chilly, with wind sneaking in between cracks in the hundred-year-old block wall. Sure, it was a bit musty too, but if George noticed any of these minor conveniences, he never said so. You see, spending hours with trains had been in his blood for seventy years or more; he'd even put in a brief stint with the real locomotives, shoveling coal on the Pittsburgh and West Virginia Railroad steamers many years back.

A classy, low-keyed, and truly delightful gentleman, George years ago had opened his layout each Monday evening to all who wished to join in. The basement fairly bustled then, as George did his best to help young boys develop an interest in model railroading. Steam power was the order of the day; since those new-fangled diesels were not permitted to turn a wheel on George's railroad.

Slowly and inevitably, the years changed the Gateway Pass. The loud excitement of Monday's club nights now was but a memory. George's three children grew up and moved far away. His wife was busy with community activities almost every night. Each evening after supper George would head to the basement to spend a few hours tinkering with his passion. Those few fortunate folks like me who visited his railroad might notice the plastic buildings were coated with dust. Painted background scenery on the old block walls had faded and was rife with water stains. George would laugh about the spider webs that clung to the front of his beloved steam engines after they'd gone through a tunnel. Old eyes didn't mind time's changes.

George's evenings were spent downstairs in Molesville, as he called it. Once he turned on the power to the tracks, he'd grin widely, toot the whistle twice, and instruct his H.O.-scale engineer, "Harry," to get the Gateway Pass Limited out of the depot on time.

One day a few years ago, George took a nap on his living room couch, and never got up. The Gateway Pass was silenced; its owner gone to glory. As a friend of the family, I volunteered to liquidate his railroad assets and dismantle his layout. Thus, at a train show a few months later, George's beloved steam engines, cars, and buildings were sold off piecemeal to bargain hunters, each unaware they were taking home a part of a man's life and dreams.

Dismantling the Gateway Pass proved to be a formidable and gut-wrenching task. He had built it carefully and solidly. With each thrust of the pry bar, another section of trackwork was loosened. Feeling like I was breaking windows in church, I thought of George continuously; silently apologizing to him with each thrust of the hammer. Plaster-of-Paris mountains came apart in explosions of dust. Bundles of wiring hung down uselessly. With each rumble of the reciprocating saw, another wooden support tumbled to the concrete floor. Eventually, the job was completed. A few pieces were salvaged, but much of his layout ended up in a junk pile. Sorry, George.

On his wife's piano, you could still see a photograph of George's ear-to-ear smile, as he sat behind the control panel of the Gateway Pass. Alas, nothing else of his railroad remains. That is, except for late at night in the dark and empty basement. If you listen closely you can hear two toots on the whistle. Rest easily, George. Harry has the Gateway Pass Limited out of the depot on time.

Sound Familiar?

I've heard you say it, too. "Geez, I wish I was in better shape!" When we look back at photos of us from years past, we notice a different body shape than today's. We were trimmer, probably because we were more physically active. How about you? You looked pretty good then too, huh?

Staying in some kind of shape through the years has been challenging. When we were young, we didn't even think about "being in shape." It just happened normally. We guys played a lot of ball, rode our bikes, and kept busy doing whatever chores mom and dad said we needed to do. School days were active, too: gym class and all. You young girls rode bikes and kept busy also. Once marriage and delivering babies began, you gals faced a greater challenge than us menfolk. Perhaps an even bigger roadblock was having the time available to involve in active exercise when your little curtain-climbers were zipping around the house tossing your pots and pans about.

Through the years, various attempts I've made at staying physically active have proven less than fruitful. I'll go through a bunch of them. In the early Seventies downhill skiing seemed like the way to go. Fast, exciting, colorful, and glitzy. My bud Howie likes to tell about the first time we were on downhill skis. We had been out of college for a few years, and feeling adventurous. It was at a popular ski area about an hour from where I was living at the time. After renting skis and strapping on those twenty-pound boots that cut off all circulation below your ankles, we stumbled around laughing at each other. The renter guys directed us to the beginners area. Yup, the bunny slope. We felt embarrassed to start our skiing careers amid the five-year-olds wearing their Smokey the Bear hats, their fathers running alongside of them, encouraging them onward. I give Howie credit; he did amazingly well for a gawky dude, but I was borderline out of control, legs wide, skis pointing outward when I tried to stop. Enough of that; I needed a bigger challenge. More speed would help me stop, I reasoned.

We lined up for the "t-bar" to take us up one of the big-boy slopes. For those of you not familiar with a t-bar lift, it is this curved piece of metal that hangs down (roughly in the shape of a "t') connected to an overhead cable whereby a machine whisks you up to the top of the slope. No problem, right? Well, I'd never seen one before, and I heard no instructions as we waited to get on. I was super-charged, too excitedly chatting to pay attention to directions anyway. I remember it being a sunny winter Saturday morning, with maybe two feet of snow everywhere, and a Kodak sky. A perfect day for skiing, and the lines were crowded. We had to wait our turn, and then grab onto the t-bar in motion as it headed up the slope. Many skiers were in line behind me. When it was my turn, I grabbed onto it, and sat down on the t-bar. That's when things really turned south. You weren't supposed to sit on it. Who knew? When I put my weight on it, there was nothing to support me, and I immediately fell on my back, right in the t-bar line, my skis askew and me facing upward toward the blue sky. The lift operators stopped the t-bar machine. That got the other waiting skiers grumbling. I gathered myself, recovered my poles, stood up, and motioned confidently to the operators to start it again. When they got the cable moving, once again I tried to sit on the t-bar. And once again I immediately fell, causing the operators to stop the lift once more. I heard irritated cries from other skiers anxious to get up the trail, admonishing me to "go home," and "get off the slopes" (those being the most thoughtful of the comments). The two lift operators, angry now, hustled over to me. One grabbed my arms as I lay prone, the other grabbed my ankles, lifted me up, and threw me, skis and all, over a snowbank. Right about then I'm thinking this skiing thing isn't what it's all cracked up to be. Ol' Howie almost fell over laughing. In fact, now fifty years later he still has conniptions laughing about it.

In the mid-Eighties, running became very popular. For some inexplicable reason, I took it up. I did fairly well at it; I would start jogging in Pennsylvania, run up through New York state, then finish up back in

Pennsylvania. Fortunately, Linda and I live only a quarter mile from the state line, so I only had to jog a half mile to complete that run. To others, it sounded like I was a real road warrior. Try as I might, I never was able to experience that elusive "runner's high" that was supposed to anoint me with vigor, peace and mindfulness. It was time to try something else.

Around '93 the hospital where I worked offered a Wellness program to do aerobics after work. Why not? Aerobics were the rage, the music was rockin', and it looked like fun. It also afforded me the opportunity to see the girls I worked with jumping around in their underwear. What I didn't account for was all the stretching that was part of the routine. Jeez, that was hard. My grunts echoed off the walls. I hung with that for a few years until the aerobics class lost its fancy. Then I gave yoga a brief but unsuccessful try. Very brief. Yoga took stretching to a whole new level of torture. Water-boarding couldn't be that painful. Nope, scratch yoga off the list.

When I was in my early fifties I thought it was time to join an athletic club to work out regularly. The YMCA was where most of the guys went to lift and use exercise machines. But it was located too far out of the way for me. There was, however, a small club not far from work, where I could go directly after work, thereby not allowing myself the opportunity to come up with excuses to skip the workout. Otherwise my thoughts might be "I wonder what kind of birds are at our feeder this afternoon?" or other weighty reasons to hurry home and relax on the porch with a cold drink.

There wasn't as much stretching at the athletic club, but Sue, who ran the club, had her own brand of torture. You had to lift these heavy hunks of scrap metal in every possible direction. Then, while you were lying there straining with gobs of perspiration running down your forehead, in the most vulnerable position possible, she would let you have it with a verbal barrage of how many vegetables you should be eating. The woman was a Veggie Vigilante. "No hot dogs!" she'd warn. "And no french fries!" She had to be a stockholder in a broccoli company.

One thing that I quickly learned was never to look over to the next guy who was doing a similar exercise. I'd be on my back, struggling with weights roughly equivalent to that of a Campbell's soup can in each hand. The guy next to me looked like he was lifting the engine from a Buick. Even a quick glance can do untold damage to the fragile male ego.

If you kept your membership up for a year, she would award you a t-shirt with the name of her Athletic Club proudly displayed on the front. Sue gave me mine, but requested that I not wear it in public. With my pathetic body she feared it would look bad for her business.

Maybe I'm running out of time. My next plan is to go down to the local nursing home and join their intramural bedpan league.

Just A Stroke of Luck?

The summer of 2010 was one of the hottest on record for us up north. Down south it was even hotter. Mid-July in Charleston, South Carolina brought 90-plus degrees. Linda and I had gone down to that historic old city to visit family. Thick humidity blanketed us every day. One such day at noon we were in downtown Charleston with my nephew Mike. The mercury hit 95 as we hustled down the crowded sidewalk to a computer store. Despite the humidity, I had been feeling fine. So good, in fact, that the day previously we spent hours hiking through the Francis Marion State Forest, located just north of the city.

Once inside the store, I leaned against a counter as Mike helped Linda answer computer questions. I'm not sure exactly when, but I began to feel "spacey." Without realizing it, I dropped my backpack to the floor. Nothing unusual about that. But when my glasses slipped out of my hand and fell to the floor, Linda turned to me with a scowl. Then she noticed a facial droop on my right side. She reached over. My right arm hung weakly. My right leg couldn't support my weight. She realized I was having a stroke.

Mike ran to the store manager to have him call 9-1-1. Meanwhile, Linda sat me down on a stool. In minutes there was a commotion outside the store. I saw a fire truck at the front door. Still spacey, I thought there must be a fire across the street. Then, firefighters came running right toward me. Soon an ambulance crew relieved them and began prodding. Minutes later I was wheeled out of the store in a gurney to the ambulance. I remember glancing up at the crowded street and feeling bad because emergency vehicles had backed traffic up during the busy noontime rush. I was rushed six or eight blocks to one of the most prominent stroke centers in the South.

Up until that event, I had been proud of my physical condition. Every morning I had been taking long walks with the dog. Linda and

I had been bicycling regularly. We had done canoeing and volleyball only weeks before. Of the eight major risk factors for a stroke, I had zero. At age 62, I was not taking any medications. But all that meant nothing. Today in Charleston I was experiencing a major stroke. Having a stroke means that a blood clot has blocked the flow of blood to the brain. Severe strokes often lead to serious life-long disabilities, or even death. The docs rated me 9 out of 10 on the scale of severity. Has my time come?

The emergency room had been alerted and was ready for me. Several specialists were waiting. Linda was told I might need surgery to break up the blood clot. The operating room was readied. They would first try a clot-busting wonder drug injection called TPA. Linda was told I had only a 30% chance that it would be effective, given the severity and location of the stroke. Meanwhile, urgent phone calls were made. Family and friends began praying for me. Even some folks I hardly knew dropped to their knees.

Waiting for the injection, and while lying on an ER bed, the doctor showed me a ballpoint pen. He asked me what it was. I couldn't get the words out. I tried to tell him it was something to write with, but those words couldn't make it out of my mouth either. Next he pointed to his wristwatch, and asked me what it was. Again, the words wouldn't come. In my mind, I knew what it was, but the words were stuck somewhere between my brain and my lips. I tried apologizing to the doc for not being able to answer, but I suppose I was babbling.

Soon the docs began the injection. Two hours had elapsed since the noontime stroke. Within thirty minutes of receiving the wonder drug, I once again began being able to express myself. Strength returned to my arms and legs.

Two doctors returned to my bedside. They asked me the same questions as before. This time when I answered, they nodded approvingly. Linda knew I was in a recovery mode when I asked for pen and paper. I needed to write down this experience while it was fresh in my mind.

Later that afternoon I was admitted and moved upstairs to a hospital room. Every fifteen minutes through the night I would be awakened, and the nurse would ask me where I was. She'd follow by asking me if I knew what happened. Then she'd test strength in my arms and legs. I'd be rolled down the hallway to get MRIs, CAT scans, and lab tests. My recovery continued. The doc appeared in the middle of the night, and called my recovery "amazing." He said I was a "poster boy for TPA." But why did I have a stroke when I didn't have any of the risk factors?

During my second night in the hospital my heart monitor started beeping oddly. It revealed that I had developed a periodic heartbeat disorder that more than likely caused the stroke. The docs were glad to have found the cause. I had something I had never heard of called atrial fibrillation.

Within three or four days of leaving the hospital and beginning on a blood-thinning medication, I was on my way home to Pennsylvania. Linda even let me drive part of the way. Sometime on that long road home, I realized I had become the beneficiary of a miracle.

In retrospect, I had never considered that I would have a stroke. I considered myself to be in the best of health. Others who knew me thought the same. But still it happened. I learned strokes can occur to anyone. Risk factors include smoking, being overweight, having diabetes, heart disease and high cholesterol. Lack of exercise, alcoholism, drug abuse, and family history of strokes also increase one's likelihood of having a stroke. I had none of those factors.

Those of you who fit any of those categories need to be aware of potential strokes, and share those concerns with your physician. And if you are over 55, the likelihood of a stroke increases; even more so for folks at age 65. It also is wise for all of us to recognize the signs that someone else is having a stroke; facial droop, weakness in one side of the body, and being unable to express oneself clearly are just a few of the signs. Once signs of a stroke are suspected, it is critically important to contact 9-1-1 immediately, and to get the person to a hospital. The miracle drug injection that worked for me, I learned, is only effective if it is administered within three hours of the onset of the stroke. For those living in a rural area, that time can go by mighty fast before reaching a treatment facility able to administer the drug.

So what have I learned since that close call with a severe stroke? First of all, to be thankful for every day and every simple blessing that comes my way. Secondly, I am most appreciative of the skill and compassion of first responders and medical professionals. And I'm indebted to Linda and others who were doing all they could while on the sidelines.

But was it just "luck" that my stroke occurred when I was within a few city blocks of a leading stroke center? Or that Linda quickly identified it as a stroke? Was it luck that the medical staff was ready to treat me with the best of medications? Or was there another reason?

The answer, I suspect, lies far deeper than a simple stroke of luck.

Preserving The Signs of Our Times

Lately you hear a lot about people making a "bucket list." Just in case you've been trekking through Greenland for the last ten years and haven't heard, it's a list of things folks want to accomplish before they go "boots up." One of the most important pursuits on my bucket list is a desire to preserve signs of historic value. You can find signs like this along a highway, on an old building, in an old railroad station, or just about anywhere. One of the best I've seen was a political sign, "Mudd for Montana," out west. Sounds great, huh? But the dang thing was out of reach, way up on a pole and is probably still hanging there. Only a few years ago, a fellow named Ulysses S. Grant was running for office in Virginia. I'm not kidding. That sign was crying out to be preserved, and indeed it was. I'm not sure how many signs I could fit in a bucket, but I'm still working on it.

As you may have determined, I have been known to remove a sign from its original placement to mount it in a more secure location for future generations to appreciate. It's just a service I'm doing for humankind, and I don't need any special recognition for it. That new location may include historically significant places like our garage, the basement, or our screened-in porch. It also may include passing them along to a history-minded buddy (to safeguard his identity, we'll call him "Al"). Al has a museum in the basement of his home. Al's focus is on political memorabilia. He is a nut on preservation too, and has even removed classic political signs from their perch in Ireland, brought them home as carry-on luggage, and preserved them in his museum. For that he won the first annual International Sign Preservation Award.

Me, I have never acquired a sign from outside of the U.S. The closest I came to an international preservation was when we were in Hawaii eons ago. While leisurely strolling across a golf course, I came upon a sign that was literally crying out to be saved forever. What made it attractive to a preservationist of my caliber was that it was written in both English and Japanese. This was no run-of-the mill metal sign. Guys, this baby was granite. Could I possibly haul it home? Fortunately, this all happened years before 9/11, back when you could carry a samurai sword onto a plane. If memory serves, hauling that sucker through the long corridors of the Honolulu airport in a duffel bag was enough to lengthen my right arm by about four inches.

As mentioned above, Al's specialty is the saving of important political signs. And it's become an activity that brings his whole family closer. You see, together with his sons and daughter, they have perfected the "Barf and Grab" process. When Al sees a sign in need of preservation, he pulls his van over near the trophy in question. Then "Dave" or "Mike" jump out and feign stomach sickness when other cars are approaching. As soon as the coast is clear, they make their move and ready the sign for eternal preservation. Even his daughter "Amy" has developed similar skills. As we all know, the family that grabs together, stays together.

There are other signs we pass by every day, but are not of sufficient import to be selected for preservation. Although they may indicate one thing, they really mean another. For instance, have you driven through a town and seen a sign that reads "Historic District," with an arrow? You'd best avoid going that way. Why? It simply is pointing to the sleazy, run-down part of town. Or how about the one that reads "No Through Traffic." That one actually points to a shortcut to avoid red lights, but the town residents don't want you or any other outsiders to know about it. Or what about the sign you see everywhere that reads "Bridge Freezes Before Road Surface." Not only do you see them up north, but you see them in places like Louisiana and Florida. Listen, friends, if you don't know by now that bridges freeze when the temperature drops, you shouldn't be driving. It's sort of like saying "Ice May Be Slippery." I've done considerable research on this particular subject, and if they were to take all those "Bridge Freezes" signs down and line them up next to one another, they would make a line that would stretch from Camden, New Jersey to Standing Water, South Dakota.

One more thing about signs; they really have changed a lot over the years. Back when you and I were young, if your dad was driving down a road and you saw a sign on a building that said "Schenectady Chair Company," providing you could pronounce it, you knew you were in Schenectady, New York, and you knew what they made. Today you could pass a similar building and it might say "Horizon Products." Does that mean you're at the horizon? Could you be approaching the Twilight Zone? And what the heck do they make? Are they too embarrassed? Another one that kills me is when you're driving down an interstate and you get passed by a speeding truck that reads "Innovative Logistics" in big letters. Years ago, that one would have read "Ralph's Trucking Company." Wasn't that simpler? Or how about when you go through a big city, and a huge building has a sign on it that says "AGFA". Now what the heck is that? Can't they tell you what they really do in there? Maybe they don't know? Maybe they don't want you to know?

It's no wonder no one stops to do a "Barf and Grab" on an AGFA sign, even if it was within reach. And, heck, it wouldn't fit in your bucket anyway.

Our Window Tapper

Birds. They're lovely; fascinating to watch. Linda and I are not true "birders" in that we don't travel to distant forests to glimpse that elusive Two-headed Teal Ratbird. Nope. We just like watching them at our feeder and at the ponds, but right now I'm talking about one individual winged creature.

We "lovingly" call him Mr. Cardinally. Yes, he's a bright red male cardinal and to many people this dude is a beautiful example of birdhood. He is all of that, I admit. But there's more to the story. It began three years ago in the spring when he would tap on our windows occasionally. That was okay, since after reading about him we learned he was either trying to protect his nest, or trying to ward off other male cardinals whom he saw as a threat in his window reflection. I got it. We allowed him to do his occasional tapping, expecting it would soon stop when he tired of it, when nesting season was over, or when his beak finally fell off.

Well, spring turned into summer, then into autumn. The tapping continued, increasing in frequency; intensity too. Then it was winter. Although it might have been ten above with snow blowing fiercely, that didn't deter him from his daily routine. Tap. Tap. Tap. It got annoying. He's still at it.

Yes, we did all the regular stuff. We tried turning lights on and off, mounting a fake owl in the window, hanging aluminum foil near the windows, making faces at him through the closed window, telling cruel jokes about Mrs. Cardinally, yadda yadda yadda. Everyone on the internet seemed to have their own correct answer, but nothing has kept Mr. Cardinally from beginning his tapping at first light. In the winter, it was around 7; in summer it's 5:30. It goes on all day till early evening, every day. Almost all windows are fair game; basement and all.

To get inside this dude's little bird brain, I'm thinking his day goes something like this. Mrs. Cardinally wakes him dutifully at the first hint of morning, and sends him out early to fetch a few dried up whatevers clinging to our plants and trees this time of year. He brings the breakfast back to the nest, then readies for the day's work. "Today I need to keep working on my window tapping; it's just something I gotta do" he tells her as he flies off, aiming for our house. "Don't be late for dinner!" she chirps. "And remember we're having Charlie and Chelsea Chickadee over for sunflower seed casserole." Hubby only nodded as he squeezed off a few white droplets over our truck, heading toward our windows. His plan was to attack the bedroom windows first, since it was now getting light and he wanted to leave his timely wake-up marks on the glass, and to assure no one overslept.

If you want to know the truth, Mrs. Cardinally has been worrying about him. She thinks he spends too much time attacking the windows, and not enough time doing improvements to their nest. "We could use some more dried grass," she reminds him almost daily. But he's oblivious. Obsessed. And he has virtually no time for the baby chirper she's nesting. Recently she's noticed that his beak is not as sharp as it used to be, but hesitates to tell him. She heard there might be a special herb to help, but he may be too embarrassed to try it. And his crown has virtually disappeared. She wonders if he's drinking too much puddle water. One of the blue jays at a neighboring nest loudly spreads rumors that Mr. Cardinally is developing a case of CTB, the brain damage that pro football players get from too much head-banging. Personally, I think the blue jay is right. But how to intervene in a therapeutic fashion, rather than using a .22 ?

We've checked out a passel of suggestions. One bright idea I've seen is to cover all windows with newspaper. I agree that it would likely keep Mr. Cardinally at bay, but would make the house look like we were hiding a meth lab. Same as the suggestion to put plywood over the windows. Who comes up with these ideas? I saw an advertisement to buy "bird repellent spikes" at $31 a package. That sounds like a good deal for the guy who is selling them. Mounting aluminum foil didn't work for us, so buying "metallic bird tape" probably won't faze Mr. Cardinally either. Another idea is to "soap your windows." I thought that should only happen on Hallowe'en. I'll file that suggestion away, along with the one that says "keep your windows dirty." Hey, we live on a dirt road that produces clouds of dust with every pickup truck that barrels by. Our windows rarely ever stay clean, despite Linda's determined efforts.

Another suggestion is to run sprinklers over your windows. All our windows? For 16 hours a day? Our well will dry up. One of the more low-key ideas is to "be patient; wait for breeding season to end." That won't work for Mr. Cardinally, who apparently knows no end to the breeding season.

One site that lists suggestions on how to deal with problem birds gently finishes by reminding the world that "birds should never be harmed." Well, I agree with that in principle, but I must confess I've had numerous fantasies about this flying critter and how to counter his incessant tapping. One of them involves my throwing him in a microwave for thirty seconds on high, just to teach him a lesson.

Mr. Cardinally, be ye warned!

Thanksgiving Traveling: A Look Back

Every year we hear the same news story. Millions of Americans will be traveling over Thanksgiving. Today, flying and driving are the way to go. But what about in years past? Let's journey back in time to 1931.

The full effects of the Depression were hitting hard throughout most of the country back then. Few families had autos. For those who did, gas money was hard to come by. Most intercity travel, if you could afford it, was by train. Flying was in its infancy, and perilous indeed.

Warren, Pennsylvania, is located in the northwest part of the state. A town of some 20,000 souls, it's situated about 400 miles from New York City. Let's replay what it would have been like if you were planning to travel from there to New York City for the holiday.

It's Wednesday evening. Tomorrow is Thanksgiving. It's blustery and biting cold in Warren. A few inches of snow are on the ground. Due to the weather, your next door neighbor offers to drive you to the depot in his big Nash on his way to work. Once again you re-read the note from Aunt Jo and Uncle Harry inviting you to visit them in New York City over the holiday weekend. "We'll meet you at Macy's Parade, then we'll go to our apartment for a turkey dinner. And pumpkin pie for dessert!"

You shivered as the sedan slowly made its way to the Pennsylvania Railroad station, over on the west side of town. You checked your pocket watch as you approached the depot. A quarter past eight. You had at least fifteen minutes before train time. You waved a thanks and a goodbye as the car pulled away. After stomping the snow off your boots, you struggled to open the heavy oak door into the waiting room. As soon as you entered, you felt the welcoming blast from the coal stove in the corner. You were glad you had spent a few extra dollars and bought a ticket good for a sleeping car. You set your suitcase down next to the dark-stained oak bench. Pulling the schedule out of your pocket, you see the train left Erie two hours ago. It was called the Southern Express, Pennsylvania Railroad train #580. Minutes later you heard the soft chuff-chuff-chuff of the steam engine approaching as it slowed for the depot. The Pennsy was right on time.

With excitement anew, you hustled outside onto the concrete platform. The damp cold off the Allegheny River was bracing. Moments after the train screeched to a halt, you glanced at the pulsing black locomotive that was now blocking Pennsylvania Avenue amid a cloud of sweet-smelling coal smoke. Mesmerized by the panting and wheezing engine, you walked toward it, and noticed the number 1120 in gold paint on the side of its cab. A half dozen dark red passenger cars curved around behind the engine. The ding-ding-ding of the crossing gates filled the air. The conductor, a silver-haired man in his 70's, looked immaculate in his gold-trimmed black uniform. He helped you up, as you climbed the four stairs with your suitcase. You then stowed it on an overhead rack. Although the car lights were dim, you had no trouble finding a seat. Due to holiday traveling, the car was nearly full. Its steam heat had the temperature plenty warm. You removed your overcoat and took a window seat next to a prim white-haired lady. Later you learned she was from Corry and was traveling to Harrisburg to spend the holiday with her daughter. Soon the conductor called out "All Aboard," and moments later you felt a gentle tug as the train pulled away from the depot. You settled into your plush velour seat and introduced yourself to the lady. The engine's exhaust quickened and you heard the clank-clank-clank as the train rumbled across the Allegheny on the steel trestle.

In a half hour there was a brief station stop at Sheffield, then later you could feel the train slow as the engine labored up the long winding grade toward Kane. At each highway intersection, the gates were down and warning bells were ringing. The flurries had ended. In the moonlight, you could see the snow had deepened. The porter came through and pulled down the beds. You climbed in, and felt warm under the tan wool Pullman blanket. It was almost 11 by the time the well-lit St. Mary's depot came into view.

The rhythmic rocking of the heavy car made it tough to keep the eyelids open. Soon you were fast asleep as the train continued through the darkness past Driftwood, Renovo, Lock Haven, and tiny settlements along the Susquehanna River. Sometime later you felt the train stop. You rolled over and peeked out the window. Rubbing the sleep out of your eyes, you noticed you were in the dimly-lit train shed of the Harrisburg station. It was 5 AM. Then again you dozed. You hadn't realized the steam engine had been replaced by electric power.

"We just left Lancaster," commented the porter as you passed him in the narrow aisle. It was time for coffee. You walked through two cars, getting a blast of cold air as you stepped between the rumbling cars. Although still dark outside, the lights shined brightly in the dining car, amid the fragrant aroma of coffee and bacon. The steward, a white-jacketed, cheerful black man, pointed you to a seat at a tiny table and asked you to write down your order on his pad. "Can I pour you some eye-opener this Thanksgiving morning?" he offered, grinning widely.

After a delightful plate of eggs, toast, bacon, juice and coffee, you returned to your seat, since the porter had now taken up the bed. Philadelphia was soon behind, and the train gathered speed in the last gray moments of dawn as it headed north towards New York.

You glanced at the headlines in the Inquirer, then nodded off again. When your eyes opened you were crossing the wide flatlands of the Jersey meadows. In the distance, you could see the sun reflecting off the top stories of the huge Empire State Building, which opened only six months ago. Then the speeding train ducked down into a long black tunnel under the Hudson River.

After a brief ray of sunlight, you were in the darkness of the chasms below Penn Station. As the train gently pulled to a halt, you grabbed your suitcase down and stepped out onto the platform. The underground station was chilly and damp. After climbing the stairs to street level, you noticed as you made your way through the holiday throng that your train had arrived on time, just before 9:30. You turned up your collar at the crisp morning wind, but the atmosphere was festive as you walked crosstown the three blocks to Fifth Avenue, following streams of parade-goers.

Before this, you'd only seen photographs of Macy's Thanksgiving Day Parade, and now you were actually here, on 42nd Street, enjoying it all in person! To add to your holiday thrill, you'll soon be seeing the smiling faces of two very special people, Aunt Jo and Uncle Harry.

You were mighty glad you decided to make the trip here from Warren!

The 700 Pound Gator

I saw a news photo showing some guys in Mississippi who landed a record 730 pound alligator. You probably saw it, too. The darn gator was huge and ugly. It looked like a dinosaur on steroids. In reading the article, the most amazing thing to me was that these guys were out hunting gators in the middle of the night, latched onto the big one, and decided they needed help to land it. So they called a buddy or two in the middle of the night to come help them, and, amazingly, they showed up to help! Makes you wonder how many phone calls they made before someone actually appeared. Perhaps one of those calls went something like this:

"Hey Boonie, this is Lem. Sorry it's the middle of the night, and you can tell I'm out of breath, but you won't believe this! Me and Red are out in the river, and we just shot this huge gator. The dang thing must be thirteen feet long and weighs maybe 700 pounds. It looks mean as heck. I think he's done for, but we're not sure if he's dead. We need you to come down and help us pull it in to shore."

Silence.

"Boonie, are you there?"

"Yeah, Lem, by the way, what time is it?"

"Three A.M. Whatcha doing?"

"I guess I fell asleep in my chair watching Hollywood Squares."

Lem is adamant. "We need you down here right away! It's one helluva huge gator!"

"Oh dang," Boonie replies, then hesitates. "I'd like to help you guys out, but I just remembered tomorrow is Aunt Clara's birthday, and I should run down to the convenience store and get her a card."

"At 3 A.M.? A card? You gotta be kidding me."

"Yeah, but this is a special birthday. It's her 93rd."

"Boonie, there's an all-night store right on the way to Pokie's Dock. You can pick up the darn card, jump in your jon-boat, and meet us in the middle of the river. Then you can help us pull this whopper of a gator into shore."

"Are ya sure it's not too cold out?"

"No, Boonie, it's humid as heck, and hauling in this monster gator will keep you plenty warm!"

"Dang it, Lem, I just thought of something else. I promised Ernestine I'd make up a big pot of sauerkraut for her."

"At 3 A.M.? And didn't you tell me she left you last week and took up with that plumber guy?

"Well, she did, but if she comes back, I really ought to have a pot of fresh kraut ready."

"Boonie, you ain't wimping out on me and Red, are you? This is one heckuva big gator, and he may be mad as hell being nailed. I think he still has one eye open."

"Me a wimp? Heck no, no one calls Boonie no wimp. Where exactly are you?"

"Drive down to Pokie's right away, and we're straight out from there. You can see us waving our flashlights. Don't come behind our boat, because the gator is there. He may be chomping at the bit to get loose."

"Durnit, Lem. Just remembered I can't get there. The Chevy is at the shop. Got a bad modulator or something."

"What about your pickup?"

"Uhhh . . .Ernestine took it."

"And the Harley?"

"The plumber took it."

"Boonie, you're wimping out. We need you right away!"

"Lem, what about you calling Melvin? He's usually up late, and he's strong as a moose. He'd never turn down a friend in need."

"We just tried calling him. He has a toothache."

"And Digger?"

"His wife answered. Woke her up. When we told her about the gator, she said he's out of town at an ax-throwing tournament. Boonie, we need you bad!"

“What’d ya say? Huh? Lem, now I’m having trouble hearing you. You’re breaking up.”

“I can hear YOU just fine, Boonie.”

“You’re breaking up.”

“Boonie, we need you, guy!”

“Can’t hear ya, Lem. I’ll call you in the morning to see how you made out. Good luck with that big ol’ gator!”

The Tractor Chronicles

Those of us silver and gold guys who live out in the country need to have more than just an old pickup truck and a riding lawn tractor for toys. As Hank Williams Jr. said in the song, we need to have a "shotgun, a rifle, and a four-wheel drive." Without a doubt, we country dudes have to show that we are real men. Hank Jr. only touched the nostril of the possum though; we gotta have more than that. We need a big-ass tractor . . . like the real honest-to-goodness farmers have. I don't raise alfalfa, plant kidney beans, lasso Holsteins, or anything like the real guys do, but that's not important. Tractors are where it's at.

When Linda and I first moved out to the country many moons ago, we didn't have a tractor, just a wimpy little red riding mower. One of those K-Mart jobs made of tin and plastic. My neighbor Johnnyboy already had a big tractor (at least it seemed big to us). As I putt-putted around mowing the front lawn, I would look over longingly at his blue and gray Ford. He was perched high on his tractor as he ran his brushhog back and forth over his fields. Sigmund Freud would have diagnosed me with a severe case of Tractor Envy. After a few years of dealing with that malady, at a farm auction I bid on and purchased a vintage Allis-Chalmers WD tractor. In its faded orange, it looked like it had sat out in the sun much too long, was weary, and ready for Assisted Living. Real farmers haven't used those old girls since barns had "Mail Pouch" painted on them. But it was one we could afford. More significantly, I didn't know any better.

It was time for tractor problem number one. The auction was twenty miles from home, I had to drive it back, and I'd never been on a real tractor. Before leaving the auction, its owner thankfully took a couple minutes to show me how to shift gears. He said something about the brakes, but I was trembling too excitedly to take it all in. The tires looked old, cracked, and shaky, but it was a tractor. No K-mart piece of crap here. A real tractor. We named her Beulah.

It probably took three hours to drive it home at a perky 5 mph, rumbling over hill and dale. Linda followed behind me in our little red 'vette with the four-ways flashing. Just to clarify, this was not a Corvette. Just an embarrassing little Chevette. The downhill sections were white-knucklers as Beulah's big rear wheels shook the tractor like a bronco with stomach spasms. I guess what the guy was trying to tell me about the brakes was that they didn't work real well.

Somehow I made it home without having to call 9-1-1. Eventually we kept Beulah around for seven years or so, cutting grass with her belly mower and proudly hauling a little trailer back and forth around the yard. But Beulah had problems. One of her main issues was that on most days she didn't want to start. She just sat there and made a whirring sound when I tried to get her going. Other times she just coughed. And then there were days I couldn't even get her to belch. My mechanical skills couldn't save the day, since I didn't know the workings of a starter from those of a salad shooter. But when the stars were aligned and she did catch, cough, and get running, I was one proud dude sitting up there in the afternoon sun, her acrid exhaust blowing back in my face and down into my lungs.

Both Beulah and Johnnyboy's sleek Ford only had two-wheel drive. That led to problems, especially during mud season (which, in this part of the country lasts most of the spring and summer). But we both came to revel in the challenge when one of us would hustle over to the other breathlessly, saying "My tractor is stuck!" Such an event called for dragging out the tow chains, and heading for mud country.

When you have a tractor stuck, the first thing you have to do is "figger." You need to look everything over, and decide the best way to yank it out, so that the second tractor doesn't get stuck worse than the first. After figgering out the slope of the land and where the ground is solid, it's time to get to work. A chain gets wrapped around the stuck tractor's axle, and then both guys get on their tractors and fill the air with ear-shattering noise and exhaust fumes. Usually we have to rock the tractors, and that always leads to copious amounts of mud being slung all over jeans and t-shirts. The face, too. Then we yell to one another over the commotion of the engines, and send each other hand signals, which are interpreted as "slow" to one guy, and "gun it" to the other. After the air is totally fouled and we're splattered with mud, the next step is to move both engines to idle, dismount, and try to figger another way. This whole process gets repeated about six times. An hour later the stuck tractor is free. Huzzahs ring out! Our thirsts get the best of us, and it's time for a cold lemonade, or whatever the drink of the day may be.

One time my dad, a suburban guy from New Jersey, was visiting and watching the spectacle as Beulah was trying to yank Johnnyboy's Ford out of the muck. My dad was shouting instructions, all the time with a serious look. He didn't get it that we were having so much fun being stuck it didn't really matter how or when we freed it.

The years have passed. Dad is gone. Beulah got traded in for a spankingly sharp New Holland compact tractor. Johnnyboy upgraded too. Our new machines are both four-wheel drives, so, sadly, we're not getting stuck near as often. But I suspect ol' Hank Jr. would be proud of us, as we reminisce about our mud-splattered days of yankin' tractors. Hank would say we made it. Two true country dudes!

We're Going Where?

After a long, cold, and snowy winter, most of us northerners seeking a change of scenery in March headed south to Key West, Cancun, or Hilton Head. Not us. We headed to Sweden. Huh? More cold and snow?

It was our first trip to Sweden, long planned because Linda has been wanting to visit the land of her ancestors. Most Americans who visit there do so in summer, when according to unconfirmed rumors, it can actually be warm. But, I need to warn you. Don't go then if you want to see anyone. In summer, Swedes aren't home. They're all on vacation to the U.S., the Caribbean, or other sunny locales. So I'm not sure who would be left to visit. I also wonder who might be running their airports, or their country for that matter. On second thought, Swedes don't need anyone to run their government, with everyone on "holiday" so much of the time.

During the rest of the year, on Saturdays and Sundays you'll find them at ease, amiably chowing down on butter, coffee, and sweets all day, while speaking gibberish to one another. You've got to hand it to them, though. They have a special day nationally for sweet rolls, and even one for waffles. (It should be noted that the Swedes have a six-syllable name for sweet rolls that cannot be pronounced by human beings). During the few days in the year when they are not on vacation, Swedes are busily paying their taxes.

Never having been to Sweden before, we didn't know what clothes to take along, or how cold it would be in March. We decided on a colorful array of warm duds. One of the first things we noticed once we were walking in town was that Swedes are color-blind. In Stockholm, everyone was dressed in black coats and tight-fitting blue jeans. Linda's bright red winter coat stood out from the crowd as if she just escaped from prison.

Our question on clothing was not the only one soon answered. In Stockholm we expected to see folks skiing to work, and toboggans everywhere. Wrong. Many folks bicycle to work in March, or to town for their sweet rolls and butter. Joggers and walkers are out exercising everywhere. Surprisingly, we found that it rarely snows in regions of the country where most Swedes live. While folks in Boston and New York were up to their eyelashes in snow this winter, most of Sweden only had an occasional dusting. Northern Sweden is another story. We were "up north" for only a few days, and their climate looked like the Yukon in January.

Northern Sweden also has its own local culture, and their own cuisine. One of the local food favorites is spelled something like "Surstromming" (many Swedish words have funny looking dots over their vowels, like they had extra ink in their pens they needed to use up) Anyway, I would describe Surstromming as a small uncooked fish, a little bigger than a sardine, marinated overnight in fresh cow manure. Upon opening the can, you could clear out a hockey arena. Fortunately for them, they only eat it on special occasions, like an Olympic curling triumph over the Canadians. They have other curious local customs in Sweden. While we have the lovable Easter bunny in the U.S. laying colorful chicken eggs, Swedes celebrate their holiday with Easter witches (yes, that's right) that fly in on their brooms from an island called Bla Jungfrun. Rumor has it the witches rub spices on their broomsticks, but that's all I'd better say about that. Bla Jungfrun can best be pronounced with a mouthful of moose goulash. Another curiosity is that in northern Sweden the locals talk to one another without opening their mouths or moving their lips. Honest! I can't figure out how or why they do it. Maybe they don't want frost on their teeth?

Everyone thinks that going to Sweden is expensive. Guess what? It sure is. But folks who live there say it's cheaper than Norway. (I thought I'd share that helpful bit of information in case you were planning on a couple months north of Oslo.) I checked with the Norwegian Tourist Board and have confirmed that only eleven people have come to vacation in Norway ever since Leif Erikson and the missus brought the grandkids back to see the farm in the summer of 1018. But where, I ask you, can you go nowadays where it is cheap to vacation? North Korea?

On a more positive note, there is much that we can learn from our neighbors across the pond. The Swedes have stayed out of wars for 200 years. Think about that one. Also, the Swedes are low-keyed, and don't experience the daily tragedies that are regular fare on American newscasts. Random shooting deaths are unheard of. The same for controversies of police and skin color. Drunk driving is practically unknown. For sure, folks drink their share, but they take not a swallow if they are driving. We didn't hear a single Swede complain about the weather. Sure, it was overcast, drizzly, and 40, but they just took it in stride and went about their lives. And we don't know how they do it, but their roads are all in excellent condition, pothole-free, wherever we traveled. Best of all, we felt welcome everywhere, even if they talked funny.

So next winter, forget about the Caribbean. Book a flight to Stockholm. You'll love their sweet rolls.

America's Game; Wherever You Lived

When we silver and gold boys were kids, the fields were brimming with us young fellas. I'm not sure where the girls were then, but they sure weren't with us. And we didn't care.

I won't get into how times have changed: electronics and all. You know about that. What is remarkable is how we kids came up with rules among ourselves for the game we played, and how the rules were universal no matter where you lived.

I had a number of phone chats recently asking how other guys remember ball being played back then. I called my buddy Flash who grew up in Virginia; with Howie (from the Pittsburgh area): with Randy (rural Pennsylvania); and Willie (South Jersey). My kid years were spent in North Jersey. Judging by the similarities in how we played, we may as well have all been playing together rather than spaced throughout the East.

Here's what I found. There were no written rules or books anywhere about what is now referred to as "sandlot baseball." We just called it "playing ball." Little League, Pony League, and other adult-supervised games were just catching on.

Back before adult-organized leagues, we kids arranged the games ourselves. No grown-ups were involved at all. We would ask kids at school if they were coming. Or maybe it was just understood that we would be down at the field after school was out. There were no van rides to the field (oops, I guess there were no vans yet) and . . .heavens to Betsy. . . nobody's mother was there to watch.

We'd ride our bikes to the field; often with a bat across the handlebars and a ball glove hanging there too. Once at our field, we'd quickly drop our bikes to the ground and run out to start catching fly balls. Locking our bikes? That was unheard of.

None of us wore shorts; it was either last year's school pants or dungarees. Heck, we slid into bases over rough ground.

When we made up teams, we tried to make them even.

When the game was ready to start, we used a bat to decide which team was up first. It was hand-over-hand; if your fingers were at the top of the bat and you could still hold it, your team was up.

If there weren't enough players for each position, the batting team would supply a pitcher and/or catcher.

If there was a close play at any base, we kids might argue for a few minutes, but we'd come up with a decision. Soon the argument would be forgotten, and the game would go on without hard feelings.

The last guy picked would play right field. The best kids played shortstop or center field, or maybe pitched if there were enough of us.

When there weren't enough outfielders, hitting to right field was an automatic out (or you could "call your field").

No matter how inept a kid was, he was still given a time at bat like everyone else. If he hit the ball well, a cheer went up.

If a youngster came without a glove, when he was in the field he could use a glove from the team that was at bat.

If a fella was a lefty and there were no left-handed gloves, he'd have to use a right-handed glove.

Stealing bases was not allowed.

Anyone's bat could be used.

We hoped someone would bring a ball. If a ball was hit into the brush or the woods, the game was temporarily paused and everyone went to find it. If the cover came off the only ball we had, one of us would take it home and wrap electrical tape around it, and we'd use it again the next day.

Getting a brand new white baseball out of a Rawlings box was almost unheard of.

During the first games in the spring, it didn't matter if it was so chilly there were "bees in the bats." We still played. And if it was glaringly hot in the summer, we played anyway.

There were no water bottles or water breaks. If you were lucky enough to have a nickel in your pocket, you might get a Coke on the way home.

The game continued until it was time for supper.

Everyone got plenty of exercise, and while riding our bikes home we all felt good about ourselves.

OK, you the reader might say "here's just another feel-good story about the old days." Well, in retrospect, there was considerable value into how this universal game was played. We may not have recognized its merit at the time, but we kids made group decisions, initiated activities on our own, worked out differences among ourselves, and developed teamwork which often led to long-term friendships. No grown-up was telling us how to do it. There was an overall sense of fairness while demonstrating good sportsmanship. Those qualities came from inside us.

Back then, whether it was "the Sandbox" in Oil City, a church field in Virginia, a former pasture near Pittsburgh or Vivyen Field in my hometown, we had to make do with poorly-maintained playing fields. Grass on the infield? No way. The field may have had a backstop, but the screen usually had holes in it. Nowadays the ballfields are maintained by the towns and are in much better condition, but guess what? They sit idle on warm afternoons.

So, perhaps you're thinking I'm merely reminiscing about the good old days. Maybe I am. Or have we lost something more than just a slice of Americana?

The Future of Naming

I've been doing a good bit of driving lately, and there's some stuff I need to talk with you about. It's all about how things get named, and the future of our national naming policy.

Let's begin with bridges. When bridges were first built, they were named for the river or creek they spanned. Made good sense. Then some folks got together and decided that wasn't enough, and our naming industry was born. Bridges started getting named after people like George Washington, even though it's highly doubtful he ever walked across the one in New York City. And you've heard about the Golden Gate Bridge. In New Jersey there's the Pulaski Skyway. Buffalo has its Father Baker Bridge. All named for historical figures, grand vistas, or other generally good dudes. The Verrazano Bridge in New York has a rolling melodic sound to it, even though it's hard to spell. I think he was either an explorer, or the guy who built the first Indy car. All of those names are okay with me, but here's a question for you. What's the most impressive bridge named after a woman? Hmm. I can't think of one right off, and maybe we need to build a huge bridge somewhere, even if we don't need it, just to recognize a lady. The "Mom Bridge" would sit just fine with me. It's a bridge we could all relate to.

Next, let's talk about roads. Highways often memorialize someone. I've driven recently on the "Lincoln Highway," the "Bud Shuster Highway" and the "David Zeisberger Highway," along with a ton of others. That's separate from their official highway or interstate number. I admire "David" for his wonderful journal of explorations throughout our area many years ago. "Bud" was a politician known for his pork projects. Since he helped get a zillion highway building dollars, I guess that's okay too. I'm hoping you already know who "Lincoln" was. There's a "Blue Star Highway" not too far away. I never figured out what Harry Blue Star was known for.

With all the big bridges already named, a number of years ago the medium-sized bridges were next in line to get names, such as the Vietnam Veterans Memorial Bridge. Almost every town has one like that, and it's great to memorialize our national heroes. Next, some even shorter bridges got names. For instance, many overpass bridges on the interstates are named for heroic state troopers who lost their lives while on duty, or individual servicemen or women who made the ultimate sacrifice. I'm all for that. Lately I've been seeing some really short bridges have names, even township bridges. In some cases, the names are longer than the bridges. Well, that's okay with me, too. Might as well throw a name on it, plus it's good for my buddy Jerry, who's in the sign-making business.

Recently I've been noticing they have begun naming highway interchanges after people. There's one in Erie that has a name; Harold somebody. Not sure who he was or what he did. I'm thinking that's a bit of a stretch. Probably nobody thought to ask Harold on his death bed whether he would like an interchange named after him. I can't picture a kid today in high school pondering his future, and daydreaming about his name being honored by a highway interchange some day. But the movement has already started, and I think in a few years every major interchange will be named after someone. There must be a committee somewhere that makes the decisions. They probably have discussions like "should we name it after Marvin? How about ol' Donny? He was a good guy; used to shovel my mom's sidewalk. Or maybe Buster? He opened the first tavern in town."

Another option would be for the highway department to sell naming rights (like they do for stadiums). When that happens, I expect your GPS can be programmed to "turn right at the Luden's Cough Drop Interchange." I suppose if it brings in money for the state highway department to fix potholes, that would be all right.

Along the interstates, some of the roadside rest areas now are named. I assume it's for folks who gave their lives, did some noble deed, or was the first to use that restroom.

Looking to the future, here's tomorrow's problem. What next? What will carry names once all the bridges, highways, roadside rests and interchanges are named? So far, I haven't seen names on smaller rest areas that only have those temporary stalls on them. Are you thinking we should name each temporary toilet stall after a politician?

In future years there still will be more heroic servicemen and women who give their lives, or state troopers or firefighters who die in the line of duty. What will carry their memory? I'm thinking that culverts are next in line, but it's hardly fitting for a hero. So instead, maybe companies can put their names on them for advertising. You might see a sign designating the "Log Cabin Maple Syrup Culvert" appear along the highway. I doubt there are many of us who would like a traffic light or stop sign named after us.

Here's something I just thought of: should we rename stuff that's already here, but might be long overdue for a name change? I'm sort of tired of hearing about the "Atlantic Ocean." Should we re-name it after someone, or, better yet, sell its naming rights to a company? How does the "Hewlett-Packard Ocean"sound? Neat, huh? "Lake Erie"is kind of a dull and boring name, too. Think about it. Let's name it after a famous General, one who gave his life in battle. I forget what war he was in, but we could re-name it "Lake General Electric." And that way our government can make some bucks on it, too.

Oops, I'd better get back to my driving. I almost missed that darn "Marvin" interchange . . . .

Joe's Front Porch

No, not my own porch. It's another Joe. The story started one summer morning when I hopped off my bike to chat with two young Amish men who were working a portable sawmill just down our road. "You ought to go talk with my dad," one of them offered. "He can't get around real well so he sits up on his porch all day and loves to talk to people."

That was all we needed. Despite our living here for thirty-some years, Linda and I had never got to know any of our Amish neighbors up close and personal. So one evening we drove three miles to their farm house, tentatively walked up the stairs to the porch, and introduced ourselves. Joe , in his seventies, was sitting there, perched in his favorite chair, and welcomed us with a loud "Why, hello there!" With that, we struck up a friendship immediately.

Shortly after our first visit we were hosting our friend Mikael from Sweden. We asked Joe if Mikael could come over with us and fulfill his wish to go for a buggy ride. "Why sure!" Joe bellowed. That truly opened the floodgates of friendship. Mikael left for a ride with Joe's son Joe Jr., and experienced the ride of his life! Mikael, though he speaks English fairly well, is still learning the nuances of our language. He came back smiling widely from his buggy ride, blurting out "he even let me grab the steering wheel!" We all laughed! Afterwards, Mikael and Joe Jr. sampled each other's tobacco, Mikael spoke of everyday life in Sweden, Joe answered every question about his Amish culture, and we chatted and laughed well past nightfall.

From that memorable evening forward, going over to sit on the porch to talk with Joe, his wife Lovina, and their bustling family has been a special treat. Joe entertains us each time with stories of his youth, his writings, his family, and people he has met through the years. Linda and I soon found we weren't the only "English" folks (as the Amish refer to us non-Amish neighbors) who have discovered the charm of

Joe's front porch. Just about every time we stop over, another English neighbor shows up, welcomed by a rich and warm personal greeting from Joe. We often kid Joe that he is "holding court" from his porch as he eagerly directs the evening's conversation.

For several years, Linda has been wanting to learn how to do canning the Amish way. Taking a chance, we asked Joe and Lovina if we could watch them do so. "Why sure!" Joe again bellowed. "You can join us and help!" So on a brilliant September morning a few years ago, we gathered on Joe's front porch with a box of empty canning jars along with buckets of tomatoes, peppers, and other freshly picked vegetables. Joe's daughter Elizabeth, his daughter-in-law Lydia, and our new "English" friend Jennifer all joined Lovina and Linda spending the entire day doing the cutting. Later in the afternoon when the grandchildren got home from school, even the youngest of the girls eagerly joined in. Joe sat in his special porch chair, holding court once again, yelling out instructions and tending the stoves. It was a fun and memorable day indeed. By evening, many jars of "pizza" sauce, "V-9 juice," and chow-chow had been put up. The women were exhausted from working all day, but that didn't keep Joe from his throaty laugh and barking out additional directions.

Everything canned that day was delicious! But our porch time together was growing short as the seasons changed. When snow began falling, we were invited inside to sit next to their simmering wood stove. We shared more good times, more stories, and more laughter. At Christmas, Joe and Lovina surprised us with a fine box of apples and oranges. The winter proved to be an unrelenting one, and we longed to chat again on Joe's front porch when springtime came. It was a year that spring did not come quickly.

By late April, the weather finally turned for the better. Every few days after that, we had been stopping over to spend time together on the porch. What we expect to be "just a few minutes" usually stretches past an hour or two. Through Joe's wisdom and sense of humor, he has taught us a great deal about the Amish culture and their family life. We "English" have so much we can learn from them and their simple but hard-working way of living, as shown by their strong family ties and their steadfastly keeping the faith and customs passed down through generations.

When I stop and think about it, what stands out most about the Amish and us is that we are so much more similar than we are different. And in these troubled times across the globe, we are incredibly fortunate to live in a part of our country where cultures and religions get along so well. Let's keep that in mind when we hear of what's happening elsewhere in the World.

Joe and his family have taught us that important lesson, and if you don't believe me, just climb the stairs to Joe's front porch. He'll greet you with a warm "Why, hello there!"

The Burn Barrel Chronicles

The most personally satisfying aspect of living in the country is having a burn barrel to call your own. Nothing is quite so exhilarating on a summer morn, when the grass is still wet, than leaning over your favorite barrel with wadded-up newspaper in hand, lighting a match, and experiencing the "whoosh!" Say goodbye to those never-ending credit card applications and car insurance ads you get in the mail, paper towels stained with mung, and empty Little Debbies boxes. But in a few hours that delightfully sweet aroma of country living is gone. Till another day.

Eventually, though, a question arises. What happens after you've performed that much-loved routine for six months or so? Yup. Your barrel is almost filled up. A goodly supply of rain and snow has helped congeal your residue into a solid gooey mass. So what's next? It's time to give last rites to the black gunk in the barrel and dump it. But how? Where? If you budge the barrel thinking you'll lift it, get real. You'll notice it now weighs about four hundred pounds. I suppose you can reach down in and shovel it out a little at a time, but I'd rather have my teeth busted out with a pipe wrench.

Indeed, a front-end loader can be the answer. Here's hoping you have one. Wheelbarrows? They went out with the Middle Ages. But however you get the stuff out, where to dump it? I've been tempted on Sunday mornings when my neighbors are at church to dump it behind their garage. I doubt they'd notice. But I usually end up digging a hole out back. Before I bury it for good, I get my last glance at blackened paper shards, bits of aluminum foil, goobery fragments of plastic, and whatever else is hidden in that mysterious black blob. If you're lucky you might spot the remains of a squished sardine can that got tossed in by mistake.

So now that it's buried, is it gone forever? Hmmm. Good question. Imagine if you would, that 18,000 years have passed, planet Earth has barely survived climate change and another ice age. Two archeologists have been surveying around in our area, digging with their normal caution, searching for signs of previous civilizations. Their conversation might go something like this. (Readers please note: as a courtesy, I have translated it back to our present-day English from their contemporary Ak-Wandi. Names of the archeologists are purely fictitious and should not be confused with anyone alive or dead).

"Hey Larry, I'm over here behind these darn briar bushes. My probing device hit something interesting a while ago. It was black and gunky. I've been sifting it super carefully. I think I've hit paydirt!"

"I'll be there in a few minutes, Mary, but I'm taking my morning break. Tell me what you found."

"Wow, Larry. This will ring your chimes! I found the remains of bird wings. Could be from a species like those creatures called chickens that lived here eons ago. I'm getting a distinct whiff of honey mustard on the bones. My detector has picked up a trace of ancient tabasco sauce too. And you won't believe this. I dug up what might be what's left of the oldest K-cup ever excavated! I could even make out the words. Those ancient peoples were wimpy! They drank decaf!"

After Larry took the last bite of his bagel, he wandered over to his colleague. When he saw what she had found, he wiped the crumbs out of his beard and peered down. "That's quite a find, Mary. Their civilization must have been primitive as heck. It could have happened when this general area was known as the United States. If memory serves, that would have been before that country was invaded by Belgium. I'll notify the professor back at the university. He'll want to dig around in that black gunk himself after he gets back from his beach vacation on Planet Zoltan."

"One more thing while I'm digging at this site," she continued. "I found what seems to be a number of crude ancient masks. Not fashionable at all. I wouldn't be seen in one, even getting groceries. I ran them through my automatic carbon-dating calculator and learned they came from way back in 2021. I wonder what was happening then that they wore masks?

Larry again seemed disinterested. "Probably nothing; they must have been big on costume parties."

Mary was pensive for a minute or two, then her face lit up. "No, it was more than that. I recall from an ancient history app, that was about the time they had a pandemic, and folks had to go around wearing masks. Strange, huh? But luckily the pandemic only lasted about twenty years till they found a vaccine or something."

Larry yawned, then nodded. "Yeah, I guess it was no big deal. Let's go get lunch."

That Sign in Benezette

It's a small town, but you may have heard of it. According to the latest census, the tiny Pennsylvania village of Benezette, located in Elk County, has a population of 996 souls. Its historic local hotel is well known for its fine dinners. People are friendly. The rough terrain is great for outdoor buffs. Autumn colors make it even more appealing. But that's hardly what it's known for. In addition to its humans, Benezette is home territory to perhaps 1,400 elk, the largest elk herd in the East. If you don't know what an elk is, picture Bambi on steroids. They're big critters! You have to go more than a thousand miles west to find a larger herd. Here they spread themselves out over much of the county, but Benezette is where the action is.

When autumn arrives, the male elk get frisky. It's time for the bulls to seek out the ladies, known as cows. It's also when thousands of visitors show up in the Benezette area wearing LL Bean duds, trying to catch a glimpse of the elk, as up close and personal as the elk will allow. Many visitors carry binoculars, energy bars, and bottled water. A few have cameras with lenses as long as drainage pipes.

Bull elk are big dudes; and the cows are almost as large. When the bulls start competing for female companionship, they can get in a serious spat with one another. The biggest and strongest boys win the hooves and hearts of the ladies.

Give credit to the foresight of the Commonwealth of Pennsylvania. Back in 1913 a decision was made to bring elk back here, where they had once thrived before being killed off. All were gone by the time of the Civil War. Within fourteen years, nearly 200 elk were brought east from Yellowstone. They were transported in railroad box cars. It's amazing any of them survived. When they reached Elk County, they were shooed off the boxcars into an environment totally different from their home in Wyoming, with types of food they had never eaten.

Despite that rough start, a few hardy critters made the transition. Eventually the Game Commission protected them, and by the 1980s the herd was on its way to growing it to its present impressive size. Elk became a bigger tourist attraction than Cougar Bob's Tavern in Kellettville. A superb visitors center as well as viewing areas were constructed. On a given sunny autumn day, the cars of hundreds of elk lovers, as well as curious folks like you and me, converge in the parking lots. You can even buy kettle corn and postcards of downtown Ridgway in the lobby of the visitors center.

As you drive up the mountain in your SUV or pickup, there are signs warning "Do not stop on the roadway." OK, I get it. That could cause an accident if you stopped on that winding road to snap a photo of an elk that suddenly appeared out of the morning mist.

Once you get to the visitors center, signs proliferate. As you walk on well-manicured trails which lead to good elk spotting points, every trail has a line of signs. They remind visitors not to walk on the grass, not to feed the elk, to give elk space, to stay on the trails, not to say bad words where the elk can hear you, and other things your mother probably told you not to do.

But here's the sign that got to me. It says "Do Not Name the Elk. Let Wild be Wild." Honest, that's what it says, and there are a number of signs like that. I suppose if you got fairly close to a bull elk, and you said to him "how are you today, Elmer?" the folks who put up the sign are afraid that 'ol Elmer will want to crawl into the back seat of your Volvo and come home with you to lay beside your recliner while you watch "America's Got Talent."

My guess is that will not happen. First of all, there's no data to support that elk give a darn what's on cable TV. Secondly, there's a zoo-full of other wild critters out there in the world that have been named, but remain disinterested in your living room decor. Somewhere in the vast ocean there's a famous 50-foot killer shark named Deep Blue that is not interested in your backyard pool. There's a lone jaguar in California named El Jefe who is unlikely to pee on your living room rug when you love him up. Others: an aggressive orca whale named Tilikum, and there's Sudan, the last northern white rhinoceros on the face of the Earth. "Jaws" was a fictional shark, but naming him didn't seem to make kids want to pet him. And what about Sasquatch?

As we were walking the trails in Benezette (no, not on the grass), we were fortunate in having a peak experience of getting within hailing distance of a few massive elk. With no one else around within sight, my buddy Johnnyboy called out "Hey, Esmerelda!" to the nearest cow elk. He even winked at her (there were no signs prohibiting that). I kept looking around wondering if there were any elk-naming police hiding, ready to pounce. Luckily, no. But here's the rub. Another sign said "Do your part; if you see something, say something."

Does that mean say it to people, or to the elk? I'm confused. They need more signs.

The Low Maintenance Home

Have you noticed while looking through real estate ads, seeing a house advertised as "low maintenance?" Whenever I see one, I think "who would want to buy one like that?" Some would say the term "low maintenance" in reference to a home is an oxymoron. Thinking back, I can't recall ever seeing one listed as "high maintenance." Occasionally you see properties advertised as "nice starter home" or "handyman's delight," but they don't really come out and say how much fun might be in store for the lucky buyer.

It's hard to believe there are folks who wouldn't want to spend the rest of their adult lives working on a house. By having endless work to do in your home, it saves you the trouble of trying to find a hobby. And think: if you couldn't continually work on your house, you would be stuck going to events like craft fairs every weekend. Or you'd have to stop at health food bars to sample Greek chocolate yogurt, or other foo-foo stuff. Even worse than that, you might become so bored that you get dragged to a yoga class. Who would want that? Give me a couple sheets of drywall to balance over my head to hang on the ceiling for a fun afternoon.

By having a typical high-maintenance home, you can be assured of being on a first name basis with all the cashiers at the local hardware stores. Instead of wasting time developing other friendships (which would take time away from your beloved home projects), you can simply invite all the cashiers and stock guys over to your house for a barbecue. For laughs, you can all roll around in that pink insulation everybody loves.

Linda and I have lived in our small one-story home for 36 years. By my latest calculation, I am about one-third done with all the planned upgrades. I'm figuring I'll need to live to be 208 to get everything done.

That is, of course, realizing that remodelings already completed will need to be repainted and refurbished. So there's much to look forward to.

To really round out your life, you need to have huge lawns and fields to mow, as well as big gardens to keep trimmed. Having them will take up plenty of time, so you won't have to be doing unpleasant things like going to movies or concerts, or sitting in the sun working on a tan. Having a piece of property will allow you the pleasure of cutting brush every spring and fall, and the joy of sawing off low limbs that nearly knock you off the tractor while you're mowing. And if you live in the country, you can make big brush piles to burn, sending friendly plumes of smoke throughout the neighborhood. And don't miss the opportunity to throw an old piece of carpet on the burn pile to keep it smoking all day. Try to do it when your neighbors are hosting a family reunion.

Remember that cute little silver maple tree you planted out behind the house 25 years ago? For years you thought it would never grow. Now it's become so huge that it's threatening to yank off your down-spouts. That gives you the opportunity to spend gorgeous autumn mornings balancing precariously near the top rung of your ladder, leaning over while trimming with your pruner. For the afternoon, there will be plenty of joy cleaning out the gutters, then raking up leaves. No need to watch boring football games.

If I haven't yet sold you on the excitement of a high-maintenance home, this might be the clinker. For an extra bonus, have a pond or two out back. That gives you the opportunity to weedwhack around the pond banks every couple of weeks. It's fun indeed, especially on a humid af-ternoon. If you don't think it's an opportunity for exercise, then you've never tried swatting at deer flies that land on the back of your neck while keeping the weed whacker from slicing into your ankles. If it's a calm day when you trim around the ponds, all the clippings float merrily out into the water. That provides the opportunity later to "rake the lake" to clean them off. More healthy exercise! And speaking of being physi-cally fit, having a pond allows you to jump out of bed every summer morning at dawn to dash outside in your jammies. There you can flail your arms to chase away the herons, who come like clockwork to gorge themselves on the fish you've tried so hard to get established.

And folks, here's the real money-saver. Having your own high maintenance home takes away the bother of having to decide where to go on a vacation. Not to worry; you won't have to time to go anywhere. Cut the grass in the summer, rake leaves in autumn, plow snow in the winter. And if the snow gets deep on the roof, you can remove it with that delightful invention called the snow rake. A word of caution; using it for more than thirty minutes will cause your shoulders to fall off. Or, you can leave the snow where it is and let it ice up underneath. That will allow you the challenge of replacing your kitchen ceiling after water drips down through the light fixtures. When those leaks appear, it also provides an opportunity to hear from the guy down the street who tells you what you should have done instead.

So keep alert to find that "high maintenance" place of your dreams. You'll stay too busy to even think of regretting it.

Behold The Ancient Mound Builders

Just a week ago, I was walking through the living room past the TV while Linda was watching a History Channel program. This show was on the ancient mound-builders of Ohio. I paused as I was munching on a pretzel and watched for a few minutes. Amazing stuff! The TV host was saying they still don't know why they were built, but it may have happened back in caveman days.

Perhaps the problem with this type of historical question is that we are trying to figure those things out from our perspective, not theirs.

I didn't give it another thought, but you won't believe what happened. It was the next morning. Talk about an incredible coincidence! I had stopped at one of the first yard sales of the spring, and was picking through stuff. It was out in the boondocks, on a dirt road in front of an old frame house that looked the worse for wear. A lot of the stuff for sale was really old, and covered with dust. Some boxes came complete with mouse droppings. Reaching underneath a few Donny and Marie Christmas ornaments, I saw this 8-track tape. I hadn't seen one in a while, so I took a chance and stuffed it in my bag. An old lady in her '70s had the sale, and I got her down to a quarter for it.

After I brought the recording home, I ran it through the tape player in Grandma's '63 Dodge Dart. At first all I heard was static, then a sound like a wolf howling in the distance. Then, voices. As I listened, I was astonished to hear the actual voices of two cavemen thousands of years ago. I knew 8-tracks were old (rumor has it some had been found in King Tut's tomb) but I hadn't realized how long they had been around. As I listened in amazement, here is what they said, as best I could make out:

(first there was the sound of chewing; not sure if it was a guy or an animal, or an animal chewing on a guy). Then a belch. Then static. Moments later, a voice:

"Hey Grinny, what are you up to today? Ya hungry?

"Well, Zim, I already munched on leftover Stegosaurus innards for protein, and I was thinking about gathering some grain, even though my medicine man says it's not really good for me. And cholesterol is a concern. How 'bout you?

(another belch)

"I already had a salamander salad. I could use some exercise. I was thinking about rolling some really big stones. Gotta stay in shape, y'know. Wanna join in? Should be fun."

"Would you be rolling them uphill, or downhill?"

"Uphill doesn't work so well, I found out. I'm gonna try going down this time."

"Good plan. Oh man, Zim, you sure know how to have a good time. I'd like to join you but I'm cooking up some lizard brain for a Happy Hour snack. You and Sophie ought to come over and check out our new reclino-rocks.

"Actually, Grinny, I'm gonna change my mind. I rolled stones just last week. Maybe I could build a mound."

"A what? Did you say a mound?"

"Yeah, a really big one."

"What would you make it out of?" Grinny's voice sounded in-credulous.

"I was thinking perhaps dirt and stones. Maybe add some mud for effect."

"Yeah, I suppose that would work. But why build a mound?"

"Well," Zim continued, "I don't have any hobbies except catching snakes. Sophie and me just moved into our new cave. It was in ready-to-move-in shape, so I don't need to bother doing any remodeling yet or anything. The rattlesnakes skittered out as soon as we got settled. So I'm kinda bored."

"Don't you need to go foraging for food?"

"I sent Sophie and the kids out berry-picking. If they don't get trampled by some critter, they should be home before dark."

There was a minute or two of blank space before Grinny's voice was heard again. "Where would you build this mound you're talking about?"

"Down there by the river. I'd rather build it on a big mountain, but Ohio doesn't have any. Ohio doesn't have much of anything . . . "

"Zim, don't you need to get permission from our king guy to build something big like that?"

(another belch)

"Chill out, my friend. I already checked with Big Thor. We're good. There's ordinances against open burning and on separating garbage, but nothing on mound building. C'mon, it would be good exercise."

Again, Grinny hesitated. "Well, I suppose I should get my body moving around. I got my cardio by chasing down that hyena on Tuesday, but I guess I could do some upper body. By the way, what would you call your mound?"

"Hmmm. Good question . . . I think I'd call it a monument."

"I didn't think monuments were invented yet."

"There's no time like now, Grinny."

"A monument to what? There's nothing here in Ohio that's noteworthy."

There was more blank space on the tape till Zim responded. "Well, we could build it, then sometime later maybe someone could decide what it's for."

"Okay, now I'm tracking with you, Zim. In the future when our grandbabies have their own grandbabies, they'll have nothing to do on summer mornings but spread llama dung on their lawns. When they see this mound it'll give 'em something to think about. They'll wonder what we were up to. Heck, you and me, we're just staying in shape. You've convinced me. I'll take the lizard brains off the fire for awhile. Then I'll be ready to help."

At this point, the recording got too grainy, and I couldn't make out anything more. Then, an unexpected noise, startling me. Stretching, I reached over and shut off that ringing nuisance.

After I find where I put that tape, I'm gonna send it in to that TV show.

Another Lost Art

About a dozen years ago, our local YMCA sponsored a "Business To Business Challenge," in which local industries and businesses formed teams to compete against one another in contests such as volleyball, "frisbee soccer," swimming, running and other athletic pursuits. The team coordinators at the hospital where I was working assessed my physical condition, and entered me in the competition they felt I could handle. It was the Spelling Bee. It turned out to be a lot of fun, but I lost out to the eventual champion when I messed up on "humidostat." (If you must know, I substituted an "i" for the "o"). My buddy Johnnyboy never lets me forget that one.

News stories surface a couple times a year about an eight-year-old kid winning the national spelling contest correctly spelling some word with about twenty syllables, like "cymotrichous." It's always a word no one in this country has ever even seen before, no less spelled. The winning contestant usually is of an international heritage, so maybe it's a word they use everyday over there. Maybe something like "Good morning, would you like cymotrichous in your yak juice?"

Winning a national spelling contest is a tremendous feat for those youngsters after studying long and hard. In today's world, it's like finding raccoon feathers, because it appears as if we are producing a generation of young folk who not only cannot spell correctly, but don't feel any particular need to do so.

Unlike the younger generation, many of us graybeards haven't gotten comfortable with sending electronic messages Dick Tracy-like on phones or wrist radios or what have you. Proper spelling on them is not expected, or even encouraged. Contractions like "u" or "lol" are the norm. What would have happened if we used that stuff back in fourth grade in Mrs. Lockwood's class? Yup, you guessed it.

I can't just put the blame on young folks for poor spelling. It's adults, too. And you see it right here in our little part of the world. For example, we live on a road that begins in Pennsylvania, and changes names when it enters New York. So there's different street names on the signs on each end. Here's the rub. Both are spelled incorrectly. In New York, we have "Colemen" when it should be "Coleman," and in Pennsylvania "Darylmple" when it should be "Dalrymple." Maybe I'm too much of a stickler on what spelling should be. Perhaps no one else who has traveled our road hundreds of times has even noticed. Or cared. Maybe I need to look for a hobby.

I have a clipping stashed away that my brother-in-law Al sent me. It's a photo in front of a college building in New Jersey, where they recently erected a fancy welcome sign at the entrance of the campus. The sign reads "College of New Jerserey." There had to be some red faces about that one. Mrs. Lockwood would have made the speller stay after school. I'm sure you've seen other such goofs that have made the news.

And don't even get me started about apostrophes. Whenever I travel down a road just south of here, I have to close my eyes when I pass a big sign on a barn that says "Vietnam M.I.A.s-Your Not Forgotten." I agree strongly with the message, but some night I'm going to sneak down there with a paint can and add an apostrophe after the "u" and an "e" after the "r." Another sign that really bothers me is on a store where I go with some frequency to purchase libation. The sign reads "Now Open Sunday's." I keep wanting to cause a scene just to get that darned apostrophe removed, but if I do, I'm afraid they won't let me back in to make next week's purchase.

It seems that hardly anyone is despairing over today's ho-hum attitude toward spelling miscues. It's beginning to look like in tomorrow's world that correct spelling won't matter. Sort of like studying Latin, or learning how to use a Slide Rule. Or taking Calculus (whatever that is, or was).

But I hope they continue holding national Spelling Bees, because it reminds us of a lost art that some folks somewhere think is still important. And if you ask me, the kid who studies hard and wins it deserves national attention. Even if the papers spell their name wrong.

The Puppy Chronicles

Were we ready? It had been more than a year since our beloved Mattie-dog had passed on. Linda and I both missed having the company of a pooch around and underfoot. "I want a puppy, one we can train ourselves" was her mantra.

Over the previous twenty years we had brought two rescue dogs into our home. Each had come with their own issues based on whatever nightmares their lives had been beforehand. Overall, they had worked out superbly. But Linda's dream this go-round was to have a pup, one to train ourselves. Her breed of choice was a Labradoodle. We learned that breed doesn't shed; that was a big drawing card to Linda, since she is in charge of our household vacuuming department.

The biggest question was: could we handle the daily chaos of puppyhood? Were we ready for a return to needle-like teeth puncturing our fingers? Newspapers on the floor? Where will we put everything that looks remotely chewable? The last time we had a pup was eons ago, when we had oodles more energy. Then we were more naive about the amount of time and commitment that was needed to bring up and train a pup. Despite these lingering questions, as Christmas was only days away I gamely kept up the search for a Labradoodle to call our own. Late one night, while checking online, I found a female pup that was being offered at a much lower price than the others I had seen of that breed. Was that because she only had one leg, I wondered? Or was she the worst terrorist pup in Ohio? We took a chance and made a commitment to the breeder, with the pup staying at its breeder's till we had finished a trip and (hopefully) puppy-proofed the house.

Four days after New Year's we drove four hours to meet her, seal the deal, and bring her home. We were told the pup had spent its first three months of life on a farm, one of a litter of sixteen, and was the only one left. When we first saw her, the breeder's granddaughter was cradling her. Hmmm. I looked at Linda and observed "Her paws look pretty big, don'tcha think? How heavy did you say her mother was?"

Readying for the adventure ahead of us, we placed her in a cage in the back seat of our pickup and started home. Five miles into the trip, she hunched over and presented us with a steaming pile in her cage. Just nerves? Geez I hope so! Fortunately, the rest of the trip was much easier on the nostrils, with the pup napping most of the way. Once home, she needed help learning how to climb the two steps into the front door. But other than piddling on the mud room floor when she first walked in, she did fine. Her initial night went better than expected, with only a half-hour concert coming from her cage.

The next day was her first full day with us. Hey, did she grow overnight? She sure looked like it. Or maybe at first glance we hadn't gotten a good look at her legs. They looked as long as my buddy Johnnyboy's. But she was lovable and soft, and doted at the slightest attention. In twenty-four hours she had cut down her mistakes, and was eager for frequent excursions through the snow-covered yard. Now the next big question: what to name her? After spirited discussions, we decided on calling her Fika (FEE-kah), an upbeat Swedish word. In that country, if you plan to meet good friends for a morning sweet roll and coffee, it is called going out for Fika. So the name seemed to fit. With boundless energy, she began learning some of the household rules. Fika chose to learn some better than others. "Don't bite!" was one she was slow with. Later in the day, she had her first meeting with Bottle Rocket, the neighbors' full-grown Lab, a docile hound much-loved in the neighborhood. Since he was more than three times the size of Fika, our pup cowered from him at first, but soon was jumping up, nipping at his ears and his plumbing.

We hadn't thought about it until we brought her home, but we began wondering if Fika was the product of a puppy mill. The lady from whom we bought her gave us a couple different versions of our pup's heritage, and we never got to see the alleged farm where she spent her first three months of life. And after more research online, duh! Ohio has got to be the world's capital of puppy mills. Well, I guess the people in that state have to be number one for something. Maybe it was a puppy mill she came from, maybe it wasn't. Be that as it may, Fika was ours. Maybe we saved her from puppy mill life.

Newspaper acquisition suddenly became a priority. In Fika's first few months, we went through bundles of them spread on the floor in the mudroom. She seemed to unload most on photos of politicians. Good girl! Looking into the future, I'm concerned that folks in the U.S. aren't getting their daily news from the papers like they once did. I guess the day will come when we'll see puppy owners spreading computer paper on the floor to catch doggy pee.

Thanks to Fika, there's no need for Linda or I to join an athlctic club. She forces us to stay active. I hadn't run the hurdles since high school track days. Now I'm back at it, hastily tripping over barriers as she grabs for food crumbs, dirty socks, and well-worn sneakers. Each of the frequent trips outside is an adventure of balance and fortitude.

And what was that we had read about Labradoodles not shedding? What's all this black hair on the floor? Neither of us had read the fine print. Some Labradoodles don't shed. Some do. Guess what we got?

It's been almost a month since Fika joined us. Has it been worth it? Hmmm.

The Lineup

Remember the first use of the Lineup on TV? It was on Dragnet in the Fifties. At the end of each episode the unfortunate crime victim would peer carefully at six unshaven, unsavory characters lined up against a wall. The victim would look up and down the lineup, and their eyes would widen as he or she identified which one was the perpetrator. They would give an over-sized nod to Sgt. Friday, who would move in and usher the bad guy away, as a refrain of "Don-de-don-don" would be heard. Who could forget it?

I don't watch the tube much anymore, except for coverage of natural disasters and weather extremes. But at times I tune in if there has been a mass shooting or other heinous act. You probably have noticed it already, but they all have something in common when there's a big announcement to be made. It's today's version of the Lineup. This time it's grim-looking authority characters behind the person at the podium.

In the case of a horrific crime, be it a mass shooting or whatever other awful event happens these days, standing behind the main speaker are representatives of law enforcement agencies involved in the incident. They're never sitting. So the intent, I'm guessing, is to show solidarity with the main speaker. For many of the law enforcement or government agencies today headed by men, the lineup on the stage primarily consists of Caucasian males. As the speaker provides the information, the Lineup guys all compete to display the most serious face. If you watch these events with family or friends, try this. Put whatever horrific event aside for a few moments. Try to find the guy showing the Ultimate Frown. Hint #1: look for furrowed brows. Hint #2: look for pursed lips. Find him? I don't know about you, but just once I'd like to see one of these stony-faced dudes reach over and pinch the next guy on the bum.

With political figures, the makeup of he Lineup is quite different for the "Big Announcement." Their intent is to show the world how inclusive they are. No all-white guy show here! If the main speaker is a Caucasian male, in the Lineup you'll see several women, at least one African-American, a Hispanic, an Oriental, and sometimes a religious figure if one can be found willing to associate with the politician. And of course, there is the person doing the signing for the deaf. If we get more inclusive in the future, perhaps you'll see a dwarf and an Eskimo join the throng. I'm good with that. Or getting a person from the opposing political party to stand in the Lineup. They would be easy to spot, since they would be the only one rolling their eyes during the announcement.

Something I'd like to see during one of those political announcements is one of the guys in the Lineup trying to suppress a giggle. You know how hard that can be when something just strikes you as funny? Remember when you were a kid in church, and ol' Mister Potter let one fly against the pew, and it reverberated? You almost turned purple trying to keep from busting your cork. I'd like to see someone in the Lineup trying to suppress their mirth while the speaker is going on about the National Debt Limit.

Which brings me to a related point. What if the political figure making the announcement inexplicably let loose like Mister Potter did? Can you picture the Lineup folks behind the speaker begin coughing, grimacing, waving at the air, or pinching their nostrils shut? You can bet that scene would make it around the world on the web in about eleven seconds.

Recently there was a news item that occurred during a presentation a state governor was giving at a grade school. It seems a young student standing behind him in a version of the Lineup actually fainted. That's a true story. Fortunately, the kid was fine afterwards. Knowing how riveting the governor's speeches are, I would have to say that the kid made an excellent move to seek medical treatment rather than to listen to the remainder of the speech.

But getting back to the Lineup on TV, be alert for the next time you see a speaker tramp up toward the microphone with an entourage lining up behind him (or her). Watch them carefully. The ghost of Sgt. Joe Friday is lurking somewhere nearby. Remember, he started this whole thing.

Don-de-don-don.

Remembering Summer Camp

You may have gone to summer camp a few years back. It may have been a faith-based camp, a Scout camp, or a private one. It's fun to reflect back on those fun-filled days.

I lived only a few miles from New York City, so camp for me meant going fifty miles away to a Boy Scout camp in the mountains. We Scouts had started saving our quarters for camp the previous autumn. Twenty bucks for the two-week stay was a lot of quarters to come up with, what with other important personal expenses like baseball cards and Cracker Jacks, all coming from a rather pathetic cash flow.

When July finally arrived, how exciting it was to board the chartered bus, all in our Scout summer uniforms, heading off for camp! We sang "100 Bottles of Beer on the Wall" at the top of our lungs, told goofy jokes, and yelled back and forth the whole trip.

It seemed like it took forever to get there, but once we arrived at camp we were shown to our assigned lean-to in what seemed to be the middle of a deep and mysterious forest. Remember, we were not country kids. We broke up into "patrols," which we had to name. One group called themselves the "Bear Patrol," another was the "Tiger Patrol." We named ours the "Too Bad For You Patrol."

Each morning we dragged ourselves out of our sleeping bags at the sound of Reveille. Then we lined up at attention in the parking lot as a scratchy bugle over the loudspeaker heralded the flag being briskly raised. Our knees were knocking in the chilly mountain air wearing our Scout shorts, so we were glad when the last note was played. Then we took off at full speed towards the mess hall, which was even louder than the bus ride, what with the din of dishes and heavy silverware banging, and a hundred young kids jabbering excitedly. Once finished with our Sugar Crisp and milk, if you wanted to practice for your swimming merit badge, you changed into your swimsuit. It was still wet from yesterday because you left it in a pile on the floor near your sleeping bag. Your teeth were chattering, waiting to jump into the water off the dock. That mountain lake felt like it had ice floes in it! Shrivel city!

There were other merit badges to work on, like Reptile Study. It was the first time I picked up a snake. No, it wasn't slimy, but it canceled urges for me to pick up any more of them in my lifetime. Another activity you could sign up for was the Mile Swim. After several brief attempts that ended with coughing and lungs spewing out lake water, I decided to leave that badge for others. Just after lunch came the highlight of the day. Going to the trading post! I'd pull out a couple dimes and nickels to buy an ice cream sandwich, and a package of Fizzies to pop in my canteen (heaven only knows what might have been in those little pink tablets that made your water all bubbly). If you had an extra nickel, you could buy a postcard with a camp scene on it. My first day there I sent one home to Mom and Dad, sort of like in the Camp Grenada song we remember.

After a week of frenetic activity had passed, Sunday meant it was visiting day for parents. Our scoutmaster reminded us that morning to brush our teeth and comb our hair. I recall standing anxiously by the gravel parking lot waiting for my first glimpse of Dad's green Chevy coming into view. I had so much to tell my folks! Shooting a rifle for the first time, holding that snake, going hiking, canoeing, playing softball in the evening, and feeding a raccoon outside our lean-to at night. All so exciting! At least I thought so. And I was hoping that Mom might slip me another fifty cents or so for spending at the trading post, to assure an uninterrupted supply of Fizzies.

That was maybe sixty years ago. I don't know if city kids still go to summer camps in the country, but I doubt it's as popular as it once was. Giving up their electronics for two weeks might be too much of a sacrifice for today's kids to make. In retrospect, those weeks we spent at summer camp were a great opportunity to pal around with other kids in the great outdoors, experience some new things, and to live away from your folks for a few days. Parents probably needed that break more than us.

The canoeing I learned there became an important part of my life. About twenty or so years ago I was doing a week-long canoe trip up in northern Canada with Linda, my buddy Johnnyboy and his wife Connie. While taking a pee break on shore, we were passed by six or eight canoes with teenage girls from a wilderness camp. Their main camp was many miles from any town. At these wilderness camps, kids spend a full six weeks in the outdoors, the last two or three weeks on a long canoe trip out in the Canadian bush. They paddle all day. They cook their own meals, and carry their gear from lake to lake in big, bulky wooden boxes strapped to their backs. In that part of northern Ontario, it's not unusual to go a couple days without seeing anyone else. In their flotilla this day were two girls in each canoe. They may have been fourteen years old, along with their leaders in a separate boat. It was cloudy and cool in mid-morning and had rained earlier, which would have made morning cooking a challenge. As they were paddling by, we cheerfully called to a girl asking what they had for breakfast. "Peanuts!" she yelled back with a snarl. "All we had were peanuts! I don't call that a breakfast!"

That young girl is well into motherhood now. I wonder if she sent her kids to summer camp . . . .

'Tis the Season

One of the prime reasons a lot of us country dwellers love living around here in the early spring is that we can't get enough of what that time of the year brings. Mud! March means mud, and plenty of it. Oh, and April, too!

We country folk crave mud so much that we liberally coat the sides of our cars and trucks with it, just to show off to city dwellers that we live out where Mother Nature intended us to. This is a great time of the year to stroll on our dirt roads, and our fields as well, just to have that heavy clay goo stuck to our boots. Why bother going to a gym to do leg exercises when you walk in the country and lift an extra five pounds with each step?

What I find amazing about our annual crop of mud is that I don't remember planting it. Yet each year it comes up, thick and juicy as wet concrete. If only our flowers grew that well. But as Spring continues on, each year we are faced with the dreaded dry season that follows. That darn sunshine is bad news for our mud. As spring wanes, I find myself heading out in the morning, turning on the garden hose, and wetting down the mud to keep it healthy as long as possible. Every additional day with mud is a day in paradise.

I should report a setback I had a couple years back. Just as mud season was beginning to peak, I was summoned away and missed almost a whole week of prime mud. I had to fly to Key West for a bachelor party. Bummer, huh? I was getting homesick down there because I saw no sign of mud. On the beach, I looked at the girls closely and saw no sign of mud on their bikinis. Trust me, I looked closely.

During mud season back here it's fun to fire up the big tractor and drive it back and forth through the lawn, trying to see how deep I can make the ruts. And that squishing sound adds so much to the ambiance!

Linda always remarks at the sight of mud streaks on her dark slacks as she gets out of the car. She knows that it marks her as "country."

Mud means money, too. Peak mud season always brings plenty of out-of-state vacationers to our local roads. You can't help but notice them peering out their car windows as they bump and bounce along, searching for the deepest, thickest and wettest browns that our area can provide. All the while they're snapping photos before heading back to Florida and Frisco, where they brag to their neighbors about the beautiful browns they saw.

Speaking of money and tourists, I need you to hear this out. Just like on CNN, you're hearing "breaking news" right now. I'm taking this opportunity to announce I am accepting cash donations for the development of the International Mud Wrestling Hall of Fame, which I think is a perfect match for this area (cash only; no personal checks, please). The location I have selected is on my buddy Johnnyboy's property, since he has enough space for it. I intend to let him know about it the day construction starts. With the Hall of Fame being located here, that will encourage local residents, young and old, to get out in our bountiful mud and start wrestling.

There are good reasons others of us love mud, too. My neighbor Jimmy owns a car wash; you can tell why he adores this time of year. And then there's a friend who operated the township's heavy equipment. He loves to play around in it with all his big boy toys, making brrm-brrm-brrm noises with them.

Alas, all good things must come to an end, and spring lasts not forever. By July most of our mud is only a fond memory. With a tear in my eye, each year on the Fourth after returning from the parade I scrape the finely-aged mud of March off the truck with a propane torch and a kitchen spatula. But I know with a quiet confidence that our mud season will be back again before long.

It's Senior Tuesday!

For you out there approaching your silver years, I have good news! You have the opportunity to save a few bucks on groceries every "Senior Tuesday." At least that's how it works at the grocery store where we shop.

To make the most of this, you need to hit the store early, before it starts crowding up by mid-morning. Getting there by eight, I only have to share the aisles with a smattering of other old fogeys. You can tell who we are. Call us "The Morning Dudes." In winter most of us wear blue or dark green jackets to go with our blue jeans and sneaks. Once the temp hits 50, shorts become optional for those of us who have the illusion that our legs still look athletic. We wear ball caps to hide the sorry remnants on our heads. We carry a small white slip of paper in hand with a bunch of words scribbled down on it like "eggs, cookies, beer." We don't waste time; we're on a mission. We know where our stuff is. We don't buy tofu. We hustle down the aisles quickly, decisively grabbing cans and boxes, then getting to the registers as soon as possible. We "Morning Dudes" don't have coupons. We don't ask for "cash back" at the checkout. Then we're gone.

As the clock moves towards ten, another crew appears. It's the silver and gold ladies, either alone or dragging their husbands along. You know who those guys are, too. They follow meekly around behind their wives, dutifully heeding instructions to put the right brand of coffee and the right kind of crackers into their carts. They are likable folk, these "Old Marrieds." They actually talk to one another. Or maybe mumble. They take time to visit with other couples they run into. Maybe it's their neighbors down the street. Or it's folks from church. Often it's someone vaguely familiar, but they can't remember who. You can't help but overhear them. Most conversations begin with an update on their latest trip to the doctor. You won't hear them re-hashing last night's football game.

A number of years ago when my parents were in their late 80's and living in a supersized retirement community in New Jersey, when we visited them Linda and I always offered to do their food shopping. But on Senior Day we dreaded shopping for them at their local market. And it usually was that day, because my mom watched her nickels to the end.

Let me set the scene. First of all, you couldn't find a place to park despite it being a lot the size of many National Parks. I usually ended up finding a spot next to the bank, almost out of sight from the store entrance. You had to dodge the other arriving shoppers as they erratically jerked their shiny full-size sedans up and down the lanes, their eyes barely above the dashboard. They were on a search for their elusive Holy Grail, that empty spot right outside the door. Once you were lucky enough to make it safely inside, it was constant chaos, almost as if the store was giving away free prune juice.

Many of them were old enough to know Calvin Coolidge personally. But it didn't appear any of them had ever owned a drivers' license the way they mishandled their shopping carts. How they managed to get them consistently stuck crosswise in the aisle was mind-boggling. They would stop to visit with everyone they smacked into, whether they knew them or not. On the days my dad went shopping with us, he was the worst. He would always try to make a joke with disinterested shoppers standing nearby. That added to the painful experience, and left me rolling my eyes.

One of our first stops was always the deli counter, where they were lined up about four deep. You had to take a number, and ours was usually something like 32 when they were only on 11. There often was only one clerk there, a hardscrabble 50-ish woman wearing a red cap with a rolled-up brim. She had the personality of a tugboat deckhand. When their number came up, everyone would order about nine items. "What kind of ham do you want?" the clerk would blurt, impatiently. There would be a delay, and the white-haired shopper would motion to the side of their head. "My hearing aid batteries aren't working. What did you say?" It only got worse from there.

When your cart was finally loaded, and you got disentangled from the others, then you had one last dreaded obstacle. Yup. The checkout line.

There were usually about eight carts ahead of you, some piled high with what appeared to be a decade's supply of toilet tissue and Depends. It was a perfect location for my dad, because he had a captive audience; they couldn't escape listening to his stories without forfeiting their place in line. Strangely enough, most of the other patrons seemed unaffected by his discourse on what he thought were interesting subjects. He'd converse on how he rode the trolley from North Bergen to Lyndhurst back in the Twenties, or how he had dug up a few dandelions in the neighbor lady's yard that morning. Maybe they couldn't hear him, so they just kept smiling. What made checking out even worse, was that every senior felt a need to pay with exact change. I'm guessing it was a matter of local culture. Ladies would reach deeply inside their handbag to find the right number of pennies hidden far down at the bottom of their purse, or men would reach into their pockets and, with a look of manly satisfaction, count out the ninety-seven cents before giving the handful of coins to the gal at the cash register. Ugh. Each one of those fifteen minute shopping excursions took at least two hours.

When I look back at going to that crowded supermarket with Dad, the memories now have mellowed, and it's all good. The years have taken him from us, and we've long ago made our last trip there. But today here at our local market, keep an eye out for us "Morning Dudes." You'll know us. Just don't get in our way.

The Bug In The Horn

The year was 1956; maybe early '57. So I would have been eight or nine. My hometown was split by a busy railroad line four tracks wide belonging to the West Shore division of the vast New York Central system. Today, only a single track remains. But back then, on those four tracks, the rumbling long freight trains and short commuter passenger trains of the Central rode behind black diesel engines wearing a bold "lightning stripe" paint scheme. The mile-long freights pounded through town at 40 mph, rattling windows, shaking the ground, and leaving a lifelong impression on youngsters like me.

But there was another train, too, this one in odd colors. Once a day a lone diesel in faded gray and orange pulled a short string of freight cars south through town, much slower than the Central's trains. Such was the New York, Ontario and Western; a decrepit railroad perennially teetering on the brink of bankruptcy. The Old & Weary, as it was affectionately known, ran on the Central's tracks through my home town to its terminus by the Hudson River at Weehawken.

Dad's bus driving schedule meant he had to get to work by daybreak to haul commuters from New Jersey to New York City. Then he had a layover of a few hours at home before going back to carry commuters home again. That worked great for me in the summer when school was out. Though a youngster, I was an eager train-watcher. I was oblivious to railroad schedules, so I thought it was just by chance that when Dad and I were heading to the hardware store in the green Chevy that we'd hear it. But he knew.

"It" was a diesel horn much different from the powerful growlers of the Central. I recall it being a muffled sound, somewhat off-key, like a novice taking his first blow on a trombone. It sure sounded funny. I'm not sure which one of us named it, but Dad and I called it the Bug-in-the-Horn. We'd be heading to town near the Church Street crossing, and Dad would bring the Chevy to a halt next to the tracks. The muffled diesel horn would blow, and the gray and orange diesel would rumble slowly through with its boxcars swaying. I'd be wide-eyed, grinning. Moments later the tracks would be still again; the caboose's marker lights disappearing down the tracks. Dad would start up the car and we'd finish the errands.

The "Bug-in-the-Horn" was a secret between Dad and myself. Heck, it would have been of no interest to anyone else. How many times did we share the experience? Though I've replayed the memory a thousand-fold, maybe it only happened a dozen times; perhaps less. Years have a way of changing perspective. Phrases like "bonding, "generation gap," and "quality time" were decades away from popularity. This was simply a young kid, a proud dad, and a train with a funny horn.

The Old and Weary finally gave up the ghost in '57 and went bankrupt. Its gray and orange diesels were sold off to other railroads. Dad lived to be ninety-one before going to glory. The night before he died, I held him as he lay in his hospital bed and thanked him for everything he did for the family and me through the years. I thanked him for working so hard to support the family, for taking us on vacations, for the love he showed us every day, and for being the unselfish father that he was. Maybe because it was such an emotional time, I regret that I forgot to thank him for one thing . . . .

The morning sun is shining brightly as we head to town. Suddenly, I hear it. I look up to see Dad knowingly smiling back as he quickens the pace. We exchange our special glances. In front of us, the crossing gates slowly drop as the warning bells sound. Dad pulls over and shuts off the motor. To our left a headlight draws closer. The ground shakes as The Bug-in-the-Horn and its string of boxcars rattle across the Church Street crossing, drowning the ringing of the warning bells.

Too soon, like life, it vanishes into the distance. The gates go back up, the bells become silent, and Fords and Chevvies once again cross the tracks.

Someday Dad and I will meet up again: at least I hope we will. I'll have a lot more to tell him then. And this time I'll remember to thank him for those sunny days years ago when the sound of a funny horn brought a father and a son closer together.

Ethel and The Witch Doctor

It wasn't too long ago I was sitting peacefully in a quiet place, paging through the "Bathroom Reader," when I saw a list of the biggest hit songs of 1958. I noticed hit #6 of the year was "The Witch Doctor," credited to David Seville. If you listened to your transistor radio back then, you may recall it even reached #1 on the weekly charts for a month or so. I know you've heard the tune; we all have.

If you're an old fogey like me, the song is stuck in your brain like super glue. You know how the chorus starts "ooo-eee, ooo ah-ah." Altogether there are 22 "sounds" that make up its chorus.

You may be interested to know that after extensive research and interviews, I've found that 85.4 % of folks in their 60s and 70s are familiar with the tune and can repeat the first two sounds, and 38.2% can even recite the whole 22-word mantra. Those amazing statistics reveal that it ranks second only to the percentage of those who know the correct words to "This Little Piggy Went to Market."

Why is that? And how did it happen?

First of all, "David Seville" is only a stage name for a guy we'll call Roger, who actually wrote and performed the song.

Secondly, how did he come up with his 22-sound chorus? And with that chipmunk-sounding voice? Can you imagine him trying line after line in his living room, to get one that was just right? His wife Ethel (I'm not using her real name to protect her identity and her money) had to sit through his many attempts. The conversation between the two of them after several hours each night may have gone something like this. She starts:

"Roger, or David, whatever your name is, stop all that nonsense. Put that guitar away and just be quiet for awhile. Or, better yet, go take a look at the washing machine. It's making that banging noise again . . .

"No honey, not now . . . I think I've got it . . . "ooo-eee, ooo-ah-ah, ting-tang . . . . "

"Oh Roger, here we go again with that foolishness. Why don't you put that thought away and write a love song? And did you hear me about the washing machine?"

"Just a minute, Ethel, I'm getting closer!"

"Roger, that stuff doesn't even rhyme. You should try something catchy like "Ramma-lamma ding-dong.""

"No chance. Someone already did that, Ethel. Wait . . . I've got it. Walla-walla-bing-bang."

Then an hour passes as Ethel watches "Ozzie and Harriet" and the next show, while Roger continues to fiddle with the chorus. Having heard enough for the night, she storms up from the sofa. "Roger, if you don't get off this stupid Witch Doctor kick, I'm going to take you to one of those head doctors. There's something not right with you."

"Walla-walla ooo-ah . . . oops, that's wrong. I gotta start over."

"Roger, did you forget to take your meds this morning?"

"No Ethel, I took them. And I'm getting close. Real close."

"You said that same thing last night at 3 A.M. Even our dog Alvin heads to the basement when you start with that dumb verse again and sing it like you're a squirrel in heat."

"It's gonna sell a million, I know it will. Have faith in me, honey."

"Hrrrmph. And, Roger, you promised me one more thing when you were finished with all this goofy Witch Doctor stuff."

"Uh, what was that again?"

"It's my flower garden. You said you would do something about it. My garden is overrun with chipmunks. They're digging holes all over it."

"Chipmunks, huh? That's got my creative juices flowing even more. Maybe next I could come up with a tune about them . . . ."

"For heaven's sake, Roger, get hold of yourself. And, for one more time, please go downstairs and take a look at the washing machine."

"Hmmmm . . . chipmunks . . . thanks to you, honey, I've got it!

A Childhood Thrill!

As a kid I loved to get postcards in the mail. My parents always managed to put food on the table, but couldn't afford to take my sisters and me to any fancy places, let alone on exotic vacations. I was more fortunate than some of my friends, though, since I had aunts and uncles who traveled. When Aunt Jo and Uncle Harry did their annual trip to Bermuda or Venezuela, they always remembered us kids with postcards. What a thrill to get them! Somewhere in our attic, I know I still have a few stashed away. They would also go to the lake at Deposit, NY, for a week each summer. My sisters and I would get postcards showing pine trees and old wooden inns around Oquaga Lake. They never forgot us. Many times I have taken those postcards out to read them again. There are even some postcards from childhood of which I remember their wording. When my cousin Billy and his parents went by ocean liner to Europe back in '56, he sent me a card mailed from the *SS United States*. I remember it well. It showed a side view of the majestic ship, and Billy wrote that "British planes have been flying over us all day." Even some less exotic cards are still etched in my memory. When we were about ten, my buddy Giz went to the Jersey Shore with his parents for a week. He sent me a postcard written in pencil that read "Yesterday we went fishing. Today we are going to the beach." I probably still have that one stashed away somewhere, too.

By age twelve I was starting to grow up, and I finally went somewhere by myself. Yup, I was shipped off to Boy Scout camp for a week in the summer. Now it was my turn to send a postcard! My first day there I found one at the camp's trading post. I printed it out in pencil, stuck a three-cent stamp on it, then sent it to Mom and Dad. Naw, I wasn't homesick or anything. Hah! It probably pictured a lean-to like the one we stayed in, or canoes on the lake. Or maybe a bear, even though we never saw one. I'm sure the message told them how icy cold the swimming was in the lake, or about the raccoon that got into my buddy Ralph's Hershey bars. My mom kept the postcards for years, then gave them to me just a few years ago before she died. And yeah, I still have that one in a box somewhere.

People don't send postcards anymore. Why should they? They take along their Smartphones, tablets or whatever, and effortlessly snap a selfie on the beach, and email them or Facebook them or whatever. But it's not the same as getting those wonderful old postcards, which took more effort to send. When you got one, it meant you were somebody special.

Today we take what used to be called "living color" for granted. Everything is in color now, including a lot of things that shouldn't be. We forget that prior to 1940 or so, the only color scenes to be found were paintings or hand-painted/hand-tinted postcards. A lot of us kids collected postcards, and some are still saved in albums. It's also a business, too, as you can see by checking online. Postcards that show turn-of-the-century buildings, railroad depots, women in their Sunday-best hats, or Main Street with trolley cars are considered valuable because they show what colors those things once were and what everyday life was like. Comparatively few of those cards were sent; even fewer were saved. On the other hand, postcards that show Florida orange groves are not as prized, because everyone seemed to have an Aunt Millie and Uncle Ed who vacationed in the Sunshine State in February and sent them back to shivering family members up north. And then there are scenes that haven't changed. Postcards sent from Gettysburg in 1920 showing Civil War monuments look just like the ones for sale today.

Even before picture postcards, there used to be message postcards. Back around 1900, other than Western Union telegrams, postcards were the only way to get a message to out-of-town family. They were blank and cost one cent to send, and often bore tragic news. Here's one that I have saved: "I am sorry to tell you that Papa is ill, and will not make it. We are heartbroken." Addresses back then were often simple, such as this one: "Miss Susan Conover, Bayonne, New Jersey."

Today you can find vintage postcards at flea markets, antique stores, or in a shoebox in your aunt's closet. They are fun to look through, and to read what was sent. They tell of events that were important back then, but seem so mundane today. Here's a message on an old one I picked up somewhere: "Having a great time. Will be in Binghamton tomorrow." How about this one: "Car is running real good, but oil is running right through the engine." Or this card, showing a long gone luncheonette in a small town: "This is where we had lunch today." Messages like that were important, back in the day. But times have changed, and we have, too. Folks traveling today rarely bother to send postcards. Few places sell them anymore. We're in a different era, that of social media. Maybe we're just too wrapped up in ourselves to share a thought, or an event, with others in our life. Or we tap out so many messages and photos that everyone is overloaded.

Indeed, postcards are going the way of the typewriter and the rotary phone. Another slice of American life has passed on. Maybe I'll be the last person to miss them.

Geezer's Choice Awards

One of our regional newspapers asks us locals to name our favorite businesses in the area. They call it the annual "Reader's Choice Awards." It's an interesting contest, and it's become an event that generates a lot of buzz every year. The winners in each category get an official certificate signed by someone who works at the newspaper.

"Favorite Restaurant," "Favorite Auto Parts Store," and "Favorite Hairdresser" are some examples. "Favorite Place To Eat Chicken Wings" is one that gets more specific. I see they didn't list "Favorite Politician."

The only problem with asking for favorites from everyone who reads the paper, is that the results are too general. What the paper should try to identify is favorites for certain groups of people. "Reader's Choice" winners for young people (those under 55) may be quite different from our group of folks. To wit, I'm suggesting the newspaper begin a "Geezer's Choice Awards" contest so the whole world knows what makes us Seniors tick. Some of the categories might be:

Favorite clothing store to buy plaid slacks

Favorite location to tell stories to no one in particular

Favorite store to use their restroom

Favorite restaurant to spend an entire morning drinking coffee

Favorite barbershop to discuss this year's corn crop

Favorite doctor's office to tease the nurses

Favorite parking lot to take a nap in

Favorite radio station to listen to Kingston Trio tunes

Favorite highway to drive down at 20 miles per hour

Favorite used car lot to hunt for an AMC Gremlin

Favorite location to leave your glasses

Favorite store to buy prune juice

Favorite sports bar to watch Petticoat Junction reruns
Favorite store that's now a vacant lot
Favorite restaurant to buy oatmeal
Favorite store that you can't find anymore
Favorite downhill slalom course to test your walker

If the paper started this kind of contest today, a lot more of us would be interested in submitting our choices. Now, let me see, where did I put that entry form? I know it's here somewhere . . . .

Running Out of Time

Hey there! Take a look at that 'ol calendar. Days are passing too quickly, aren't they? Forget about all that carrying on down in Washington. Before today's game comes on, get your buns outside and get working on that house painting you've been putting off. I've heard the same story before. You've had a busy summer so there's no way you could possibly have done it then. When was the last time you painted the trim on your place? You're guessing offhand maybe three or four years ago? Think again. Try eight years ago. Maybe ten. More? Could that be why you're avoiding looking at it?

So now you've been shamed into taking on the project. Good start. Remember to factor in the prep time it takes. Maybe you already bought the paint. So that's Step Two. But where did you store the can? There it is; you found it in the basement. You recall you had it stirred by the machine when you bought it. Again, good move. But that was weeks ago. Or was it last year? And if you're really sharp, you remember where you put the wooden paint stirrer that came with it. Oops, it's got crap all over it. When the mood finally hits you and you get the urge to get the job done, you open the can. Ugh. After quickly wiping the stirrer with your sleeve, you stick it in and it feels like it's half full of wet clay. So you gotta work at getting it stirred. It slops around some, and now you notice some drops on that pricey t-shirt you got down at the Shore. Darn it! And you can't wear those new sneaks, can you, and get crap all over them? Where's that old pair? Dunno. Lost another half hour looking for them. For a lot of trim jobs at our house Linda reminds me to use tape to keep the paint lines straight. No need, I'm thinking, with my artist's eye and nerves of steel I can save time by not bothering with tape. That usually turns into a "discussion" after midway through painting trim, I get a momentary spasm, and the brush goes all bockety.

Jumping back to square one, just picking out the right paint is a struggle. When you read the tiny print, every can says it might cause cancer in California. With all those wackos out West, it doesn't surprise me. So you make an executive decision and grab the brand that promises you only need to use one coat. Why not? That's saving time and money. Good move! You save more money by buying an inexpensive brush. Oops, what's this? It was made in a country you've never heard of. After a few hours, one coat is on and you step out into the yard and check it out. Not bad. Will it pass muster? In my case, Linda says "Nope." She does all the Quality Control in our household. "One more coat should do it." Should? So it's back to the store for more "one coat covers all" paint to slap on. What time is Happy Hour, anyway?

Ours is a one story home, so that makes it easier to reach most places. A number of years ago when I was helping to paint a house that was almost three stories high, I was petrified. I climbed the rungs like my arms were made of jelly. The knees were knocking like a pair of castanets. Took me five minutes just to get up there. When I finally got to the top where I was supposed to paint, I couldn't figure out how to do it. Since I needed to hold onto the ladder with both white-knuckled hands, how was I supposed to handle a paint brush too? With my teeth? And reaching out to the side to actually spread paint? You gotta be kidding me.

At our place we have a roof over a storage room that leads outside from the basement. Unfortunately it has only a small pitch, so it can't be shingled. We had an addition many years ago done by our builders. They said I need to put a new coating of aluminized goo on its roof every year. Not wanting a leak, I've been dutifully slapping on a new coat every August. Each can I've used says the coating is good for seven years. With all the coatings I've put on, I multiplied 7 times 30 years, so I really shouldn't have to do it again for 210 years. I would probably need that many years to find the correct time to do it, since the directions say to only use it when no precipitation or dew will occur for 72 hours. Are you kidding me? When is the last time it's been that dry around here for three days? They might as well say don't use it on a month with four Tuesdays.

When you're finally done with the day's work, it's time to clean up. According to the can, it says (using their gentle terminology) to clean up with mineral spirits. That makes it sound like after a full day of painting, you might end up with a tiny spot of white paint on your thumb. Yeah, right. What the can should say is "Remove all clothing, totally immerse yourself in a large tub of kerosene and rub all parts of your skin vigorously with a wire brush for twenty minutes." Then, "Repeat." Whenever I paint something I seem to have remnants from where the hairs on my head used to be, down to my shoes. And after my initial cleaning I still find traces on the back of my arm, or on parts of my body that never came in contact with the brush.

But despite going through all the headaches involved with painting, you know you can't put it off any longer. It's time to get outside while it's still warm enough to get the job done.

On second thought, maybe after I get the can stirred, I'll just watch a few minutes of the first half. I can always finish painting tomorrow.

I'm Granny Yeager's Rocker

Bwank-bwank-bwank

I don't mean to frighten you, but that's the sound I make when I rock back and forth. The calendar on the wall says 1889 and I've just been born from a tall oak tree. Muscular, loving hands created me in a woodworking shop amid the aroma of fresh maple and cherry shavings. There was some stinky smoke, too, but I didn't mind. I feel young and strong!

Bwank-bwank-bwank

A few months have passed. I've been bundled up, and now I'm in a house in a little village. The big willow tree outside the window keeps me cool on warm afternoons. When I came here it was snowing. They placed me across the room from the big black coal stove. It was so cozy when it sizzled! Sometimes a friendly dog lies against me; his name is Jippy. His fur is soft and fuzzy against my legs. Granny Yeager is the nice lady who takes care of me.

Bwank-bwank-bwank

Many years have passed. It's 1921 now, and I've moved upstairs into Granny's sitting room. I've been here for a long time, and I feel so loved. Granny bakes a fresh pie every morning, so the house always smells so delightful!

I live in a dark red company house, just down the hill from all that racket at the coal tipple. So much noise out there: endless lumps of anthracite rattling against the conveyor belt, and those smoky steam engines clanging their coal cars together all night long.

My favorite time of the day is when that little girl with the curls, Lorraine, sits with me in the late afternoon sun and keeps me company while she plays with her paper dolls. Sometimes she whispers to them.

And Granny wipes me off with a damp cloth every evening to get the dust off. That's so cool and refreshing!

Bwank-bwank-bwank

It's a long time later now, 1979, and I've been here in this dining room for thirty years or so. I was bundled up a long time ago, and moved far away from Granny. I don't know what happened to her. But it's OK, because I'm still with the little girl. Lorraine has grown into a woman, a mother, but she still loves me. A nice man lives here too. He doesn't pay much attention to me, but he makes Lorraine smile. She carefully lays her finest quilts on me, and her favorite needlework. They keep me warm. But not today. All the fabrics have been gathered up and put in a box. I think I'm going to be bundled up again. Strange men, young and reeking of perspiration, are here. I think they will be lifting me into that big truck parked in the driveway.

Bwank-bwank-bwank

Twenty years have passed. The calendar says 1999 and I live in a different house. It's only a tiny home, but Lorraine likes it. I spend my time in a crowded room next to her bed. The nice man with her has become sick. Lorraine worries about him so, but she still cares for me. When she feels well, she rubs a soothing oil on me. It seeps into my skin and makes me feel young again. But I can feel Lorraine's hands are growing weaker. Late last night I could hear her sobbing into her pillow. I'm afraid I will be bundled up again soon.

Bwank-bwank-bwank

It's only four years later but I have a new home once again, after I was bundled up. I've come to like it here, though it's so far away. I'm at Joe and Linda's house , and . . .good news . . . I'm back in the living room again! There's a friendly cat that jumps on me, but she gets yelled at when she does. Her fur tickles me; I kind of like it. I'm feeling better. I've got an artificial hip so it doesn't hurt as much when I rock to and fro. It's hard being away from Lorraine. I don't know what happened to her. Maybe someday she'll come visit me. I hope so; I miss how she softly caressed me, and how she'd talk about Granny.

Bwank-bwank-bwank

The calendar reads 2027 or 2028, I'm not sure. I'm so scared. I've been bundled up again. It's cold up here. I'm so alone. There's nobody here that I know, or who cares about me. No warm fur. No one has rubbed oil on me for a very long time. I'm up on a stage, it's loud and there's all these strange faces down there. They are holding up little white cards with numbers on them. A lot of them looked closely at me and poked at me. I don't know who they are, and I'm scared.

Now the man with that loud voice is pointing at me, and cards are being lifted in the air. I'm so alone.

I wish the little girl and her paper dolls were still here with me . . . .

Which Way is North?

We seniors can find lots of ways to criticize younger generations, much as our parents found fault with our long hair, bell bottoms, and the Beatles. I'm one of the first to point fingers. My latest soap box speech has to do with knowing where we are in the world around us.

Okay. Once again, I'm reminded that times have changed, and I need to be in step with the 21st century. Today many of us have the luxury of GPS technology (global positioning) while we're driving. When we're in unfamiliar locations, having GPS at our fingertips to find our way can be a fantastic help. Linda and I rely on it when we're driving in a strange city. My role is to white-knuckle the steering wheel as rumbling 18-wheelers and SUVs zip by in the passing lane at warp speed. She is glued to her iPhone and tells me how far it is to our exit, which lane to switch to, or the name of the next road. It's truly a form of magic. Clark Kent would be impressed. So would Henry Ford.

Her navigation has saved us many times over from going around in circles, or wasting time trying to locate an address. I get it. It's something we have come to rely on in today's world. But is it a good thing to be dependent on GPS wherever you go? On trips with people in the younger generation I've been noticing they rely on that technology every time they hop in their Honda, rather than trying to familiarize themselves with their surroundings. What's up with that? And what about maps? They seem to have gone the way of manual typewriters. Is that a good thing? Not always, I'd venture.

Here's an example. A few years ago I was with a number of American Red Cross volunteers driving through the Florida panhandle headed for Panama City, which had been obliterated by a hurricane days before. Its fierce winds had knocked out electricity for many miles around, and flattened cell towers. Many roads were blocked off due to trees being down. Nobody's cell phone could connect with GPS. Trying to find the way to Panama City would have entailed many more hours of frustration and danger had I not added a Florida road map to my backpack. Several of the others with me were surprised I brought it along. One of my colleagues looked at it like it was from an antique store. But it worked. It got us safely through the chaos.

Whatever the younger people are known as these days (Generation X or Y?) they seem overly dependent on GPS to get anywhere when they're driving; even if it's only across town. And if they're away from home visiting friends or perhaps hunting for a watering hole, they let their Uber driver find their way rather than figuring it out for themselves. Heading north or south has become meaningless. Many of us who grew up years back had a much better sense of where we were in the world, what direction we were going, and how to get there.

There were a lot of reasons for that. First of all, as kids many of us loved to look at maps. Before Dad backed the old Chevy out of the driveway, my sisters Carol, Lynn and I would have a road map out to see where we were going on our trip. We'd know, for example, that in going to visit cousins in Massachusetts we'd be heading north of Connecticut and east toward Boston. Then we'd follow the map along as we went. We'd actually look out the car windows to see where we were, rather than sitting with our heads down, focused on a smartphone or GameKid. Does that happen at all these days?

There were other ways we knew more about the world around us. Riding in the back seat, we'd be looking out the window with eyes wide, reading town names and committing them to memory. We learned we lived in a huge, mysterious and wonderful country. When Dad would bring the car to a stop in their driveway after the long trip, we'd have a sense of landmarks and towns reminding us how we'd get back home.

Today, if some rogue country or terrorists knocked our GPS satellites out of commission, most Americans wouldn't have the foggiest idea of how to get anywhere.

I think I'll hold onto my roadmaps.

Saving Your Local Post Office

Perhaps you're old enough to remember needing only a three-cent stamp to mail a letter. That was back in the stone age, before the advent of email and tweeting, and texting. Indeed, people actually wrote letters to other people back in the day.

You who live in rural areas also remember there were many more village post offices than today. A few years back as a cost-saving measure, hundreds of the smallest post offices were closed. Not only did that cause hardship for folks who lived in the boondocks, but their closure caused even more of a loss within those little towns. In many cases, with the closure went the whole sense of community around the village. In the good old days of Americana, the post office was a gathering place to share all the local news, like hearing that farmer Brown was the first to get his hay in, and the juicy gossip, like the widow Carlson's mysterious late-night caller.

Many changes have occurred since the long-lost days of the three cent stamp. We now have a forever stamp. What was once the Post Office has now become the U.S. Postal Service. Some tragic incidents have happened at post offices in the last twenty years. But one fact remains constant: the postal service is losing money. A lot of it.

We hear periodically that extensive federal budget-cutting efforts are on the horizon. Our two political parties joust over it. The USPS will take their turn on the chopping block, even though they no longer are a direct federal agency. Rumors abound in Washington that another round of closures could occur. Undoubtedly that will affect some of our smaller communities. That's such a shame for a more personal reason, too. The clerks at the rural post offices are usually nice, chatty, helpful folks. They know most of us by name. Those at the big-city post offices just growl when you finally get to the front of the line and humbly ask to buy a couple stamps. Or they roll their eyes if you dare ask to explain the difference between Priority and other rates.

Fortunately, there is a solution to this upcoming post office closure crisis. And the good news is that it's easy to do, and won't cost you and I anything. It won't raise our taxes one cent. But you're the one who has to do it!

Here's how it goes. Every day in your mailbox you receive perhaps four or five pieces of mail from companies trying to sell you stuff you don't want. Maybe you get twice that amount. Traditionally it's been magazine publishers, but recently there's been a run on auto insurance offers. Satellite TV networks are close behind. Or else it's from banks or credit card companies wanting you to take advantage of their latest offer. One thing, though, is in common. Many provide postage-paid envelopes in which to respond. Those companies are later billed by the Postal Service by the number of envelopes people return.

Many of us routinely just glance at junk mail, and toss it in the trash. My friend Judy said she always opens her mail over the waste basket to save time. But don't do it! if you toss those out, you won't be saving your local post office. What you need to do is to take a few moments, open each piece of mail, and set aside those with postage-paid return envelopes. In the one from the insurance company, enclose the ad from the septic tank pumping company, seal it, and mail it. In the postage-paid envelope from the credit card company, put in last week's grocery list, seal it, and mail it. You get the idea.

Do it, and the big companies will cough up the loot to keep the Postal Service in the black. Our local post offices will be saved!

I'd like to think I came up with this magnificent plan myself, but I have to give credit to my brother-in-law Al. He's a life-long Democrat, and whenever he gets mail from Republican candidates asking for donations, he adds a colorful comment on a scrap of paper, stuffs it in the postage-paid envelope, and sends it back unsigned. I'm sure they enjoy reading his replies.

Anyway, back to what you and I have to do. I've done some rough figuring, and I figure if everyone in the United States sends back four pieces of postage-paid mail each day, it will raise revenue for the Postal Service by 6.2 kazillion dollars per year.

That is more than enough additional revenue to save all our rural post offices. I double-checked my figures, and although I haven't taken any math since I got a "C" in 5th grade, I think the numbers are accurate.

But remember, you and I have to do it. And there's no time to waste. Hey, here comes Susan the mail carrier pulling up to our mailbox right now . . . .

World War II: Still Very Personal

How easy it is to forget how miserable war can be. In the news these days we hear about a potential conflict with North Korea, or with Russia. Maybe Iran. Are we out of our gourds? You guys who went to Vietnam know what it was like. Same for you Korea, Gulf War and Afghan vets. Back in 1861 when the Civil War broke out, thousands and thousands of men immediately signed up on both sides, imagining war to be a grand adventure. Then came the horror. Haven't we learned from all this?

Today Memorial Day is a time to enjoy a three-day weekend and plan picnics, camping, boating, golf, or softball tournaments. To young people today, World War II may seem like ancient history. Do they even teach it in high school any more? Do youngsters know what D-Day was? To those of us in our silver or gold years, that awful war remains very real. Almost every one of us has some kind of personal connection.

To my good friend Randy, it was his father. He landed on Normandy's Omaha Beach while enemy shells were still falling everywhere. As part of the Army's 28th Division, he hiked his way through France, Belgium, Luxembourg, and Germany, fighting for the freedom we all take for granted today. Along the way, Charles Witmer earned a Silver Star and Bronze Star for bravery. During one major battle, his unit became surrounded by enemy tanks. He assembled his anti-tank weapon, fired, and disabled enough tanks to allow his unit to escape the trap to safety, saving many American lives. After the war was over, he came home to Oil City, worked in the Post Office, and rarely mentioned his contributions to our country.

My buddy Johnnyboy's father was equally as brave, and just as low-keyed about his service. He flew 25 missions in a B-17 bomber over Germany. It may not seem so dangerous to us living in peace 75 years later, but one in every four fliers in those bombers never made it home. Enemy fighter planes and ground fire made every mission dreadfully dangerous. On some missions, half our bombers were shot down. Harold Hibner came back to his hometown, raised a family, started a business, and put his heroic service behind him.

At the same time those B-17s were flying their perilous missions, my college bud Flash's father was a radio operator on B-24 bombers. He also managed to survive 25 missions on some of the most dangerous missions of the war over German-held territory. He came home, began working, and rarely mentioned the horrors he had experienced in seeing other planes in his squadron shot down in flames.

Linda's father did his part too. His role was on hospital ships in the Pacific, where their crews provided compassionate care to soldiers injured in battle or suffering from disease. He lived into his 90's and talked little of the time he spent doing his part during WWII.

My good friend Howie's father was a Navy Seabee. Working in a construction battalion, he built runways on remote Pacific islands for American bombers that helped bring the war in Japan to a close. He was on an island called Tinian when a B-29 bomber took off from the runway he helped build. It carried a special payload; an atomic bomb.

Many of you reading this have your personal connections to World War II. Maybe you fought in it, or maybe you stayed on the home front doing your part during this terrible time. Or your dad or uncle or grandpa put on a uniform. Women took important jobs wherever they could. Everyone made a contribution.

Uncle Bob fought in the deadly Battle of the Bulge in 1944. He was a forward observer, which meant he went, often alone, ahead of most other troops to locate enemy forces. In that battle, thousands of our soldiers died fighting in the snow. How many more would have perished if not for his scouting work? Uncle George served in the Pacific theater in a supportive capacity. Uncle Howard packed parachutes to save the lives of flyers. These brave men returned safely home and lived into their 80s, but Uncle Chet was not so lucky. He gave his life when, as a fighter pilot, he was shot out of the sky by enemy anti-aircraft guns. It is for Uncle Chet, and all the other brave men and women who served and gave their lives for our freedom, that we celebrate Memorial Day.

As you enjoy your holiday weekend, take a few minutes to remember the sacrifice so many fine young people made to help us have the freedom we enjoy today. And let those lessons keep us from sending today's young people off to war.

Why Are the Ball Fields Empty?

Spring, those glorious months of the year when we hear the crack of the bat, and watch the ball streaking out to center field. Ah, baseball. America's Springtime passion! That was then. The Fifties. Those halcyon days of Willie Mays, PeeWee Reese, and Mickey Mantle. Fast forward to today. Welcome to the electronic game age. Or maybe it's the "soccer mom" age.

Have you noticed how many times you pass a well-manicured ball diamond now on a Spring afternoon, and see it deserted? In the evening, adults will be filling the dugouts, hitting the softball as their pickup trucks sit parked outside the fences, coolers brimming with cold drinks. But what about the afternoon? Why isn't the backstop ringed with bicycles, and youngsters clamoring about?

It wasn't always that way. Back in the Fifties and Sixties, you had to get there right after school to claim the field. Kids would hurriedly drop their books off at home, grab a glass of milk, yell to mom that they were going to play ball, and pedal furiously over to the field, balancing a bat and glove across the handlebars of their dependable old Schwinn.

Back then, we kids knew how to get a game going without an adult standing around to coach us, or to tell us who was "out" and who was "safe." We'd arrive at the field in a flurry, wearing our dungarees and white tee shirts, and "choose up" sides. Nobody liked being the last guy picked, but everybody was chosen, and everybody played. Those of us among the last picked knew better than to gripe.

Back in my home town we named our sandlot team the Ungies. None of us can remember where that name came from. Everyday after school when it wasn't raining, we'd be off to the field. My best friends Gunnar and Giz were always there with me. Giz may not have been the most fleet of foot, but we always found a spot for him to play. Usually right field. Back then if for some reason there weren't enough guys, we played without a right fielder, and Giz would move in to play catcher. He couldn't do much damage there, and he knew it as well as we did. He would have gone to first base, but that was Gunnar's domain. Without a right fielder, if you hit to right field, you were out.

We Ungies would play ball till dinner time, most every day through the spring and into summer. Finding an empty ball diamond on a warm afternoon was as rare as finding an empty casino parking lot today. Perhaps you might say these observations are merely the forlorn lament of an old geezer, but think again. Getting together to play ball was more than smacking line drives and making a nice catch. We didn't realize it then, but we were learning how to organize. How to make rules. We'd share ball gloves. We learned to schmooze those who weren't sure they wanted to play today; heck,we needed them! We learned how to negotiate among ourselves. How to be fair. We learned that some of us were better ballplayers than others, but our buddies at the bottom of the batting order still knew they were a member of our team, and were counted on. Giz may have been slow getting to the ball, but that boy could hit liners. Adults? They would have only got in the way. This was our game. Girls? We didn't have time for them.

But time moves on. Many of today's youngsters have benefited greatly from Little Leagues, and soccer has taken off like dandelions in the outfield. Soccer? Back then, we vaguely knew it was a dumb sport they played in faraway places like Italy.

Now as I pass empty ball diamonds, I can't help but wonder where today's kids are learning how to negotiate with one another, how to make rules, and how to follow them. How do they decide who should be hitting clean-up? Can they plan games themselves, or do they have to wait for adults to do it for them? Or, are games played only on electronic gadgets?

You can't turn back the clock, but I'd feel better if today's kids knew the importance of always making a place for Giz in right field.

Cutting Brush

If you live in rural America, you know all about the springtime routine of cutting brush. To those of you who live in town, you may wonder what it's all about. Here's the skinny:

It all begins with weed control. First, there's run-of-the-mill weeds that move into your lawn or fields in a never-ending pursuit to grow and make babies. They either can be yanked out by hand, cut down by shears or by using a variety of gas-powered machines that cost a couple hundred bucks each. You also can spread stuff that costs fifty bucks a bag over these weeds. That's providing your lawn spreader didn't get too rusty over the winter. It may take a few hours to get them under control, but they are tame as vanilla. They aren't the bad boys. This is all about our blood-thirsty foes; the ones that attack you.

Briars. A real enemy of mankind. In researching their real scientific names, I found misleadingly comfy names like Dewberry and Sweet Briar. That's akin to seeing a 20-foot python coiled up outside your front door, and calling it "only a worm." These briars have sharp barracuda-like thorns to cut you to shreds. We country folk call them by hyphenated names. Gardening experts humorously suggest wearing "thick gardening gloves" when you cut them back. Hah! What you really need is a Tin Man outfit from the Wizard of Oz.

That's not all. You may have heard that in Washington, the CDC recently announced new guidelines for us guys who go out to do a face off with briars. They strongly suggest wearing a Kevlar jockstrap. I'm not sure what they came up with for the ladies. These briars won't just destroy your hands, they gouge your forearms, shred your legs and rip your earlobes. They can reach out with vengeance and scar your cheeks. Their goal is to sever your aorta. When you come inside after surviving the battle and look into the mirror, it appears you fell into the path of a runaway snowblower on steroids.

So how to get rid of them? I suggest you go down to your neighborhood Army-Navy store and pick up a few hundred gallons of surplus defoliant Agent Orange. Pour it into that attachment you saw on TV for your garden hose, turn that baby on, and let them have a heavy blast. If by chance the store is all sold out to others in your neighborhood or township, some well-placed explosive devices might do the trick. Use them liberally.

The gardening "experts" (again, humorously) say the way to eliminate them is to cut down the stems and paint them with 41% glyphosate. That deadly elixir is also known as Round-Up. It's the same toxic stuff that's the subject of lawsuits across the land, since using it has been identified as causing cancer. Not just in laboratory mice, but also in humans who garden a lot and spread 41% glyphosate on briars. My guess is those experts don't have any objection with using Agent Orange. If you inadvertently overspray it onto your neighbor's azaleas, they'll eventually forgive you. Maybe.

And guys, here's another option for you. If you still harbor revenge in your heart from a traumatic event that occurred decades ago, try this. Dig up the briars' root balls in their entirety. It's not easy; you may need to use a backhoe. Load them into the back of your pickup. Next you'll need to wait until total darkness. Drive over to where that girl lives who turned you down for a date to the junior prom fifty-plus years ago. Yeah, I know she's aged a bit. So have you. Sneak over to her garden and plant the root balls among her prized orchids and roses. Tip-toe back to your truck, then go home and get a refreshing night's sleep. Drive by in a couple days and see if she is out there feverishly digging away, with red streaks on her arms and legs. Trust me: you will feel so much better.

You may recall that years ago when George Bush (the younger) was president, every Spring he would go down to his Texas ranch on vacation. The squadron of photographers who accompanied him would have a photo op to snap pictures of him cutting brush while trying his best to look like a normal country dude. But no sullen look for the prez. He'd be wearing an eighty dollar button-down shirt rather than an old blood-stained gray sweatshirt, and without a single Band-Aid on his cheek. It doesn't take an expert to see he wasn't doing real brush-cutting. If so, he would have been accompanied by the Surgeon General riding along in a half-track.

The news gets even worse for country folk. There are other denizens out there, threatening to take over. Multi-flora rose bushes grow like gangbusters, and they too have an attitude. Just ask my buddy Johnnyboy. Death by brush-hog is one answer. If you choose to cut them back with pruning shears, you won't win. Too tame. Try sharpening an ax, drink three cups of high-octane coffee, get all fired up and hack away at those buggers like you're doing an O.J. Simpson imitation. You may not kill them, but it's good for the soul.

I know it's not easy out there. But we country boys are tough. Give it your best shot. Winning is everything.

Not So Silent Night

Recently I was lying awake on a frigid night at home, with a great shroud of snowy silence hanging over everything outside our window. The only sound I heard was the flushing of the toilet in the International Space Station when it passed overhead.

The silence made me daydream about a warmer time, recalling a summer night about twenty years ago when our crew was on our annual canoe trip in Ontario, well up past North Bay. We had been out paddling in the backcountry, and hadn't seen any other humans in a day or two. Just critters. I recall that the quiet that night was overwhelming. I was lying by myself in a one-man tent perched on the shore of a good-sized lake. It was well after midnight. The buzz of the mosquitoes had quieted, and the only sound to be heard was the haunting tremolo call of a loon on a lake a mile or so away. The tiny tent I had brought must have been designed for the infant child of a dwarf. Being the first to clamor out of our canoes in the late afternoon, I had claimed this prime tent site that offered a grand lakeside view. Our group's three other tents had less scenic sites, bunched together further up the rocky hill. Now in the thick of night, the only light was from the parade of stars overhead. The night was calm and silent. And peaceful.

Until I heard the noise.

What was that? It was the sound of a critter at the garbage bag where we had gathered our non-burnable trash. But what was it? I could hear metal cans clinking against one another. In an instant I was fully awake. I realized I had stupidly forgotten to hang our trash bag in a safe place; from a tree limb. At least I should have stashed it closer to the others' tents. It was closest to mine. Then I heard the noise again.

Was it a grunt? Or my heartbeat? I couldn't tell. I went through the possibilities. I started with the smallest. Mice were out of the question: too small to make cans clink. Perhaps a raccoon, foraging. A skunk, hungry for a handout, waiting to unload on anyone who came near? Maybe a black bear. Egad. Will I be torn to pieces, the subject of a harrowing story in Reader's Digest? Or could a huge moose have gamboled into camp? We had seen signs of them earlier. They were around. The more I thought, the options were not all that good.

I wondered if any others in our group heard the critter. But their tents were further away, and after a hard day's paddle they all were making big time zzz's. Since I don't carry a firearm, my only weapon was my flashlight. I reached around for it, and shined it around inside my tent. Okay, I said to myself, use your voice. I yelled "Get outta here!" Then I waited. Silence. The chorus of zzz's continued from the other tents. What to do?

Just to be safe, I rolled out of my sleeping bag, where I was humped up like a baked potato, and reached over to put on my boots. All was quiet. The yell did it. I breathed a sigh of relief, and shoved my boots aside..

Then I heard it again. Cans rattling. Whatever it was, it had to be big enough, and it didn't scare easily. I figured that pretty much ruled out a raccoon.

By now the excitement had put additional pressure on my bladder. I gathered intestinal fortitude, zipped open the tent while still on hands and knees, and shined my flashlight in the direction of the trash. My heart was pounding. I saw no eyeballs. Nothing. Our trash bag was hidden behind some jackpines, and the black night swallowed the light before it reached far enough. I couldn't see anything. A few mosquitoes buzzed over to lay claim to my blood, so I zipped the tent door shut. I hovered on hands and knees inside the tent door, my back up against the nylon roof, my bladder readying to bust. Think. I had to figure out my next move.

Perhaps the flashlight beam scared it away. But I hadn't heard any heavy footsteps retreating into the bush, so maybe it was still there . . . . a black bear or a moose couldn't be seen in the dark, nor would it be easily spooked.

What was that? Another grunt? Or my imagination?

I thought about calling out to my buddy Johnnyboy for help, but he could sleep through a propane explosion. Fellow trekkers Dennis and The Chief were both calmly snoring. Maybe Connie would hear me. But what could she do? And if it turned out to be my imagination, I would be the subject of incessant ribbing for the remainder of our trip. That could prove more hurtful than a bear attack.

I laid back down for now. Quiet returned. Soon I heard the loon's call again far in the distance. Maybe the critter was gone. I knew I'd have to get out of the tent soon, since my bladder was growing bigger than a football. I wondered if sleep would ever come this night. A long paddle and several portages awaited us come morning, so I needed major sleep.

Then I heard it in the cans again. Louder. Okay, that does it. With a testosterone rush, I grabbed my flashlight, unzipped the tent, stumbled, then stood up and headed barefoot bravely into the dark for the trash bag, and the confrontation. I shined the light behind the jackpines where I knew the bag was. And there, licking out our cans, was the critter. A big ol' rabbit.

Boy, I'm glad I didn't yell for Johnnyboy.

Forgotten No More

The last of the gray morning clouds scudded past, as the crowd gathered on a grassy field in the Nation's Capital. It was Flag Day, a few years ago. Sunshine highlighted the Armed Forces color guard as they lined up. Just over the hill was "The Wall," that black granite memorial listing the 58,272 brave Americans who lost their lives in combat during the Vietnam Conflict.

But the final toll of that ugly war is far from complete. This day families and friends have come to honor 121 more victims; soldiers, sailors and air force personnel who gave their lives for our country, not in active combat, but years later as a result of Vietnam war-related causes.

Among these latest casualties lies my good friend Lynn. He enlisted in the Army in 1967, as the war was ramping up. An infantry soldier, his battlefield was a trackless jungle. The enemy was hidden every-where. On many occasions, Lynn was exposed to Agent Orange, that poison dropped from the sky to defoliate the jungle. Lynn didn't turn and run. He completed one tour, and re-upped for another. He fought honorably.

A few years later he was out of the Army and back in Pittsburgh, working as an accountant. He wrote a history of his hometown which was published. Then he researched and wrote a book delineating his family genealogy stretching back to Charlemagne, and started a ski club, among his many personal accomplishments. At one of those ski club gatherings he met Eileen. They were soon married, and moved into an apartment. Later they bought a house north of the city. Lynn's first attempts at mowing the grass ran into unexpected problems. He would break out in a severe case of acne each time. They didn't think much of it at the time. Eileen cheerfully took over the yard work, and they laughed it all off.

When Lynn was close to 50, they welcomed a daughter, Erin, into the world. He was a devoted and proud father, and adored every minute with her. But this storybook tale was soon to take an ugly twist.

Lynn's mood began wavering. Then one Sunday morning in church, Lynn couldn't get comfortable in the pew, his back was hurting him so badly. The condition worsened. After trips to the Emergency Room and a specialist, Lynn was given grim news. Cancer was found in his lungs, his liver, his back, and his brain. Although devastated, Lynn kept his trademark sense of humor while agreeing to every possible experimental treatment available.

Ten months after being diagnosed, Lynn's last hours were spent in bed in a Pittsburgh hospital. I was fortunate to be one of his many friends who circled around. Though thin and drawn, Lynn remained spirited. Just two days before the end, he was wise-cracking and laughing about past follies. But life soon ebbed out of his body, leaving Erin at age seven without a father, and Eileen a widow.

The government didn't dispute claims for Agent Orange benefits. Eileen was forced to move on with her life, keeping her full-time job and managing the house while raising Erin. As families lined up this sunny Flag Day morning, Eileen and Erin both stood proudly behind his photograph, next to so many others.

Lynn's name likely will never be shown on the Vietnam Wall. But his story, and those of all 121 who were recognized, will not be forgotten by the families these brave men and women left behind. This day the microphone was passed to each family. Some identified the fallen as "my dad," some as "my husband," and one as "my twin brother" until all names were read to the crowd. Then the color guard came to attention. The sound system played "Forgotten Heroes," followed by a soloist singing the National Anthem. In closing, the president's own bugler played Taps. There wasn't a dry eye among the assembled family members and friends, each clinging to their personal collage of memories.

Efforts are underway to memorialize all of the Vietnam veterans who made the supreme sacrifice for our country. The war that divided our country may have ended so many years ago, but it's a war that is still taking casualties.

We Americans cannot let the fallen be forgotten.

A National Wildlife Refuge?

Everyone needs to have a grand dream in their life; some signature accomplishment that they will always be known for. You know all of these: First Man on the Moon—Neil Armstrong . . .development of a vaccine for polio--Jonas Salk. . . .first person to floss while skydiving—Arnold Pinckney.

For me, the watershed event of my life would be to take thousands of otherwise worthless acres in rural northwest Pennsylvania (like where we live) and turn this huge tract of land into a National Wildlife Refuge for Plastic Easter Bunnies. Think about it. For decades, Congress has set aside humongous amounts of land for the buffalo to roam, for ducks to land, and for antelope to gambol about (or whatever they do). I'm sure most homeowners wouldn't mind giving up their land and homes, knowing it's for such a noble cause.

The sad truth is that the typical Plastic Easter Bunny spends most of its life being forgotten. Except, that is, for a brief few weeks of the year when they can be seen everywhere happily decorating front lawns from Boston to Bismarck. What happens to them the remainder of the year? Talk about ego issues! Most of these lovable and colorful creatures are so emotionally deflated the rest of the year that they can't even stand up. They are tossed aside, stuck in closets, shoved ignominiously into drawers next to ribbons, bows, and mismatched Get Well cards and envelopes. The air has literally been taken out of them. It's incredibly demeaning. Don't they deserve dreams of their own?

My guess is that we need to act quickly to get legislation passed that would designate our area for the Refuge. Rumor has it that Pennsylvania's neighboring Elk County might already be in the forefront for the honor. If you've ever driven down to I-80 through towns like Brockport and Penfield, you'd see that those people take their love of Plastic

Easter Bunnies seriously. Hardly a house or mobile home is without a multi-colored flock in their yard.

Speaking of locations, until recently scientists believed that Plastic Easter Bunnies remained in one place for the long months when they were not displaying themselves proudly during March and April. Last year, though, a Federal grant was approved, and a high-tech electronic transmitter was attached to a Plastic Easter Bunny that had been caught in the early spring. They nabbed a healthy male quickly, just before dawn. He had appeared on the lawn only the day before. It happened just outside a home belonging to Omar and Gladys Gertschner, in the tiny hamlet of Busti, New York. The Gertschners had agreed beforehand to allow state and federal wildlife officials to do the trapping. The entire area was safely secured by the State Police. First responders were standing by. The trapping was completed without incident, and without injury to the bunny. In minutes, an electronic tracking device was affixed. The bunny was released. Time passed.

When data from the transmitter was studied, it confirmed that the bunny eventually migrated south some 18 miles, crossing the state line into Pennsylvania. The bunny, who we will call "Harvey" (not his real name), was tracked to a crowded garage just outside Youngsville, Pennsylvania. Curiously, the date of the migration coincided with the date the Gertschner family had their annual yard sale.

This proposed Wildlife Refuge would allow Plastic Easter Bunnies of all colors and sizes to roam freely on land they could call their own. Isn't that what America is all about? Freedom? Let's allow Purples, Whites, Pinks, Reds, and Yellows to intermingle freely in an open society. And, before you ask, those up-and-coming Teals would be invited to join too.

Just think of its effect on local tourism! Carloads of families from places like Utica would be filling parking lots at area restaurants, hotels and motels. Happy kids would gladly toss their electronic games aside, joyfully get in step behind their parents, and march into grocery stores and Walmarts to stock up for the adventurous foray into the Refuge.

And think about this: until now, how many folks have been able to get their pictures taken in July or August with Plastic Easter Bunnies? You got it. Zip-zero. People, if you have vision and support this noble cause, this all can change. When school is out for the summer, families will put aside their plans for a boring beach vacation and head for the Refuge. The number of visitors to the Refuge will multiply astronomically.

Just like the bunnies themselves.

The Aglet Movement

We have seen how old ideas and old inventions come back to life with new names and a new purpose. It happens all the time, like today how we're using familiar old words like "mouse" and "windows" in ways that our parents never considered.

I'm guessing this is tied into the whole recycling movement. In fact, the word "recycle" is not even listed in my 1983 Webster's Unabridged Dictionary. That was then. But nowadays "recycling" is everywhere.

Much of the recycling of old words is the result of the computer age. Back when I was younger, Mom would scream if there was a "mouse" in the house. Yours probably would have too. Today's moms are OK with it. Another example is "icon." It once stood for a statue, a sacred image, or representation of something important. For example, famous trend-setting or heroic people were once considered as "icons." Those were people like Mother Theresa, Ronald Reagan, and Soupy Sales. Today, every computer screen is full of "icons," which seem to be odd-looking designs. Well, maybe that does describe Soupy after all.

To our moms and dads, "windows" meant something made of glass you looked through to see how hard the snow was falling. Today's usage can be totally different. So does "default," which my 1983 Webster's defines as "failure to pay money due," or "to offend."

Is the movement today to recycle old words due to having run out of new words? Could this be the next major crisis facing America?

One of my pet peeves is when the right word has yet to be invented. For example, when listening to the weather forecast, during winter when it is getting really cold, the weather person will often say "temperatures tonight will be down in the single digits." Single digits? Why don't we have one word to capture that temperature range, like we use when the temperature dips down to the "twenties" or "thirties?" Think of all the energy, time, as well as printing ink (and trees) that could be saved if we used only one word.

I'm suggesting that we recycle a word that's already out there in circulation to replace "single digits." How about a word that's underutilized today? As you might expect, I have one in mind already. Why don't we use the term "aglets" to refer to single digit temperatures? Do you know what an aglet is? If you don't, you're among friends. An aglet refers to the metal or plastic part on the end of a shoelace. Not many of us use that word at cocktail parties or in everyday conversation. Consider this: if you're watching the weather on a brisk February night, and the weather girl predicts that "temperatures will be down in the aglets tonight," it actually sounds downright frigid. I suggest that if more and more people agree that we need to start using "aglet," that the movement would gain momentum quickly and would soon spread across our country like wildfire (or, more appropriately, like a blizzard). Of course, I suspect it would be more frequently used in Minnesota than in Georgia. And who knows? The Aglet Movement might be the next social phenomenon in our country.

Once this new usage gains popularity and becomes common in everyday conversation, there are some other words that I think need to be brought out of the dictionary, dusted off, and recycled. One that I find fascinating is the word "tumblehome." Don't you agree that it's a great-sounding word? Kind of soft and welcoming, huh? For those of you who don't use "tumblehome" frequently, it refers to the part of a canoe that curves inward from the bow. Or something like that anyway. But I haven't figured out what to use it for. To replace "adult incontinence product?"

Maybe I'm onto something.

Sam's Story

Once again I am reminded that everyone has a story to tell. You just have to keep your ears open. Some tales are more fascinating than others. Not too long ago at a neighborhood gathering, our friend Sam had his turn. Then a vibrant 85, Sam reflected thoughtfully on a story from his childhood. I was so captivated with it that we invited him over for coffee to tell me more.

Seventy years previously in 1944, as WWII had the world fully engulfed in strife, fifteen-year-old Sam and his two buddies ran down a street in Jamestown, New York, to catch a ride on a trolley car for a fun afternoon at Midway Park's attractions. He remembers wearing a brown blazer and tan slacks as he ran. It was a gorgeous Saturday morning in August, just a week before Labor Day weekend. Sam, along with friends Joe and Sherwood, were eager to get to Midway to use their free tickets for a picnic and rides sponsored by a local furniture company.

They had to run six blocks or more before they hailed the burgundy-colored Jamestown, Westfield & Northwestern streetcar. The motorman, Lew Hoadley, who stood at the controls in the front of the car stopped the trolley telling the boys he already had a full load of picnickers. When the boys looked crestfallen, the motorman had second thoughts and said "Okay, you can ride up here next to me in the baggage compartment." The three pals eagerly jumped aboard, and grabbed what space they could squeeze into, against the side of the car. Joe was a quiet young man, as compared to the more boisterous and outgoing Sherwood. They were all good ninth grade students. The boys were sweating profusely from running to catch the trolley. All around them, happy commotion abounded from folks anticipating the fun day ahead of roller skating, hot dogs, and ball-playing in the summer sun.

The trolley sped north along Chautauqua Lake toward Greenhurst at full speed on the single-track line. The windows were open allowing a refreshing summer breeze to blow through. Overhead electric wires powered the heavy 60-seat car as it hummed along. Hoadley waved to a friend as he stood right near the three boys, the trolley cruising at 35 mph. In an hour it would be noon, and the picnic would be in full swing. No one knows why he didn't slow the car when he should have.

Sam has no recollection of what happened next. Unknown to anyone in his car, another trolley was rolling along southbound on the same track. As they both came around a sharp curve, the squeal of brakes grabbing steel rails stung the air. The two trolleys met head-on in a grinding crash. When Sam came to, he was lying on top of his friend Joe, with pieces of the trolley's wooden flooring and wall all over him. Joe pleaded, "Get off me, please!" But Sam couldn't move. He saw the sole of a leather shoe sticking up at an odd angle, facing him. He reached for it, and to his surprise he found that his own leg was attached to the shoe. Another shoe was sticking up at a curious angle: his other leg. All around him was a wild frenzy. Women were screaming. Folks were in shock, hollering "Where's my skates?" "Where's my lunch basket?" A small fire broke out from the overhead electric wires. Truly, it was bedlam.

The fire was quickly extinguished. After part of the wooden debris was moved away, two men picked young Sam up. He pleaded for them to be careful. They laid him on the ground outside the wreckage of the streetcar. With at least 50 passengers injured, a hasty call had gone out for all available ambulances and doctors. When they went to lift him into the ambulance, it was already full, so they laid him on the floor.

He lost track of his two friends. Later he learned that Joe's skull was fractured in the crash, as was his leg. The fun-loving Sherwood, who was squeezed tightly next to him, was pinned against an emergency brake wheel and suffered massive injuries. His foot had to be amputated, but all was for naught. He died shortly later. Sherwood was only fourteen. The kindly Hoadley, who made room for the boys was instantly crushed by the collision of the two steel cars.

The first surgeon who looked at Sam's legs said he would have to amputate. A second opinion was sought, and an orthopedic surgeon from Buffalo was flown down in a Piper Cub to see Sam as he lay in the hospital. One leg was fractured in seven places, the other in three. The doc arranged for some then-revolutionary penicillin to be shipped down from Buffalo. That miracle drug was hard to come by, as most of it was being sent overseas for our fighting men. Cinders, splinters and dirt were cleaned from the boy's wounds. Bone sections were transplanted from one leg to the other. The first of many casts were fitted. Sam's legs were saved. He remained in the hospital from August through December. He missed out on a year of schooling, but later regained full use of his legs. Several years later he graduated from high school.

Today, Sam sips a cup of coffee and glances at our pond out the dining room window as the details of that horrible experience are once again replayed. Then he laughs about his Army induction physical. It was seven years later, while the Korean War was raging. He recalls standing, clad only in his shorts, in front of the examining physician. The doc looked at his odd-looking legs and asked what happened. Sam told him. Then the doc asked him if he could flex his fingers and his hands. Sam showed him that he had full use of his hands. The doc responded by saying, "Well, we don't need your legs in Korea, we need you to be able to shoot a rifle, so off you go!"

Yes, everyone has a story. All you need to do is listen.

What I Don't Miss About Working

Many of us retired folks retain occasional fond memories of our past working careers, wherever it was or whatever we did. You hear other seniors say "I miss the people, but I don't miss the place." In my case, I miss the people, I miss the place, but there is one thing I don't miss. Meetings!

Most of my career was spent working in a hospital, and for those of us without any specific talents (i.e. administrators), most of our day was taken up with meetings. It started at nine in the morning, when those of us who had the nicest offices met for our Morning Meeting to discuss whatever crises occurred since we had our last Morning Meeting. The agenda could have been covered in about eight minutes, but we had a doc who loved to pontificate about anything on his mind. So our brief meeting usually lasted at least a half hour, sometimes much longer. He was a splendid doc and much respected, but due to his being headstrong nobody had the stones to cut him off.

That was for starters. The remainder of the day was spent meeting with colleagues, employees you supervised, the boss, and just about anyone else who walked through the door wanting to have a meeting. The worst meetings, though, were committee meetings. They grew like dandelions in the spring, and by their very nature keep going on and on. I'm sure the committees I retired from fifteen years ago are still meeting regularly, and probably discussing the same thorny problems we did; problems that never stay fixed.

Another phenomenon that developed was that we would have meetings about future meetings. Talk about having a life of their own! One of the most critical group of meetings occurred every three or four years when we had to get ready for an accreditation survey. We had to make sure that every "t" was crossed and every "i" dotted in all our hundreds of policies and procedures. This created untold volumes of paperwork and stress, in addition to a new series of "priority" meetings. They were critical because if we didn't pass our accreditation survey, it meant they might close our hospital. That would mean we wouldn't have any more meetings to attend.

A recent photo in the local paper of some county staff people in a meeting showed everything you needed to know. Seems a big-time politician had come to town, so that called for a high-level meeting. Nothing was spared. In preparation, the conference room had been cleared of all leftover styrofoam coffee cups from the last few meetings. No agendas from previous meetings were left lying in a jumble. Even pictures on the wall had been straightened. Although the politician dressed "smart casual" in a sports jacket without a tie, a few of the local guys, looking to impress, wore ties. I liked seeing the guys who wore golf shirts. Cool. The photo showed three or four staff with pen in hand, eager and ready to write down whatever pearls of wisdom were to come from the bigwig. The highest-ranking attendees sat closest to him at the table. Lower-level supervisors knew their place, and sat in chairs off to the side. On the table I noticed a box of sweets. They weren't those cheap-o doughnuts. Somebody had sprung for those fancy ones with sprinkles and gooey stuff on top. Wisely, no one was scarfing away when the photo was snapped. I didn't even see any crumbs on the table. Could be because the box still looked full. I know from eons of experience at meetings that it can be stressful to be first to do the reach, especially with a big-time visitor in attendance. I didn't see any napkins in the photo, which was typical, but unfortunate. Often the only choice was a white powdered sugar doughnut while you wore black. No way you could wipe off all those pesky little spots when you stood up and excused yourself to go to the restroom. I usually favored long sleeves to wipe off any mess.

Back to the photo in the paper: several smartphones were on the table. All attendees in the photo were being dutiful soldiers by not texting, watching porno, or playing solitaire while the dude was talking; at least when the photo was snapped. And no one appeared drowsy, so you know they were warned to be on good behavior. Or maybe the meeting had just started. Again, from my vast experience of attending meetings,

I found it usually took at least nine minutes before someone began nodding off. Unless it was on a Monday morning, when the walking dead would drift into the room.

In retrospect, I suppose some good things came of all the meetings I suffered through, though I can't recall anything offhand. Perhaps meeting attendance contributed to job security for all staff, as we plotted and planned how to survive as a viable organization. Quite a few years after I left, the hospital is still in business, so maybe those meetings weren't a total waste.

Crocodiles and You

Today animals and other critters help sell a lot of things you and I buy. It's everywhere. When did using animals to advertise products begin? Kids of the Fifties and Sixties remember Tony the Tiger hawking breakfast cereal. Maybe he still does. Well before that, camels had been helping to sell cigarettes back in our parents' generation. Look around: nowadays almost the entire zoo is involved.

Wall Street has found that linking a nice lovable creature with a product results in increased sales. Today you can't have your TV on for more than twenty minutes without seeing a gecko or an emu trying to convince you to buy their brand of car insurance. What's the connection there? Are geckos and emus good drivers? On a positive note, using critters has helped with animal awareness, because a few years ago the word "emu" was only found as the answer to a crossword question, or a handy way to get rid of your "u" while playing Scrabble.

If the commercials don't have a gecko or an emu, chances are they have a huggable little dog or cat to sell their product. There's one fluffy white dog that's on a lot of commercials; you've probably seen him (or her). Its owner must have hit the gravy train with that pooch. Our dog Fika wouldn't quite make the cut for most products, other than for trampolines.

What are the relationships between products and their signature creatures? As I mentioned, geckos and emus have nothing to do with insurance. Further, I'm not sure how bumble bees are related to tuna, except if you leave fish lying out in the sun, it will attract bees. Is that the connection the company wants? Who knows, but they've sold a heckuva lot of tuna over the years. A beef jerky company aims to focus on the outdoors, so they hired Susquatch to help market their stuff. I guess that makes sense.

Turtles have been enlisted to help sell car wax. Not sure about that one. Smokey the Bear has been around effectively for many years, bringing awareness to preventing forest fires. I get that connection. Lovable teddy bears have been featured in other ads too, none of which have an obvious link. In one of them, they try to get you to buy soft toilet paper. ???

So through the years, a host of animals and other creatures have been developing product identities. Alligators have gotten their name associated with sports drinks. Their cousins, the crocodiles, followed later, helping to sell leisure shoes. But does putting your foot in a crocodile sound comforting?

I've seen both a fox and a wolf selling stuff, but I can't recall what. Owls, too. Eagles help sell everything from car tires to condensed milk. Speaking of cars, mustangs and impalas have been seen on ads for their namesakes stretching back quite a few years. Successfully, too. On the other hand, falcons and hornets made an effort in the Sixties to sell autos, but maybe they weren't the right creatures since their brands went the way of the Diplodocus.

Maybe the best critter ads on the tube are for that pink bunny selling batteries. I almost enjoy watching them.

It seems there are other mammals, birds, and reptiles out there that have yet to be enlisted to sell products. Here's a few not seen yet. Would you buy "Turkey Vulture Breakfast Sausage?" Or "Python sweaters?" "Wrap a Python around your neck!" Not so good. Or "Buy a Snake Mattress, and sleep on a Snake." I don't think we're ready for that one. Mosquitoes, pigs, spiders and rats have yet to find their place on Wall Street. "Enjoy Roger the Rat Peanut Butter" might not be a successful come-on. "Relax in a Porcupine Lounge Chair" doesn't sound inviting. A line of "Happy Hippo Women's Clothing" doesn't have the right twist. Neither would an ad saying "Beautify your home with Tommy the Termite Windows" have the ring of a money-maker.

Llamas might be next in line, if they aren't selling something already. Or alpacas. I think moose help sell moccasins or something. Anteaters might be too much of a reach. "Grumpy the Grouse Potato Chips" doesn't sound right either. "Marvin the Mongoose" might work for selling rubber boots. Otters? They're already selling cell phone protectors.

Okay, enough of this. It would be fun to keep adding critters, but right now Linda and I are gonna sit down for a glass of milk and a big slice of Herman House Fly Apple Pie. Their mantra being "Us Flies Love The Pies that Momma Buys!"

Pass the napkins, please.

It's Time to Look At Stuff Again!

Not too long ago, my father-in-law passed away. He had been living independently, which meant his home of fifty years would become vacant. Suddenly it became a priority for us to get his house ready to sell. That was difficult enough to do on an emotional basis, but the task entailed even more angst when we realized everything in his house, garage, basement, and separate outdoor garage would have to go. But how quickly can we pull that off? How and where will the stuff go? To whom?

Her dad's style and furnishings weren't a match for ours, so Linda was not interested in incorporating his furniture or belongings into our home, except for personal remembrances and a few knick-knacks. But what about everything else? We'll keep his stash of aspirins and Band-Aids, and a year's supply of toilet paper. But we already had the equivalent of her dad's lawn equipment, tools, pots and pans, kitchen plates and gadgets. And there's no room for any large storage items in our home. So what to do with everything else?

We held a pair of two-day sales at his house to sell off much of what was there, and that generally went fine. But that's not the gist of this article. What was most pertinent to this epiphany of house-emptying was our need to take a hard look at all the the assorted belongings we have accumulated in our own house and outbuildings. Much of what I saw as her dad's "junk" was quite similar to the "stuff" I've been holding onto for years. Is it needed? If not, how and where can we move it along? But the biggest question: can we be motivated to really make a push? And stay with it? Maybe. Our initial target? Stuff in our outbuildings, and unwanted odds and ends lying around "out back."

Somehow I must have gotten a manly rush, and took the first steps with little delay. One pickup truck load of scrap metal was quickly gathered, loaded, and hauled off to the recycler. Then another. Then a third. How and when did we accumulate all that? Well, part of the story is that down in the barn I unearthed parts from mowers and tractors long gone; for how long now? Maybe 20 years? How about an antique tire changer that had been mounted in our garage when we moved in 37 years ago? Here's light fixtures I replaced eons ago. Old mower blades caked with rust. Metal pipe I had scavenged from somewhere. "Parts is parts" that I picked up from garage sales and never found a use for. Maybe the message is that I need to cut down on scarfing up eye-catching items: I've been like a crow gathering shiny objects. Outside the barn is a dehumidifier that went boots-up years ago. Down in the weeds behind the is a rusted hulk of something or other. Over there is a TV antenna. Oops, make that two, thanks to Johnnyboy's contribution to the scrap pile. Under a bench is an old coffee can full of bent nails. Over here on the table are a couple of tools that I never figured out how to use; might as well toss them. Big metal things with blades on them. Down on the concrete floor there's a weight bench covered with crud. Somehow over time its weights got too heavy to use. Against the wall is a bent length of iron pipe. Why did I save that? Scraps of tin I was going to use for a project. What was it? Now long forgotten. Two electric motors that I'll never do anything with. Heck, I don't even know how they work. Do we really need to keep three wheelbarrows, especially that flimsy one rusting out? Linda agreed that that one can go. What was I going to do with these odd pieces of chicken wire and metal fencing? We've never had chickens, and likely never will. Nor turkeys or llamas. Every time I've moved that chicken wire around I end up with gashes on my fingers. Enough!

Next, our township clean-up day came in a timely fashion. Another truckload. Into it went an unused roll of pink insulation squirrels had moved into and trashed, spreading pink shards into every crevice in the garage. Also from the garage came two sheets of drywall that had gotten damp and wavy in storage. Where in heck was I going to use them? Why did I save them for years? Gone now, good riddance. Rubber mats I kept tripping over. Odd pieces of treated lumber too noxious to burn. Half-empty paint cans now stuffed with cat litter. I guess I don't need this deflated football any more. On top of the load I threw in three old mis-matched tires I'd brought home from Linda's dad's; they'll take them for a few bucks.

Now to the burn pile. Through the years I've managed to accumulate a notable collection of plywood pieces of odd sizes that I've saved "in case they were needed." They look like a giant collection of weird puzzle pieces. Linda's dad had even more of those than I did; so after I hauled them home they joined the burn pile. Scraps of molding removed from a house project 15 years ago. Or was it 20? What's this in the corner? A pile of sucker rods I brought here from my old place in McKean County when we moved here many years ago. Could I still use them? Does a penguin pee on a glacier? Maybe I'll hold onto them for a while longer. Could come in handy somewhere.

Therein lies the rub.

A lot has gone. Kudos to us for hauling away all that stuff that we did. Way to go! Making those decisions wasn't overly painful. But now decision-making gets ramped up. With that mess of obvious crapola being history, how about all the rest of the stuff we're not sure of keeping?

My brain's getting tired of thinking about this.

Inside DUMM

If you've been following the news, you know there's a big debate going on in Washington about Big Government having access to our emails. Here's a personal question for you. Do you read every one of your own emails, including spam? Be honest. Me neither. If you suspect someone in Washington is being paid big bucks to read them, what follows is for you.

As a special courtesy, you are being provided with an inside look at DUMM, the Department of Unauthorized Mail Monitoring. This is a highly secret agency that few citizens know of. A well-placed source, speaking on the condition that his name not be revealed, gave me the inside scoop on the workings inside DUMM. He said I should come up with an example, and then the brainiacs at DUMM would work it through. I thought, why not? I'd begin with my own personal information, to see if it's been compromised. So I asked if DUMM has been spying on me through my emails. After finishing his coffee break, my source provided me with the following tape of two DUMM employees reviewing my personal file. Due to its confidential nature, please do not share this information with anyone.

"Hey Sam, I'm going through the emails coming into Joe's computer. He lives in some backwoods burg near Sugar Grove, Pennsylvania. I've found an email that is mighty interesting. Take a listen to this. Apparently someone is trying to sell him seamless gutters for their house. And wait; look here! Three more emails about seamless gutters. Egad. Something big is up."

"Three more? And all about seamless gutters? Has he answered them?"

"Negative."

"That's potentially interesting, Dave. By the way, where's Sugar Grove?"

"It's in the boondocks of Pennsylvania somewhere. I'm checking now on our spycam. Here it is; not near anything, except trees and deer and cornfields. Oh . . .but look at this. There's a dam nearby. A big one."

"Holy Schmoly! If he's not keeping his gutters up to snuff, what's he spending his Social Security checks on, Dave? I'm not liking this. Methinks we need to call The Committee together on this one."

"Right on. We just got directive #368-4 from headquarters yesterday, saying to be on the lookout for suspicious characters who might be using personal resources to help support those bad guys overseas. Tell me more about this Joe dude. Look up his archive file, Sam."

"Okay, I'm on it. Give me a few minutes to get into the archives . . . . okay, here he is. He's a retired guy, married, and lives out in the country. Get this, Dave . . .the dude lives on a dirt road."

"Wow! He must be one of those survivalists if he lives that way. Talk about primitive! My apartment's not ten minutes from here, just off the Interstate. I haven't heard of anyone living on a dirt road since granddaddy Amos left the hills of West Virginia way back when."

"And look, Dave, here's more on this Joe fella. Take a good look at this photo in our archival files from the '70s. His hair hangs down to his shoulders. He was spotted in some kind of March on Washington. Could be he's one of those peace nuts. I don't like it. I smell a rat."

"When was the photo taken, Sam?"

"Let's see. It was dated the summer of '72. He looks like one of those Age of Aquarius wackos. Good chance he was a radical then. Wouldn't surprise me none if he voted for McGovern and strummed a guitar. Likely still is a nutcase, living on a dirt road and all. Probably has dogs and a four-wheel drive. He could have gone paramilitary. I'm thinking sleeper cell."

"That does it! We have enough to put him on the "A" list. I'm guessing he's using the funds he should be spending on home repairs to support something bad. And don't forget, there's that big dam nearby."

"Yikes, Dave! Here's more! And this could really pound the nail in the coffin. There's a report that he was once stopped by the Fish and Game Commission while canoeing close to where that dam is. The report says they found some empty beer cans with him. But it looks like there was nothing to hold him on then. Wow! Get this! He claimed he found the empties along the shore, while he was helping to do an annual clean-up. A likely story, but not good enough to fool us with our techno stuff. We're onto him. It's all starting to come together, thanks to those tell-tale emails."

"Maybe we should talk to the boss about getting satellite photos of his place in Sugar Grove, to see what he's up to. I think we've found ourselves a hot one."

"Good idea, Dave. Let's get things in motion right away. This summer he may try to get his canoe back near that dam again. If he gets spotted out there, we can call the Pentagon to request sending a squad of Navy Seals out there right quick."

"Yup, there's no doubt he's one dangerous dude. Let's nail him before he tries to confuse our system by ordering those seamless gutters."

"And, Dave, just think. We couldn't have put this all together without those emails and our technology" . . . .

Thanks To Those Who Got It Right

We Americans remain thankful for the countless blessings we enjoy in this great land. There is, however, one blessing that perhaps most of us have overlooked. This has to do with the names of our founding fathers and greatest presidents. Hold on a minute, grab a cup of coffee, and I'll explain.

We need to be thankful that some of the most important people in our history had grand, aristocratic, melodious names. First case in point: George Washington. Because of him, we have the George Washington Bridge, the Washington Monument, and, of course, the city of Washington, D.C. They all sound strong and presidential. Imagine, if you would, if our first president had been Lefty Dinglefluff. It would have been a stretch to name all those monuments, highways, and bridges after him, and to have the nation's capital located in Dinglefluff, D.C. (on second thought, perhaps that does sound like a place where politicians gather). Anyway, thanks George, for being the person who you were. Oh, and thanks to George's parents, too, for your foresight.

Next case in point is that one of our greatest presidents after Washington was Abraham Lincoln. We all know his accomplishments were so legendary that there have been 1,500 books written about him. Like Washington, his name possesses an eloquent quality. Think for a moment, if his name had been Bubba Sniffpickle. Go ahead, figure it out. It wouldn't have worked. The Sniffpickle Memorial? Sniffpickle's Gettysburg Address? No way. Maybe they would have just called him Honest Sniffy.

More recently, historians have agreed that Franklin Delano Roosevelt (also known by his trademark initials FDR) has been one of one greatest presidents. He led our country out of the Great Depression and through the dark days of WWII. Both his aristocratic name and his initials have a solid ring to them; presidential even. Think for a moment if that same person had been born Alfred Seadog Simpletip. His name would hardly have galvanized our country during those troubled times, and calling him by his initials would have led to a host of additional problems.

States, too, have benefited from their namesakes. William Penn is one of the best examples; he had a solid, concise old English name. What if his name had been William Snoofer? Those of us living here would be living in Snoofsylvania. Egad.

You folks up in Jamestown, New York, should be even more thankful. That fine city was named after one of its first settlers, Mr. James Prendergast. What if that brave fellow's name had been Aloysius Prendergast? Aloysiustown? Hey, I can't pronounce it either. And how about that classy dude named the Duke of York, back in old England, whose name graces the Empire State? What if he had been the Duke of Prunty Commons? Oh, man, you'd need more than a zip code on that one.

These thoughts all need to be brought to closure, but not before we take a quick look at the bigger picture; that being of America itself. Many of you know that "America" was named after noted fifteenth century explorer Amerigo Vespucci. Two things could have happened that would have made our country's name more problematic. What if they had decided years ago to use his last name instead? We would be living in "Vespuccia." That sounds more like an affliction of the digestive system. Or suppose our country had been named after another famed explorer of that era, Ponce DeLeon? We would be the United States of Poncy. Ugh.

Either way, folks, let's be thankful they got it right.

Christmas Tradition, Country Style

A number of years ago, a new neighborhood tradition began out here on our little road. It began with a phone call two weeks before Christmas from my neighbor Johnnyboy. The call went something like this:

"Hey Joe, is that New Holland tractor of yours running okay?"

"Yup."

"Do you still have your backhoe on it?"

"Uh-huh. What's up?"

"Well, our septic system is messed up and we're getting backflow on the basement floor." (backflow being a euphemism for something not very good)

"Okay, Johnnyboy, I'll get her fired up and I'll be there in fifteen minutes."

We move ahead to late afternoon. The first snowflakes begin swirling down. With a heavy dose of snow expected in a couple days; we knew the work had to be done today. Not later, now. While other neighbors are merrily decorating their trees and reveling in Christmas cheer, Johnnyboy and I are staring at the ground behind his house. "Exactly where is your septic line?" I ask, gently.

"I think it's right about here." He replies, then hesitates, before pointing to the ground with his shovel. "But it's hard to say because we put that new walkway in."

"How deep down is it?" I asked.

"Not much more than three feet. Maybe four."

"And where is your septic tank?"

"It's right here too." A hesitation. "Somewhere."

"Johnnyboy, I can only reach down about six feet with this thing. I'll start digging and hope I don't bust the concrete tank with the backhoe. You keep watching."

An hour or so later, the tractor keeps snorting, and a motley collection of clay soil and rocks has been piled up and spilled over toward their patio. I'm wearing an orange ski cap, and have a goose down vest under my Carhartts as I sit high, working the digging controls. Diesel tractor exhaust lends its aroma to the dark and dreary December afternoon. Snowflakes continue swirling down. My fingers are close to numb.

Johnnyboy leans over and looks down into the excavation. "I think we're almost there," he says hopefully, as he dabs at his nose with a Kleenex.

We both get down and check it out. A thick layer of muddy clay cakes the bottom of our work boots as we slug around. He reaches for another Kleenex. We agree to keep at it.

Twenty minutes later I hear him say "we're almost there" again.

I'm now digging down six feet, almost the limit of the reach of my backhoe. "Maybe we missed it; try digging to either side" he suggests. I nod, digging further to the right and then to the left of the original hole. After another half hour he pokes down with his shovel. "It's got to be there somewhere."

Obviously.

Then we hear a "clink" as the steel fingers of the backhoe scrape the plastic pipe, busting it open.

He shoots me an excited thumbs-up! A pungent smell wafts through the holiday air, telling us we hit "paydirt."

Merry Christmas! I yell down over the tractor's din.

This event couldn't be called a tradition if it happened only once. That incident occurred twelve years ago. Then, the following year, two weeks before Christmas, in an eerie deja-vu, the phone rang once again. I'll spare you the details, but here's the skinny. Johnnyboy's other septic line was the culprit this time.

"Can't quite figure it out," he begins. "It shouldn't be doing this."

Once again I donned the orange ski cap, the vest, and the Carhartts. I mounted the tractor, breathed the fumes, and dug with the backhoe.

And again, it was a brisk December afternoon, but thankfully no snow was falling.

The same scenario played out, and eventually after several hours of digging, the backhoe scraped on the plastic pipe. And again we were rewarded by the smell of hitting our objective. The next morning, Johnnyboy replaced the pipe and filled in the six-foot deep ditch using his tractor and back blade.

Later that afternoon, he and Connie invited Linda and I over for a taste of Christmas cheer. We all laughed about the new Christmas tradition up here on our road.

And then the question became this. Will the tradition continue?

On the Ground At Panama City

The date was October 1, 2018. It was early morning in northern Florida. Hurricane Michael had torn through Florida's Panhandle only a day and a half before, as we drove gingerly westward across Highway 20 from Tallahassee toward the heavily damaged area. We four volunteers were wearing our American Red Cross vests as we searched to find a fast-food breakfast fifty miles from our destination of Panama City. Although far away from landfall, our attempts were in vain. Even the most well-known eateries were closed due to lack of power. The two-lane country road had been opened for travel only a few hours previously. Traveling was slow and perilous due to the roadway being littered with downed utility poles and trees. Electric wires hung down crazily in every direction.

Our destination was the Red Cross shelter at Rutherford High School in Panama City. Volunteers were needed there, as sketchy reports indicated that was where hundreds of storm victims had gathered. Weather reports the day before said between six and eleven tornadoes had touched down. They tore apart the area after Hurricane Michael's 155 mph winds came ashore two miles to the south, creating havoc. Damage was everywhere. As we entered Panama City, we saw off to the left on the railroad tracks where fifty or more freight cars had been blown off the tracks. Making our way carefully down the four-lane highway, we needed to avoid the right lane, which was unusable due to long strings of utility poles lying across it, wires askew.

How to find the high school? Forget using GPS; all cell service was out with towers blown over. Driving through downtown Panama City, it appeared every business was either damaged or destroyed. Tornadic winds had knocked down almost all the street signs. With no electric service, all traffic lights were out. At the busiest intersections, it was up to the Florida Highway Patrol to wave us through. At all other intersections, taking turns to move ahead was the only alternative. The sun was shining through haze with a stifling humidity in the eighty degree morning. The only other traffic heading into the city were lines of utility trucks and convoys of National Guard vehicles. Every few minutes, ambulances, fire trucks, and police cars raced by in each direction, sirens blaring. Houses and mobile homes everywhere lie crushed by fallen trees which had come down by the thousands. Only a few residents could be seen, wandering around as if in a daze. Pieces of sharp metal were lying all over the roadways, ready to puncture rubber.

Communication was impossible as we sought to find our destination. Cell phones were useless, as were land phone lines. Bathrooms were nowhere to be found. Food? Nothing was open. All gas stations were shuttered. Everything was in tatters. By stopping to ask the few locals who were out, we eventually saw the high school off to our right in the distance. As we approached it, every tree was broken off ten or so feet up, all bent over in the same direction.

This is as close to an apocalypse as I ever want to be.

The main building of the extensive high school campus was missing half its roof. All other buildings had major damage, except for the one being used as a shelter. It too had roof damage, but was usable, as long as rain stayed away. Generators were humming to provide electricity to that one structure. Milling around outside were hundreds of people, many disheveled and unbelieving, as they sought respite from the effects of Michael.

We learned there were perhaps 300 folks here, or maybe 400; no one knew for sure. Many youngsters and toddlers could be seen. A baby had been born a couple days before. Adults sat next to suitcases and shopping bags of belongings. Most had spent the night at the shelter, even though no cots or blankets had yet arrived. They had slept in hallways on the hard floor. There was no city water. To make matters even more chaotic, there were no working toilets. Portable johns had not yet arrived. In some places, the stench was dreadful. Thankfully, there was a baseball field out back.

My three companions were Red Cross nurses; they immediately took to addressing the many medical needs of those gathered here. My task was to provide emotional support. Their stories were heart-breaking. I chatted with Thomas and Cathy. They were each around 80, and had been married for 55 years. All they had worked for, lived for, and saved for had been in their house, and in their driveway. Now only a pile of debris remained. But they had each other, and were thankful they had heeded the warnings to evacuate to this shelter. Mona, 58, had evacuated but her sister stayed behind. Mona didn't know yet if she survived.

Amid the chaos, Kahlil, a young man of 26, put his personal disaster aside and was busily sweeping up bits of yellow insulation and pieces of ceiling tiles that were scattered everywhere in the parking lot. The school principal, wearing jeans and a t-shirt, had joined him and was busily picking up trash. The overall mood, despite destruction wherever you looked, was one of relief. They were safe.

During the next two days, trucks of Red Cross food were delivered, as were the first cots and blankets. Five portable toilets arrived, even as the population swelled to around 450. Two other shelters in Panama City held another 700 storm victims. Cell service remained out for another week. Portable showering facilities took even longer to arrive. Electric lines remained tangled, lying across every street. To do battle with that mess, convoys of utility trucks rumbled into town from hundreds of miles away.

Slowly, the first steps to recovery had begun.

I've Become One of Them!

A few years back, while still working full time, I heard countless retired folks say "I'm so busy now I don't know how I had time to work." I'd respond with a bemused smile and nod my head, but deep inside I pooh-poohed those comments, figuring those folks were just poorly organized, or never worked hard to begin with.

I'm here to tell you, friends, my opinion has totally changed. A couple years into retirement, and "I'm one of them." Where does the day go? How could I possibly have gone to work for all those years? Part of what's caused this epiphany is a combination of yard sales, estate sales, and auctions.

Prior to retirement, while working at least forty hours a week, I hardly gave a thought to yard sales. I was too busy getting to work in the morning to pay attention to the crudely drawn signs nailed up to telephone poles advertising a sale. And I had heard of estate sales, but I never quite figured them out. Like the rest of the working world, I drove by in a hurry, barely noticing coarsely or casually dressed folks lined up in the morning against someone's front door. Those sales were a curiosity of our local culture, I thought, something I would never lower myself to doing once I hung 'em up for good.

Fast forward to today. All has changed. In my new routine I eagerly check the mailbox on Saturday afternoon to page through the Penny Saver Guide for next week's estate sale location. And by Wednesday I'm poring through the classifieds to track down the weekend's most alluring yard sales. On Friday afternoons I have to stop by the local auction house to see what might be squirreled away in those cardboard boxes in the back room, and, of course, the prime stuff "up front."

These obsessive pursuits have made quite a dent in my lifestyle. My major household projects? They have been shoved to the back burner. You see, I've become a bottom feeder. Some people go to sales because they need to buy clothes for their kids at a bargain price, or perhaps because they want to add to their collection of salt and pepper shakers. That's all good, and I can understand their worthy pursuits. I'm looking for something I can get cheap, and then either add it to my collection of miscellaneous stuff, or perhaps sell at a profit once I store it in the basement for at least ten years.

The advantage to trolling for yard sales on Friday mornings is that if you're a skillful driver you can do a "drive by." Hopefully you won't crease a parked minivan as you scan tables of kids' clothes, pink and purple plastic toys, and VCR tapes for that special item you "collect" as you inch past at 5 mph. Then you happen to glance up to your rear view mirror and see a pickup truck about twice your size four inches from your rear bumper, closing fast, with some pissed-off dude offering a special salute.

Estate sales are the most captivating. Although you have to stop your car to check them out, you get a chance to traipse through a stranger's house, and see what stuff they had collected during the course of their lifetime. There are a number of items you'll find in just about every estate sale. Down in the basement, you'll find cans of nails (who uses nails anymore?) on a workbench shelf, paint cans with drips on the side, and rusty wrenches. In a corner you'll find a table of Christmas decorations which probably haven't been displayed since Ike was in the White House. And if it's not upstairs in the bedroom, you'll find an exercise machine down there that has gathered dust since the day it was purchased, perhaps twenty years ago.

Everyone has a small bookcase somewhere upstairs, and I can just about guarantee you'll find books on how to diagnose your own diseases, one on why you should be eating more vegetables, and one on a new approach to losing weight. You'll find them next to a collection of Reader's Digest condensed books (if they sell for a quarter, it's a miracle). And don't be surprised to find an old newspaper about the JFK assassination by the bookcase. There will be a small pile of postcards, including the one Aunt Clara and Uncle Max mailed from Florida back in '62.

The kitchen will have plastic food storage containers. You'll have to fight the ladies for those. You'll see folks going through forks and spoons, lifting them up to the light to read whether it's solid silver. And the coffee cups, too. Everyone turns them over to read the bottom, to see if they might have been hand-painted by Princess Diana. As in all rooms, there might be "collectible" stuff in the kitchen. That includes McDonald's theme glasses, vintage beer can openers, and souvenir cups from Niagara Falls. If there's a cast iron fry pan, almost everyone will turn the pan over to see if it's a Griswold.

In the bedroom there's a sewing box that might hold the one thimble that you've been searching for. You'll also find gaily-colored men's ties. Maybe worn by Gomer Pyle? A pile of nicely-folded doilies. Who uses doilies anymore? It's been a while since I've seen a Nehru jacket hanging in the closet.

Out in the garage, guys in jeans and ball caps are riffling through bins containing old hinges, doorknobs and ball-peen hammers. Close by are oil filters for cars that haven't been on the road in twenty years. Against the wall you'll find a rake, a shovel, and on the floor a power tool with a sign that says "all it needs is . . . ."

If all this stuff is so crappy, then why am I here? Folks, it's "the thrill of the hunt." Hidden behind the carburetor cleaner and brake fluid in the garage might be a rare oil can from a local refinery long abandoned. That could bring some serious bucks. Or in the bookcase, who knows? There might be a First Edition of poetry signed by Robert Frost. In the kitchen, there could be a tea cup once owned by the Queen of Luxembourg.

How could you possibly miss out on these thrills? So for those of you who have yet to retire, look what you have to look forward to!

Remembering Those Old Cowboy Westerns

If you grew up in the mid-Fifties you likely watched your share of TV cowboy shows. I'm not sure if Mom wanted me to spend Saturday mornings in front of our tiny black and white TV set, but I don't remember her complaining. That morning would find a parade of syndicated westerns featuring heroes like Gene Autry and Hopalong Cassidy. The Lone Ranger came on right after lunch; I recall those as all being half-hour shows. Once a year, though, the Lone Ranger show was a full hour. That's when they depicted how he began wearing a mask after beginning his gunslinging career as a lawman named Reed.

The epic series Gunsmoke made its appearance for an hour on Wednesday evenings, and the Ponderosa on Sundays a few years later. Every youngster had their favorite show and favorite cowboy. My guy was Roy Rogers.

His show came on at 6:30 on Sundays, and I was glued to the set every week for a half hour. Each of his adventures was so exciting that I could hardly get to sleep afterwards, even after Roy and Dale lulled me up the stairs to bed singing "Happy Trails." Today if you watch the old reruns, you wonder how they seemed so exciting. Of course, life was much less complicated back then.

No matter which cowboy program was your fave, many of the shows had to do with a band of bad guys in black hats holding up a stagecoach. It makes you wonder if any stagecoaches ever got through without being robbed. Most shows had "dance hall gals" in them. They all were good-looking, chewed gum, had perfect hair, and tiny waists. I hate to ruin that image, but vintage photos from frontier days show that few looked that way.

When my man Roy got in a gunfight, as he did at least once every Sunday night, he always won. I was on the edge of the couch each time. I doubt he ever killed anyone with his gunshots. As I recall, he would always grab one of his twin revolvers, shoot without aiming, and the bad guy's gun would sail out of his hand. The bad guy never even bled. Well, maybe once or twice into a bandana, but you never saw the blood. That sure is different from current adventure shows. On the few occasions when Roy didn't shoot the guy's gun out of his hands, he took his gun and knocked the bad guy on the head. The bad guy would immediately lose consciousness and fall to the floor. He'd wake up later on the way to jail, with no sign of traumatic brain damage. And no lawyer is taking Roy to court.

I guess Gene Autry and Hopalong did pretty much the same thing as Roy. You may remember that Gene sang a tune during each of his shows. Most of them had a sidekick, a second guy who was meant to add interest or humor. Roy had Patrick Aloysius Brady, and even though I was just a kid I knew he was a dork. Wild Bill Hickok had a sidekick with a hoarse voice named Andy, who always seemed to get in a pickle. There must have been others, too.

But the most famous sidekick of them all was Tonto, the Lone Ranger's Indian friend. I guess there's been a movie out of the same name. I heard a review of it, during which the role of Tonto was criticized as being a "stereotype" of the American Indian. Well, perhaps it was, but the Tonto I recall was one who was brave, smart, strong, loyal, and respected. I'm not so sure what was wrong with that.

I suppose the shows we watched were simple, and perhaps there were unfair stereotypes, but they had themes which helped shape our way as we grew up. The good guys worked together, and always won. The rule of law was upheld. Killing was downplayed. Even the roughest cowboys could laugh. Women were respected. Horses were run hard, but not mistreated or shot. Politics and drugs weren't even thought of. The language used was fit for dinner table talk. And despite bad circumstances, the good guys lived to fight another battle on next week's show.

I'm glad Mom let me watch them.

It's The Season For Tips

Big deal, you say. Another article on tips. Yes, this is the time of year for giving tips, and we all know it. By all means, don't forget to be generous to those who do special things for you: your newspaper delivery person, your Post Office folks, your bartender, your hairdresser, or your politician (oops, that was a misprint).

But what I'm really talking about here are the endless unsolicited "tips" that come your way this time of year. I'm referring to the everyday tips in the paper or in magazines, or online this time of year. You know them as well as I do. They include "Tips for Winter Driving," "Tips to Cut Down on Your Heating Bill," "Tips for Holiday Giving," yadda, yadda, yadda. After doing years of careful and painful research, I've determined that 77.6% of you don't even bother reading these articles, and of those who do, 94.6% don't bother following through on the "helpful" tips anyway. These tips are meant to be enlightening things you never before thought of. But it seems they are meant expressly for people who've been living off the grid for years in Mesopotamia.

For those of us living around here, let's take a closer look at the often-seen "Tips for Winter Driving." Basically, they all advise "don't drive like a bat out of hell when it's icy." Wow! What an eye-opener! When's the first time you heard that? About fifty years ago? They follow that up with "make sure you have good tread on your tires." Another shocker, huh? I'd like to see some winter driving tips that you've never heard before, like "drink at least six cups of coffee, then read the fine print on your insurance policy before driving on snowy roads." Or what I consider to be an obvious winter driving tip: "load up your favorite stuff and the family dog and spend the winter in New Mexico."

"Tips to Cut Down on Your Heating Bill" will probably tell you to "lower your thermostat to 68 degrees." Again, have you heard that before? Or, "add additional insulation to your attic." Wowzers! Who would have thunk it? How about some really new ideas? I suggest "build a toasty campfire in your living room." (Okay, on second thought, that one might be considered a minor safety issue.) I'll counter with "pedal your exercise bike all day to keep warm" (I'm gonna save that tip and recycle for my Weight Loss tips). Here's one more: "invest $25,000 in a heavy buffalo-skin robe to wear around the house."

With the holidays coming up, I'm sure you'll also see "Tips for Holiday Dinners." It usually starts off with something like "make sure you turn on the oven before you put your turkey in." I'll take the liberty to add one: "don't let your cousin from Arkansas eat mashed potatoes with his fingers." But for a perfectly jolly holiday dinner, the first hint should be "don't invite any family members to whom you owe money."

Weight loss tips come at you every day. You can't avoid them, but it's the same-old, same-old. "Eat plenty of vegetables." Didn't your mother tell you that at least a thousand times? Or a hint like "Replace double-chocolate cake in your diet with non-fat yogurt and rice cakes." Ugh. You might as well eat Cheerios soaked in kerosene. And here's a new approach for researchers out there to explore. Maybe you've heard it: "Tips for Losing Weight While Gorging Oneself on Glazed Doughnuts."

Especially at holiday time, you can't miss all the "Tips for Safe Use of the Internet." They tell you to be careful with what sites you visit, how to safeguard your credit card, to not get bilked by far-out schemes, and all the basic stuff that people ought to know anyway in the 21st century. Common sense enters into it, too.

What I'm getting at is that in the future, there should be a law which limits "tips" to subjects that have never been previously published. For example, maybe our paper should print "Tips for Catching A Walrus in Your Local Creek." I'm guessing that would be an eye-opener for fishermen. Or perhaps a more universal one: "Tips for Teaching Your Dog How to Shovel Snow." And if you're looking for a gardening challenge here's one for you: "Tips for Growing Mangoes in Your Living Room."

I've got more helpful suggestions, but I need to cut this short because I have to send money to a guy in jail in Tanzania who says he is actually a rich prince in his home country of Kranjovia. He promises to pay me back big-time. I believe him.

And I already know it. At least 88% of you won't pay any attention to this article.

Notes From a Traveler

Recently our neighbor Connie related a scenario that happened locally. She had been driving near a shopping mall, when their car coughed and sputtered at a fairly busy stop light. The light changed twice before they were able to get the car running and moving on. Several cars lined up behind them as they struggled to get it started again. During that time, Connie said not a single driver sounded their horn. Would they lay off their horns like that in Philadelphia? Hah! Or anywhere else in America?

Generally speaking, folks on the road in our rural area are more than courteous. We're downright nice to one another. We should congratulate ourselves on that. Driving down our dirt roads, I wave to any vehicles that come our way. In addition, I wave to our Amish neighbors as they buggy by us. Most folks wave back. I even catch a smile now and then.

Having recently been in New Jersey, I found that many drivers there also wave. They do a modified wave, however, using only one digit. Oftentimes they add a loud verbal greeting to emphasize their hospitality to out-of-state drivers. Our recent travels also took us to Connecticut. Drivers there don't do a full wave, or even one with a single digit. They are physically unable to wave because they keep both hands on their horn at all times. This past spring we were down in North Carolina, where drivers ought to show Southern hospitality. But down there in NASCAR country most everyone seems bent on qualifying for the weekend's upcoming race, as they zip past us at warp speed. And don't even talk to me about the highways around Toronto, where our northern neighbors change lanes helter-skelter as if they are driving bumper cars while on hallucinogenic drugs.

Our travels also took me to the skies. Not too long ago we had a two-hour layover at the airport in Philly. As I sat watching travelers hurry by, I became aware that Americans have now become a culture of the "haves" and the "have nots." No, I'm not referring to wealth; I mean tattoos. A good many of us have withstood the urge to have designs burnt into our skin. But the younger generations seem to be enthralled with the idea. If someone has indulged themselves in a "tat" on their leg, you can be sure they are wearing shorts as they zip through the airport, showing off their artwork. And if someone has a tulip, a toad, or a tarantula embedded onto their instep, you can be sure they are wearing flip-flops to display their taste. Even in the dead of winter, you'll see the tat generation in shorts, showing them off.

I guess we've come full circle when it comes to decorating ourselves. Back in my early years I'd be eagerly paging through National Geographics looking for those "special" photos. There would be natives in Africa and South America who had painted their faces and bodies, jammed rings around their necks to make them longer, and stuck needles into sensitive parts of their bodies. If you hadn't noticed, it's all happening again, but this time in our country. And now they've added purple and pink hair. It's not just kids, either. Just watch a pro basketball game. There's hardly a player who hasn't covered all visible parts of his anatomy with various symbols.

And how about earrings? Times have changed. Back when I was a teenager, the sight of a guy wearing an earring would lead to name-calling, and probably much worse. Today, beefy pro football players proudly wear earrings. I guess one of the positive outcomes of rowdy athletes wearing them is that it has cut down on name-calling and bullying.

Every generation has to make a statement of independence from their mothers and fathers. Your dad or grand-dad might have worn a zoot suit to be different. Then there was the bobby sox craze. In my era, we showed our independence by wearing long hair (before it suddenly disappeared). Bell bottoms were the thing, too. Today's young folks buy jeans that already have holes in them. My mom would never let me out of the house that way. Probably yours wouldn't, either.

So now that today's younger generation have decorated themselves with tats and nose rings, what does the future hold for coming generations to make a more forceful and original statement? Peer into your crystal balls. Will kids iron their ears? Are they wearing shoes on the wrong foot? Walk around with jellybeans up their nostrils? Coat their heads with roofing tar?

Keep your eyes open while traveling; maybe you'll be the first to see a kid with underwear on his face.

If Music Be the Food of Love . . .

You may remember that line from high school days. It was from a book or a play, but most of us could have cared less at the time. We were preoccupied with the latest from the Beatles, and the upcoming Friday night dance. Ol' Mr. Shakespeare would have encouraged the reader to "play on," but in my case that might not be the best idea. My career in music has been circumspect, at best.

Let's go back. It must have been about in the sixth grade when my perilous journey began. Here's how it started, as I recall. There was a clarinet packed away collecting dust on a shelf in our house. By this time I think my parents had gotten tired of me running my trains every night. They decided to broaden my horizons through the world of music. "Come on, Joey, give the clarinet a try," Mom said. I think my older sister played it, or maybe it was my brother-in-law's. I don't remember. But soon I found myself in the band room at my junior high school. It didn't take long to see (or hear) that this experiment wasn't headed in a positive direction. For one thing, I hardly had enough air in my lungs to make any decent sound out of it. I sort of could play an "open C" because I didn't have to finger any of those funny little metal doo-dads while doing my best to blow through it at the same time. But despite my sorry attempts to play a tune, I think my father was happy to see me as a potential band member. Maybe he was hoping I wouldn't be wasting any more of my allowance on baseball cards.

You see, the few times when my dad sat down to watch a football game with me on TV, he got the most enjoyment out of the halftime show. That was years before today's dumb halftimes. Nowadays six former athletes wearing snappy suits giggle at each other's lame attempts at humor for twenty minutes. Those dudes must take a drag of happy gas before they go on the air. If you watched football in the Sixties, you may recall that halftime shows featured high school bands marching around in formation. Dad would prefer to envision me out there, exhaling into a clarinet while wearing a goofy band uniform, rather than catching a winning TD pass.

Perhaps I made a half-hearted attempt to learn how to play that thing, but it wasn't to be. I've never seen a man so happy as when I told the junior high band director, one Mr. Martin Klibinoff, that I was quitting. I'm sure he went home and downed a celebratory margarita.

Where is this story going? Maybe you think that after giving up the clarinet I went on to catch many a winning TD pass in high school. If truth be told, I played what was called "end" at that time, but this skinny 140-pounder (wiry sounds better) never caught a single pass. 'nuff said. OK, back to music.

My singing career left quite a lot to be desired. In fact, it didn't fully mature until about ten years ago, when my buddy Randy and I did a mean karaoke version of "Honky Tonk Woman" during his retirement party at a local watering hole. I'm sure others who were there are still talking about it.

I'm getting ahead of myself again. Let's travel back almost fifty years. Shortly after graduating from college, I picked up a guitar for the first time. Another college guy down along the Gulf Coast did the same thing at about the same time. Jimmy Buffett. His results have proven to be more remunerative than mine.

I first began strumming the thing with my old friend Gunnar, who through the years has become quite skilled. My buddy Gary was my next co-star. We'd get together every week or two and play for a couple hours while staying well lubricated. By midnight we were usually sounding pretty decent. He was much more accomplished than me. He could pick; I could only strum. Not sure if that is why the big boss from Decca Records never got hold of me. Who knows? Maybe he tried to call me but my line was busy. I stuck with the guitar for about five or six years before I noticed our dog was sneaking out of the room whenever I brought out my guitar case.

Giz, my other childhood pal, started with the violin in grammar school, and just recently unearthed it again and is back playing. Way to go, Giz! Linda can play about six different instruments well, but rarely does. We're hoping now that she's no longer doing parent care that she'll have more time to do so. In the last couple of years my bud Beel always treated us to a few guitar tunes when we got together. Others' musical success stories are legion. Our friend Micke in Sweden, the most gifted of them all, plays a fantastic blues guitar.

Okay, where does that leave me today as far as my musical career goes? Since I can't sing and can't play an instrument, my options are limited. My decision has been to become a music historian. I'm not referring to being a trivia expert, I'll leave that to you others in my age group who can name The Archies' biggest hit.

My historical research effort entails studying various music themes in depth. This challenge has consumed me for the last five years. My eventual goal is to determine the exact words to the classic love song "Louie, Louie" by that iconic group, the Kingsmen. I haven't got all the words yet, but I'm getting closer. Maybe in another year or two.

After that, I'm setting my sights way higher. I want to find the deep inner meaning to the song "Crimson and Clover" by Tommy James and the Shondells. There's rumors on the web that if you play it at a certain speed, you will unearth the key to the Meaning of Life.

I hope it's not connected to playing the clarinet.

The Late, Great Hobby of Stamp Collecting

Did you collect postage stamps years ago? If you didn't, I bet your friends did. Or maybe your sister. Back in the Fifties, it seemed like just about all us kids were into that hobby. Some were only occasionally interested, but many of us put a good number of hours into it.

I was a true "stamp nerd" for a number of years. Back then, the Post Office would only come out with four or five new commemorative stamps each year. Nerds like me would know the first day that a new stamp would be sold by glancing at a flier in the Post Office lobby. As a 12 year-old I remember riding my bike a mile downtown to get the new 1960 Olympic Games stamp: red white and blue, as I recall, and cost four cents. That was the price for most of them. One day I pedaled down to get the new orange Benjamin Harrison stamp. That one set me back twelve cents. Geez, that was a lot of money! I guess ol' Ben must have been one heckuva president.

Speaking of presidents, one of the ads in the then-popular H. E. Harris stamp catalog showed President FDR, sitting comfortably at his desk, engrossed in his own stamp collection. I think he had a magnifying glass in hand, studying a stamp. I don't recall any of our recent presidents having a relaxing hobby like that. They are too busy ripping apart the opposing party.

Back in the Fifties, having a stamp collection was a great way to learn about the world. Our foreign stamp albums had a few sentences about each country. We got to know that Algeria was in Africa, and that Argentina was in South America. I never did figure out where San Marino was, but they had terrific multi-colored stamps. Triangles, I think. And how about countries like Tanganyika? The country is gone, but the stamps remain.

On the subject of disappearance, what caused the downfall of stamp collecting? I'm sure there still are many stamp collectors out there, but if you were to ask a hundred kids today who among them collects stamps, how many would raise their hand? What ruined stamp collecting for my pals and me (in addition to finding out about girls) was that countries began printing stamps not for mailing letters. They were printed so the country could make money by selling them to us stamp nerds. It took us a while to figure that one out, since the stamp companies kept their motives secret. Countries like Hungary started it, or maybe it was San Marino. Anyway, all of the sudden there were thousands of new stamps each year, and trying to "collect them all" became an impossibility.

Some of us saved only U.S. stamps. That was a good way not to have to worry about getting the 200 new Hungarian stamps that came out last week. With only American stamps, it was technically feasible to collect them all. But when we would look up the cost of a few of the 1800-era U.S. stamps in the catalog, some of them would cost a whopping five bucks or more. Even that more recent purple 80-cent stamp from Hawaii, the one with orchids on it, would set a kid back. For the rarest of stamps, it was bigger money than a newspaper route income could cover. Some of the richer stamp nerd kids bought "blocks of four" stamps, which came with a printed number on them. That would be sixteen cents. No way I could lay out that kind of jing.

In the back of magazines there were ads for getting stamps mailed to you "on approval." That meant a company would send you a couple dozen stamps. You could decide which ones you wanted to buy, and keep them. You'd send back the money for them, as well as the stamps you chose not to keep. I always wondered what if I kept some stamps that I didn't pay for. Would they track me down? Would they send some bruiser to our house to collect their stamps, and send me off to jail? I was too wimpy to take the risk.

We had this hope that our collections would someday be worth a ton of money. Every year, I would pick up a new edition of the Harris catalog and page through it, to see how much my collection was worth. I would be adding three cents to eight cents to eleven cents (or whatever), add it all up, and determine that my collection was worth about $11.72. Though it was never going to be enough to get rich, I was fortunate in what I could add to my collection.. I had "connections" to get foreign stamps, so I collected them too. You see, I had an uncle with a brother in Venezuela. I also had an aunt who knew somebody in France; they'd exchange letters and she'd bring me the stamps. But my real "ace" was Uncle George. He had access to all the stamps that came into the Lipton Tea Company headquarters. He would bring them to me in big manila envelopes after they had been torn off correspondence. That meant a lot of colorful ones from the Belgian Congo, and other countries with equally mysterious names. But when I tried to "steam" them off their envelopes, they always got crinkly. So their quality was not as good as the perfectly manicured stamps I'd buy out of Popular Mechanics magazine ads, offering "100 Foreign Stamps for a Dollar." I never figured out why my stamps came out crummy, since I soaked them, then put them on wax paper. Maybe I was supposed to soak them in turpentine.

Almost all kids today couldn't be bothered to start collecting them. Stamp companies don't advertise on MTV. One wonders if anyone will collect them fifty years from now. With today's paperless communication, Hungary won't have to put out a zillion new stamps every year. Postage stamps will go the way of the penny loafer. Even today I don't know if the H.E Harris Company still exists. Or, if anyone cares.

In retrospect, I don't regret one bit having been a stamp nerd. In addition to learning where foreign countries were located, we also got to know what a few foreign words meant. For some odd reason not all people in the world spoke English. To help, we relied on our trusty "Stamp Finder" booklets to identify which country a stamp came from. To this day, I remember that "Suomi" on a stamp meant it was from Finland. That might seem trivial, but it does have its benefits. One day, I'll actually meet someone from Finland. I can't wait to ask them "how are things back in Suomi?"

I'll bet that would make ol' H.E. Harris proud!

These Presidents Did What?

Relax folks, we're not discussing any Chief Executive still alive today. Let's take a walk back in the history of our presidency.

So you think politicians don't play well together today? Obvious perhaps, but it's nothing new. Former President Martin Van Buren brought two loaded pistols whenever he visited the Senate, in case there were arguments. That's one way to quiet your opposition. And did you ever wonder how presidential decisions are made? It's fairly well known now that when Ronald Reagan was in the White House, he regularly consulted his astrologer in San Francisco for guidance. Egad.

And what went on inside the walls of the White House? All kinds of animal sounds, for sure. President Andrew Jackson taught his pet parrot to swear. At the time of his funeral while he was being laid to rest, the parrot was uttering so many obscenities it had to be removed from the room. Our sixth president, John Quincy Adams, must have been a reptile lover. He kept an alligator in his bathtub. If one of those critters wasn't enough for excitement, Herbert Hoover kept two gators, and they were free to roam from room to room. President Harrison kept a goat inside the White House. Seems that Teddy Roosevelt oversaw what was considered to be a zoo on White House grounds. A small bear was one of the residents, but at least it was kept outside. It was noted, however, that his family pony rode the White House elevator at least once. Not to be outdone, ol' Calvin Coolidge had a couple of pet lions on the grounds to go with his donkey and bobcat.

I haven't read where any president kept his horse inside the White House but Franklin Pierce, while serving as president, was arrested for running over a woman with his horse. It seems the charges were later dropped. Political influence, perhaps? When horses and presidents are mentioned in the same context, the dude to remember was Rutherford B. Hayes. An honored Civil War officer wounded in fighting, he had four of his horses shot from underneath him as he rode in battle. Wow! That ranks him up at the top with George Bush (the elder) for bravery under fire. JFK was no slouch either. Maybe others, too.

James Garfield, who served as president only briefly before being assassinated, had an ability no other of our leaders had. He could write in Latin with one hand while simultaneously writing in Greek with his other! President Zachary Taylor, not to be outdone, was very proud of his spitting. Andrew Johnson, while in the White House, made his own suits.

Years before the Watergate scandal, Richard Nixon commented that he "was glad that he didn't live in Russia, because you never knew when you were being taped." 'Nuff said on that one.

Who was the best athlete to live at 1600 Pennsylvania Avenue? Some might say it was Gerald Ford, who played major college football. But the honors should go to none other than Abe Lincoln; before being elected, he was a wrestler. He reportedly won all but one of 300 matches. And he was known to trash-talk his opponents. So that gritty behavior didn't begin with NFL football.

Odd interpersonal stuff on our presidents? Millard Fillmore married his high school teacher. Grover Cleveland married his adopted daughter. But maybe the weirdest was Lyndon B. Johnson. He was known to give interviews to men and women while they were in his bathroom, as he was relieving himself.

Who was our best to hold the top office in the land? Washington? Lincoln? FDR? All good choices, but I submit that it was President David Rice Atchison. What's that, you've never heard of him? He was serving in a leadership role in the Senate back in 1849. He became president shortly after James Polk's term expired, and before Zachary Taylor could be inaugurated. Thus, Atchison was in the role of president, although only for a number of hours. One of the rumors about his brief time as Chief Executive is that he was partying the night before taking on the presidency, and slept through his term in office.

Maybe that should happen more often.

Meeting The Sultan

This all happened one hot and humid summer afternoon. I was hiking around in the deep woods, trying to stay in the cool shade while exploring more of our great outdoors. I had been meandering around by myself, right around the state line. But I got turned around, and I wasn't sure where I was. I had got off the path because I spotted berry bushes that were loaded with big red berries. They looked juicy and enticing. I didn't know what they were, but I gobbled down a handful anyway and continued hiking. The next thing I remember was angling down a steep rocky creek bank. I was feeling woozy. Suddenly I lost my footing on loose stones. My feet went out from under me, and I landed hard. Real hard. I was seeing stars. The next thing I felt were firm bony fingers on my shoulder. Then, a scratchy voice.

"Are you all right? I looked up to see the face of an old man. Old? He was beyond ancient. His eyebrow hairs hung down, almost covering his eyes. His facial skin was stretched thin as a yellowed lampshade over his protruding cheekbones. What few remaining strands of his white hair were curly and unkempt.

"What happened?" I asked, trying to put words together as I stared at this suddenly-appearing apparition.

He didn't answer at first. He looked me over, then said matter-of-factly "You took a tumble."

I tried to gather my thoughts. "Who are you?" I asked. I wondered if I was dreaming. Again, there was a delay before he answered.

"I don't get many strangers dropping by here." He paused again, like he was choosing his words carefully. "Just call me Sultan."

My grogginess held on as I turned to sit across from him on the gravelly bank. "Okay, Sultan, my name's Joe. I was hiking, and got turned around. I must have fallen." The old man was wearing a type of tunic, and was barefoot. His body odor was enough to gag a turkey vulture. "You live out this way?" I asked as I was beginning to get my bearings.

He was cautious again before answering. "Yes, over there, on that rocky hillside." He pointed across the creek bank to a narrow opening in the boulders.

I looked over to where he pointed. "Over there? In a cave?"

The old man called Sultan kneeled down next to where I was now propped against a rock. He chose his words carefully. "Young man, I've lived out here many years. Many, many years."

I stared back till he continued.

"Been on the move ever since I lost my job in the Depression. Good job, too. Built steam locomotives over near Albany. That was May of '31. Was a hobo for a few years. Then I took to the woods. That's how I happened upon this place. That was the summer of '47. Lived here by myself since."

I couldn't believe what I was hearing. "You've lived out here in a cave that long? That's incredible!" I used my hand to shield my face from his sour breath, but I tried not to be too obvious. "If I could ask, how old are you?"

He thought for a moment, like he was doing math in his head. "Have to think. I was born in 1911. You figure it out. I reckon maybe I'm the oldest man in this part of the World."

I was shocked. "Wow! And you're all alone out here?"

He slowly nodded.

There were so many questions for me to ask. "How the heck has he managed to live that long?" I studied his features. His fingernails were ragged, not long, but a dirty yellow-green. He had a wiry build and amazingly seemed to still be limber when he bent over.

"Well, young man, let me tell you. I've never been sick. Never seen no doctors. Eat critters that I trap. And I have a lady friend. She's only 90. Young enough to be my daughter. She comes by every day, if the weather's good. She can't come out this way when it's rainy, because she uses a walker to get around. When she comes, in her little basket she brings me the morning paper and a Margarita."

"A Margarita? You gotta be kidding me!" This was too much to believe. Is this guy putting me on?

He seemed to be growing more at ease. "Yes, that's what I live on; mushrooms and Margaritas."

"Mushrooms?"

"Yup, I grow them way back in my cave, way past where I sleep. Have four different varieties, all good."

Visions of our frigid winter weather came to mind. "Sultan, you can't possibly survive out here in the winter! You'd freeze!"

Indeed, he was getting eager to chat now. I was fascinated in looking at him; how his eyebrow hairs almost covered his eyes. He had a habit of twirling them with his fingers. "Every winter, you see, a big 'ol bear wanders into my cave. I've learned how to hibernate with them. Just takes a little patience, though I admit I've gotten a scratch or two from them. And look out if he begins to roll over." He smiled a bit for the first time, as he continued. "Me and the bear, we huddle together. Keeps me warmer than a thick quilt. Gotta admit I don't smell all that good when I finally get up and move around come Spring. So then I take a bath in the stream, in that deep pool over yonder. Water's still icy then."

I just looked at him, still unbelieving. He could barely see through the hair over his eyes. I was thinking that if I tell anyone about him, they'll think I'm batty.

"I can show you how to hibernate. Do you want to try it once you calm down a bit?" he continued. "Once you know how, and totally relax, you can sleep for four or five months. But you gotta eat up first, and fill your belly with mushrooms. I can show you. D' ya want to try?"

"Thanks, Sultan," I replied, " but I need to get home before that long. I just remembered I have to mow the lawn. And besides, my wife would start to wonder where I was after a few weeks."

"All right," he replied. "You just sit here a few minutes till you're steady on your feet, and we'll go over to my cave. I'll give you a mushroom or two."

But when I stood up, I still felt woozy. Then my knees gave out and all went blank.

When I came to, I was lying on the floor at home. I looked over to see our dog, Fika, staring back at me. Her eyes were almost covered by hair.

An Oklahoma Story

Not too long ago I was sent as an American Red Cross volunteer to a rural area in East Texas where major flooding had occurred. While there, I worked on a daily basis with a nurse from Oklahoma, who we'll call Doris. In her silver years, she is very competent, outspoken, always willing to do what needs done, and a pleasure to work beside. She has been on many Red Cross national deployments, ranging from California wildfires to Florida hurricanes to the Oklahoma City bombing, but her biggest disaster story happened in her own home town.

Doris lives in Moore, Oklahoma, a middle-class suburb of Oklahoma City. As many of you folks know, that state is prone to major tornadic activity.

On a sultry afternoon in May of 2013, Doris was a mile or so away from home doing volunteer work for another organization. Weather reports were calling for a possibility of tornadoes in that part of the state. Although locals living there take those warnings seriously, they go about their business, while keeping an eye on the sky and an ear to the radio or television. That afternoon, weather radar watchers couldn't believe their computer screens. A huge cell suddenly developed, heading toward Moore. In a matter of minutes, the warnings intensified. "Seek shelter now!" was the urgent message.

Doris was busily doing blood pressure checks for the elderly when the skies turned ugly. Her husband Dave was at work in a nearby town. Their youngest daughter, nineteen year-old Kathleen, was home alone.

The Oklahoma skies turned black as night. A huge funnel cloud roared in from the west, barreling towards Moore. Tornado sirens blared. Those who had access to underground shelters scrambled down to safety. Dave, his eyes on the sky, sped back towards Moore in his truck. Doris had to stay with the elderly folks she was with, to help them to safety. All Doris could think about was Kathleen, alone and helpless in the cross hairs of the storm.

The tornado roared like a thousand freight trains toward Moore, blasting everything in its path to smithereens. Wider than most, it was aimed toward the section of town where Doris and her family lived. Suddenly, incredibly, it was at F-5 strength, as powerful as any on record. It tore down Doris' street, mauling it with its full fury. Kathleen knew it was coming, and took shelter as best she could in a closet. The twister slammed into their house at 180 mph. Minutes later, nothing was left but the cement slab. All the wood flooring was torn off; the water pipes were stripped clean, and the bathtub, sinks and furniture had taken to the sky.

Aware that the tornado had hit their street, Doris left her elderly companions as soon as it was safe to do so. She headed towards home on foot. She had to make her way through downed power lines, overturned cars and broken glass. She climbed over felled trees and passed the remains of shattered homes and garages. It was difficult to keep her bearings, since homes, street signs, and all landmarks that she could recognize were gone. She said it seemed to take forever. Before she could get there, she got a call from Dave. He softly said "I think we've lost our little girl."

Trying to forestall panic, Doris finally reached what had once been her tree-lined street, now just a huge jumble of pink insulation, jagged sheet metal, and shattered lumber. She reached what had been her home. Nothing remained but the concrete slab. There was no sign of Kathleen. Doris feverishly dug through piles of debris with her bare hands, gouging herself on sharp nails and glass, trying to uncover some sign of Kathleen. Alas, she found nothing.

After a half hour of searching, something caused her to turn around. She couldn't believe her eyes. There stood Kathleen, unhurt but for a scrape on her arm. Doris and Kathleen hugged like never before. Tears poured down like rain.

To this day the girl has no recollection of what happened when the tornado hit, or how she was spared. All she knew was immediately after the twister passed, she was dazed and unable to find her cell phone. She heard the cries of panicked and injured children at a nearby elementary school. She went off to help.

The next day Doris put thoughts of her own wrecked home aside, borrowed a Red Cross vest, and went to help others in town whose homes were destroyed, and who had suffered injuries and fatalities in their families.

Doris' story is one beyond human comprehension. How and why was Kathleen spared? Her story provides a glimmer of hope when all might be lost, as well as a huge sense of gratitude for those who are putting their own personal needs aside to help others.

From Oklahoma, a day of disaster, and a day of joy.

On A Greyhound Bus

This all happened just a couple weeks ago. I needed to take a Greyhound to visit my aunt in Beloit. Aunt Jenny was in her mid-90s and has lived alone ever since Uncle Fred died. It was dark by the time I climbed aboard the big dog in Buffalo. It had been many years since I had taken a long bus ride like this. A snow squall was blowing up, and it was chilly as hell; the kind of damp cold that knifes right through you. I was expecting the bus to be only half full, but when I climbed aboard, I saw only one empty seat toward the back. I tried not to bump into others as I made my way through the aisle, passing several who were dozing. I tossed my backpack up on the luggage rack, nodded to the guy next to me, and sat down. Soon as I did, the driver dimmed the cabin lights and we pulled away.

The Greyhound hummed on west toward Erie, making good time. I could see from the street lights and oncoming headlights that the snow was getting serious. Not quite a white-out, but still bad. I was glad I decided not to drive it, since it might be bad all the way to Wisconsin. Some guy sitting behind me began snoring raggedly, the kind that's really bothersome. I was fumbling with my notebook, scribbling a few things down in the dim light, munching on a candy bar, and didn't glance over to my seatmate.

Without any warning the bus braked sharply, skidding slightly to the right. My notebook slid off my lap to the floor. I barely held onto the mini tape recorder I had brought along to record her voice for the folks back home. The man next to me whispered "Whoa, Nellie" as we stopped suddenly. Moments later we started up in low gear, passing red and blue police lights flashing as we rumbled by. For the first time, I noticed the other guy. He had on a gritty light sweater with stains on the front, and a short-brimmed ball cap. A fishing license was attached, dangling. He had several days' stubble. I guessed him to be about seventy. Maybe less, since he seemed to be down on his luck. Sorta mousey-looking. He smelled like a wet couch.

I told him my name. He mentioned his, but I don't recall it now. Might have been Jackson or something like that. We exchanged small talk about the snow as the bus hummed on into the night. Glancing out, I saw the squall might have let up some. I told him where I was going; he said he was headed to Montana. Didn't say where. I didn't ask. Then we said nothing for quite a while. I dozed for a bit.

An hour or so later, after leaving the bus depot in Cleveland, he jostled around in his seat. He noticed I was awake, then mentioned in a low voice "Beloit is a good town. I used to do a lot of work there." I said I hadn't been there in years. Just to pass the time, I asked him what he would be doing in Montana.

I felt him taking a deep breath, holding it in, then letting it out slowly. "I'm after an answer," he replied, like it was a big deal in a weird way. Seemed kinda spooky. My backbone stiffened. I reached down to make sure I still had my wallet. I tried to shift away a few inches without being too obvious.

"No, no worry," he said, sensing movement. He lowered his voice, looked over to me, and said "I guess I need to tell someone." His eyes darted nervously, then added "I mean everything." I wasn't expecting to be taken into the confidence of a stranger.

The guy moved closer to me so others couldn't hear. His teeth were ragged and brown; I tried not to act like I noticed. I cautiously flipped on my recorder as he began. He began. "It happened last fall, I think right around Hallowe'en. It was late at night; well before dawn." He lowered his voice, and I struggled to hear over the humming of the diesel engine. "My place is a ways from anyone's; I like it that way, y'know. The dog had been restless all night, pawin' at the bed, and then at the door. That was before the winds kicked up a storm. It began blowin' somethin' fierce." He paused for a moment, then continued. "The windows were rattlin'; I thought they were gonna bus' out. I could tell the 'lectric was gone. Then I remember there was a lull for a few moments, kinda ee-rie-like." He seemed to be choosing his words carefully, speaking slow-er. "Then something set the dog off, I didn't know what. He was actin' crazy. Then he let out a weird whimper. That's when I heard it . . . ."

(Have fun continuing this story around your campfire!)

When It Was The Only Game

When it came to sports, the Fifties was all baseball. We old dudes remember it like it was yesterday. To kids from Pittsburgh, it was the great Roberto Clemente and Forbes Field. Cleveland fans idolized Bob Feller and Rocky Colavito. If you were from the Midwest, it was Ernie Banks, or maybe Stan Musial. The West Coast? The Majors weren't there yet.

You knew all about your idols; their current batting average and home run count. Their baseball cards were imprinted on your brain. You knew the uniform numbers of everyone on your team. Growing up outside New York City, I had the New York Yankees, the New York Giants, and the Brooklyn Dodgers at my doorstep. If you were from there, you loved one of the teams and hated the other two. For this baseball-crazed youngster, it was all Dodgers. But no matter what team you followed, it was the radio that was the connection to our heroes. Whether it was Bob Prince on KDKA in Pittsburgh, or Red Barber or Vince Scully in New York, we tuned in these familiar voices whenever we could, and lived and died with their play-by-play accounts.

My Dodgers got off to a fantastic start in 1955, going 10-0. As a seven-year-old, I listened to them whenever my mom would let me. I worshiped star center fielder Duke Snider. For my birthday, my parents took me to a store and bought me a Dodger uniform that I wore proudly. I remember the store clerk quizzing me on who played second base for the Dodgers. I quickly answered "Jackie Robinson!" The clerk gave me a baseball for the correct answer! Mainly I wore my uniform in the back yard when I threw a pink rubber ball up against the second story of the house about a hundred times a night, envisioning I was "The Duke" making a great catch. I asked Mom to sew on a #4, since that was his number. I guess a few games were on television then, though I'm not sure if I watched them. So baseball to me was a compilation of the words of the radio announcer, the write-ups in the *Daily News*, and my beloved baseball cards. But mainly, it was the glue of childhood imagination pulling it all together.

One Sunday morning in the late summer of '55 my folks, my sisters, and I were downing breakfast, and Dad asked what we wanted to do today. I had been wanting to ask this for weeks, but had been too timid to ask. Not today. I jumped in and blurted out "how about going to a Dodger game in Brooklyn?"

There never was any extra money around the house, but Dad and Mom must have thought they could swing it. Soon we were off to catch a mid-morning bus to the Port Authority Terminal in Manhattan. After an hour's ride there, Dad hustled us onto the subway. It wasn't long before we rattled our way on the dark, screeching, swaying cars to a stop in Brooklyn at Flatbush Avenue.

As I bounced excitedly up the stairs from the murky subway into the bright sunlight, there towering above me was a place I had only dreamed about. The tall white letters on the stadium wall spelled out "Ebbets Field." The home of the Dodgers! Could heaven be any better than this?

Dad bought the tickets, we hustled through the turnstiles, and as we entered the ballpark, the mouth-watering aroma of hot dogs and sauerkraut filled the sunny afternoon. Hurrying inside the stands toward the seats, I got my first glimpse. There before me was the field the Dodgers played on! I looked out in awe at the greenest, most beautiful and lush grass I'd ever seen in my young life! The players were warming up on the field, with the soft thwack of practice balls hit to the outfielders. There was Duke! And Jackie Robinson! PeeWee Reese! And all my other heroes in their blue and white uniforms. The Cardinals were the visiting team that afternoon, with the great Stan "The Man" Musial in right field. I don't remember too much else, or even who won the game. It didn't matter. I was there. I was at a Dodger game!

Baseball was different then. Star players generally stayed with the same team their whole career. The sports pages weren't overloaded in the summer with other sports infringing on baseball. When there was a story in the paper about a baseball player, it was about how he played. It wasn't about his contract, his latest arrest, drugs, or the free agency that has so changed the game we grew up with.

There were better nicknames for players then, ones that sounded like ballplayers. In addition to PeeWee and Duke, the Yankees had Whitey Ford, Yogi Berra, and Moose Skowron. Other teams had Red Schoendienst, Spook Jacobs, Vinegar Bend Mizell, Windy McCall, Peanuts Lowrey, Minnie Minoso, Rube Walker, and Turk Lown. Two managers who come to mind were Pinkie Higgins and Heinie Manush. These guys sounded like they could really play the game! Today there's too many vanilla-sounding first names like Anthony, Andrew, and William. They sound like they play the cello. Why not Tony, Andy, and Billy? What if George Ruth hadn't been called Babe?

But changes the sport has undergone have not taken away what we remember about following our favorite team, day after day, in our youth. Living and dying at a called third strike. My guy smashing a homer! Then, in early October, sneaking a transistor radio into school to listen to the World Series.

The warm, cottony cloud of childhood memories. Indeed, back in the Fifties, it was all baseball.

Hurricane Heartbreak, Revisited

Katrina? We remember! Tragic scenes are forever etched in our collective memory. You may recall that three weeks after it made landfall, the Bayou State was again under siege, this time by Hurricane Rita. My memories take me back to those turbulent days in 2005.

As a Red Cross national volunteer back then, I was deployed to that hard-hit area. My destination was Lake Charles, a Louisiana city located just north of the coastal area pummeled by Rita. After my original two-week deployment ended, I agreed to spend an additional ten days there. Many vivid mental images remain from that experience, but a handful stand out. I recall them every year when I think back on that experience.

After the hurricanes hit, the Lake Charles Civic Center had been transformed into a Red Cross shelter for storm victims mostly from rural areas south of Lake Charles that had been destroyed by Rita. It was also a temporary home for scores of New Orleans folks evacuated after Katrina. As I recall, there were more than 300 men, women, and children staying there. As with other disasters, the shelter provided a safe haven as well as food and support from a host of agencies. My role, in disaster mental health, was to help provide emotional support to those in need.

As you might imagine, personal needs were immense. Some folks had been evacuated before Rita made landfall, or during the first hours of the raging winds and flooding. Almost no one knew what happened to their homes from the storm surge and winds. Separation from family members and friends was a common, critical reality. Communication down to affected areas near the coast was impossible. Contact with friends, relatives, and neighbors in other shelters was non-existent. Cell phones had not yet made their way into every household. Those who had them found their cell service non-existent.

It was a time of heartbreak and hope. A few scenarios stand out from those dark days. Thanks to notes taken then, the memories linger. At the shelter, there were many families who had brought nothing with them from their homes when they were evacuated. Some came with only the clothes they were wearing. Few children had toys. Folks in surrounding towns who were less affected tried to help out.

On one of my first days there, I was moving cases of water. Among them was a stack of cardboard boxes; maybe a half dozen in all. A note was taped to them: "To be distributed to children at the shelter." Curious, I reached in two of the boxes and saw they each contained plastic bags with a stuffed animal and a hand-written note. There must have been more than fifty individual bags. Each note read:

"Hi, my name is Mackenzie Snyder. I am 14 years old and in the ninth grade. I collect duffel bags and stuffed animals as an act of kindness for those in need. God told me that you can use a cuddly friend. So I send this with love to you. I want you to always know you are loved, especially by me. And always remember to be positive, polite, and never give up."
Love,
Your friend, MacKenzie

My heart still throbs so many years later when I read her compassionate message.

How bad was the devastation? Another memory was walking in the coastal community of Cameron and seeing how the storm surge had yanked fire hydrants out of the sandy soil. Only the shell of one lone concrete building remained standing, where there had been a hundred or more cottages. Many of those living there had relied on the shrimping industry for their livelihood. In addition to their homes being washed away, the storm destroyed many of their boats. All aspects of their lives had been terribly affected. Fast forward to 2021, and it all happened again. Although Cameron may have been spared, the storm's fury devastated other communities along the Gulf Coast.

Looking back on another unforgettable experience, this one about a week later in '05, I boarded a bus chartered by FEMA. Destination: New Orleans. In addition to a few of us Red Cross volunteers, there were perhaps twenty folks who had homes in that city. They had been evacuated out of New Orleans to the temporary shelter of the Civic Center following Katrina's deadly strike. They had no idea if their homes were still standing. We would be side-by-side with them this day as they found out for themselves.

Again, I refer to notes taken then:

Cal, a neatly-dressed black man in his 50s with a deeply-lined face, sat in front of us. He said little on the two-hour bus ride there; the kind of person who's more of a listener. The bus eventually took us to his house, a two-story brick home on a corner, in what had been a respectable neighborhood. Piles of household debris were everywhere. A green sofa was lying upside down in his yard. He walked slowly up to the front door and reluctantly peered in. He said nothing. The flood's water line was above the first floor window. We were told Cal spent two days on his roof waiting to be evacuated. "Are you going back?," I gently asked. "Nah" he said, as he shuffled glumly back to the bus.

We went to a dozen homes of our passengers. We drove down street after street past the sad remains of houses lying trashed. Many had a crude "X" marked on them. When someone cried out "there's my house!" the bus would pull over and we'd walk with them, staying a few steps behind. All were damaged, some severely. Almost everyone handled it quietly. Tears flowed.

A silver-haired woman was eager to see her daughter's house, where she had been living. She had no idea of its condition. It was on a numbered street, and she was counting down the streets by number as the bus approached. Soon, we knew it was near. Then we turned the corner. She excitedly called out *"There's my house!"* It was still standing and looked fine! Although there were no yellow ribbons on trees, just like in the song, the whole damn bus was cheering!

A rare moment of joyful celebration among the saddest of days . . . .

About the Author:

Joe Ulrich grew up in suburban New Jersey during the 1950's. After graduating from Grove City College and West Virginia University, he made the transition to living in northern Pennsylvania on a rural dirt road. Along the way, he and Linda married and together shared this country life. His career was spent at a state psychiatric hospital, and after retirement as an American Red Cross disaster volunteer. His first published book (2004) was <u>The Dust of Angels</u>, a WW2 memoir about a P-47 pilot. For the last twelve years, he's written monthly articles for a local publication, many of which are included in this book. He can be reached on Facebook at Joe Ulrich – Author.